THE GIRL
LEAST LIKELY

Also by Katy Loutzenhiser

If You're Out There

THE GIRL *LEAST* LIKELY

KATY LOUTZENHISER

An Imprint of HarperCollins*Publishers*

Balzer + Bray is an imprint of HarperCollins Publishers.

 For information address HarperCollins Children's Books, a division of HarperCollins Publishers, 195 Broadway, New York, NY 10007.
www.epicreads.com

ISBN 978-0-06-286570-0

Typography by Michelle Taormina
21 22 23 24 25 PC/LSCH 10 9 8 7 6 5 4 3 2 1
❖
First Edition

To the low-key funny girls, hopeless romantics,
and anyone who's ever felt least likely

ONE

The Best Friend Crush | Inevitable, apparently. That lifetime of platonic fun was just a cosmic ploy to get you to make out.

It should be a normal thing, sitting on Sam's couch. I try crossing my legs, slinging an elbow to one side. God, it's getting worse. It's like I've forgotten all couch-sitting procedure.

"Wanna watch something, Gretch?" he calls, walking in from the kitchen. He unloads some chips and seltzers onto the coffee table and my eyes wander his broad frame, tan arms, that one adorable cheek dimple when he peeks up and smiles.

Stop it, brain. Stop it right now.

"Sure," I say as he settles in next to me, my heart banging around in my chest like the frenzied snow outside. He tucks an arm behind his head of dark, floppy curls, clicking through the TV menu. There's a hole growing in the *Office*-themed

That's what she said T-shirt I gave him a couple birthdays back, and I frown, silently thanking the universe I didn't show up looking nice today. I had the impulse, but worried he'd notice any departure from my Hibernating Curmudgeon Aesthetic—fleece leggings, sensible socks, a whole resentful parade of *Why Do I Live in Maine?!* sweaters. (South Portland, specifically. Or "SoPo" if you want to be cute about it.)

"What'll it be?" he asks. "I'll even do a rom-com and let you commentate."

"*Moi?* Commentate?" I hope I come off breezy. Sam knows I adore rom-coms, almost as much as I adore making fun of them. What he doesn't know is that right now, I feel a little like I'm trapped inside of one.

He opens up the chips. "The last one I remember watching was *Say Anything.* When John Cusack held up the boom box outside the girl's window, I believe your words were, 'Go away, you stalker!'"

"Well, I stand by it," I say, meeting his smiling eyes. My stomach flips. Nope, there's no way I can watch hot people fall in love right now. "Actually." I clear my throat. "How about the new Marnie James Netflix special? It's really good. And I'm sure I'll be watching rom-coms with Hen and Carmen later tonight anyway—for New Year's Eve-Eve. There will be pajamas, Rice Krispies treats. We're going balls to the wall!"

Sam laughs. "Hey, where do you think that comes from? *Balls to the wall?*"

"Huh," I say, thinking. "Maybe some guy put his balls on the wall?"

"I don't know. Doesn't really capture the energy of the expression. How does putting one's balls on a wall become *balls to the wall!?*"

"Maybe it was really fun," I say, rearranging myself on the couch to face him. "Or . . . maybe a bunch of guys put their balls on the wall? As, like, a group activity?"

"Still, it's inactive," he says. "You would think to end up with a meaning like that, there would have been some real movement."

"Well, there's no reason to presume these men were just *standing* there. I think there could have plausibly been, like, a collective *dragging* of balls *along* the wall."

"So, like, a synchronized side-waddle?"

I shrug. "I think it sounds like a blast." Sam maintains his scholarly frown just a hair longer than I can. Then I snort, completely breaking, and he does too.

"Okay, how do I look?" asks Sam's mom as she enters the living room. She's in a knockout black dress and heels, clearly undeterred by the snowpocalypse outside.

"Dang, Gabriela," I say. "I don't know. Your date might feel inadequate."

"Samuel?" she says, smiling at me, and I love the way she says it. Like, *Sam-well.*

"Nope, you're my mom," he says. "I have no comment."

"Of course," she says, returning her gaze to me as she pulls on a belted jacket and reaches behind the collar to free her long curls. "I have a really good feeling about this guy." Sam groans slightly. "Sorry, sorry! Oh, and Gretchen, tell your mom I'm bringing brigadeiros to the party tomorrow. And stuff to make caipirinhas. But make her call me if she needs anything else."

"Okay," I say. "I will."

She hesitates, looking back and forth between us. I'm confused as Sam shakes his head, but then Gabriela says, "Could you two do me a favor and close for the new girl? I should leave now if I don't want to be late."

"Sure," says Sam, hoisting himself up before offering me a hand. I feel a little jolt as I take it, but repeat the mantra I've been using for months: *We're friends, god dammit. Nothing more.*

Keep Calm Yoga, also known as the whole first floor of Sam's house, does deliver on its name. It helps that it smells like dried sage leaves down here, and all those nose-tingling oils Gabriela uses to wash the mats. A class is finishing up in back, a voice piercing through some kind of techno-meets-spiritual-awakening music. *"The light within me recognizes the light within you. . . ."*

"Get ready for Amber," sighs Sam as we lean into the front counter. "She's like some kind of . . . wellness Barbie."

I make a face like, *Be nice,* then tilt my head. "Wait. Is this the one who pitched the workshop series that's just for your butt? If your mom green-lights it, I have some title suggestions. Booty boot camp? Bun-latees?"

"You think you're kidding, but you're not far off." Sam's been openly skeptical about the changes around here. For most of our childhood, Gabriela used this place to teach cat-cow to preschoolers and chair sun salutations to seniors. But as the head of a single-income household now, she's become more open to the gimmicks.

This summer they're trying goat yoga.

A loud *"Ommm"* rings out, and after a moment, the door swings open, releasing a wave of hot air. "Great class, ladies," says the instructor, her voice clearer now. She's about what I expected: elaborately spandexed and suspiciously tan for a blond girl in December, a presumably profound Chinese word branded above one hip. "Oh, and bee-tee-dubs?" she calls to the room, stacking cork blocks for patrons and tossing straps into a basket. "If you've been feeling a little wonky, trust me, it's not you."

"Let me guess," Sam says under his breath, so close it makes me shiver. "Is Mercury in retrograde?"

She looks over at us, a surprisingly perceptive glint in her eyes. "Uh, it *is* in retrograde. Like, bad. I crashed into a parked car today."

When the place clears out, we switch Amber's mix to one of Gabriela's old bossa nova CDs. The plucks of acoustic guitar are subtle, intimate, somehow bringing warmth to the cold night. It's nice not needing to talk, spreading out mats and misting both sides before wiping them down with rags. Sam sweeps; I water plants. I lower the thermostat; he goes out front to shut down the computer. When he returns to the studio, he flicks the lights. And now he's looking at me, in a clean, candlelit room.

"Hey," he says, breaking the silence. "Can we sit?" He gestures toward the waxy floor, and I nod, feeling strange as we come to face each other, cross-legged in our socks. The whole arrangement feels too serious for us. He's studying me and it's making me nervous. *He* looks nervous. But then he takes out his phone and swipes. "Xavier turned one today." He holds out a picture of his little brother smashing a cupcake into his gleeful chubby face.

"What a cutie. I can't believe I haven't met him yet."

"It's hard with them so far away," he says. "Kind of a dick move on my dad's part. I can't even be surly about him remarrying now that he made something that cute." I smile, waiting. Sam almost never talks about his dad anymore. "Anyway . . ." He lets out a big breath. "You know how they're leaving Jersey for the city because of Angela's job, right?" I nod. "Well, when I visited at Christmas, they kind of . . . asked me to come live with them, once school's out. They took me to see the place they're buying, and it's sweet. I'll have my own room—even my own bathroom. It was kind of too good to pass up, so . . ."

I open my mouth, but stop short. I must have heard him wrong. "Wait . . . you're moving away? . . . For your last year of high school?"

He shrugs, almost helpless. "It's *New York*. I always assumed I'd end up there for college. This way I can make sure I really like it before I apply. Plus, my dad said he'd pay for stage combat classes if I go. Like, real ones. Not the dinky workshops you find around here. I could spend my senior year . . . second-acting plays and getting takeout past ten p.m. It'd be a chance to bond with Xavier, too, which would be cool. I want him to know me. Especially since neither of us has much family in the States."

I shake my head. It's a lot to take in. "What about your mom?"

"That part will be hard," he says, his face falling a little. "But she supports it. And she's *back out there* or whatever now. Which, I mean. Good for her, I guess." He shudders and I manage to smile.

"When will you . . . ?"

"End of June, probably. On the plus side, I'll be out of here before all the yoga goats get shipped in."

I laugh, kind of, my brain already beginning to race. I've never known a life without Samuel Oliveira in it. Not one I could really remember, anyway. Things might be different now—really different. But we're still *Sam-and-Gretch*, with infinite shared memories, a language, practically a *universe* that's all our own.

I thought we'd have more time.

To my horror, I feel a tear spill over, but before I can look away, Sam leans in slowly to catch it. I freeze, my heart hammering in my chest. The pad of his thumb is warm against my cheek, lingering there. And now I'm looking at his mouth. I lift my gaze to search his eyes: kind, and funny, with little gold flecks I somehow never noticed. He's searching my eyes, too.

Holy shit. Is this what I think this is?

"Sam?" I whisper.

But his phone rings.

TWO

Funny Gal Pals | Your one-stop shop for all love-life analysis, ideally while doing rigorous cardio. At least one has a sass mouth.

It was a telemarketer. Because of course it was. Still, the interruption was enough to suck all the electricity from the moment. Around the world, lights dimmed over dinner tables and dance clubs went briefly quiet. Finally, Sam said, "Oh, shoot. I think the guys are coming by soon." And I said, "Uhhhhhhhhh." Okay, I don't think that's really what I said. All I know is, when the silence grew too long, I laughed and wiped my watery eyes. Then he laughed too and we both got up off the floor.

In my car parked outside, I hold my ruddy-cold hands to the blasting vents, my prehistoric hand-me-down Volvo still freezing despite the five whole minutes it spent heating while I roof-brushed and windshield-scraped and silent-screamed *WHY?!?*

I hear a buzz from the passenger seat and turn to see my cousin Carmen's face lighting up the dark. "Hello?"

"Where are you?"

"I was just leaving Sam's," I say, still in a fog. "We, um . . . He . . ." Across the street, Keep Calm Yoga is empty now, the sign on the door turned to *Closed*. A streetlamp glows out front, illuminating bits of falling snow. Sam and I stood in that very spot not long ago, until a few of the football guys came by to pick him up. I think maybe our goodbye was weird. Was it weird?

"Greeeetchen?" she says, drawing my name out curiously. My cousin doesn't know about the Samuel situation—my sister, Hen, either. Between our limited texts and their short breaks off from their first semester of college, there hasn't been a good moment. And I'd hoped these feelings would go away on their own eventually. But now . . .

Is that even what I want?

"Sorry," I say, shoving the car into drive. I feel newly awake—like I might burst if I don't get over there and start spilling. "I'm five minutes from your house. Prepare yourselves. I come bearing slumber party necessities."

"Oh," she says, a frown in her voice. "Well, we're actually still at the dorms. Today's been . . ." She sighs. "Just meet us here."

I run all four flights of stairs when I reach the residence hall, the burn in my muscles a nice break from all the thoughts. Driving over the bridge into the Old Port, I looped through strategies, only to narrow my future with Sam down to the three most likely scenarios.

One: I tell him how I feel, he rejects me, and our friendship never recovers.

Two: I tell him how I feel, he says he feels the same way, we date, later break up, and our friendship never recovers.

Or, three: I *don't* tell him how I feel, I continue to pine and fester until the day he moves away, at which time all normalcy between us has eroded to the point where it's too weird to stay in touch, and our friendship never recovers.

So yeah—I could probably use some outside analysis.

Carmen's door swings open before I even knock. "Welcome to our den of misery," she says flatly, her ponytail of blue-black hair swinging from a fun little bandanna.

"Well, hello to you, too," I say, a bit breathless. But then I glance behind her, where my sister is hugging a pillow on the bed, her face streaked with tears. "Shit." My shoulders slump. "What is it?"

Hen lifts her gaze to me and sniffs. "Lizzy p-posted a new Instagram story. She looks . . ." The word gets lost in a sob: *"Fine!"*

"Come on, Hen," says Carmen, shooing me inside. "We all

know Instagram is a lie. I'm sure Lizzy is just as miserable as you are."

"This is the hard part," I tell my sister, swapping my rubber boots for a pair of Carmen's stockpiled tsinelas—a cozy bit of home she's carried with her to the dorms. "But this is what you wanted, right? You hated being long distance."

"I know," says Hen, pulling tissues from her sweatshirt pocket. Even wrecked like this, my sister remains mystifyingly elegant, her strawberry-blond hair swept up in a loose knot, little wisps framing pale green eyes—a sort of modern-day Grace Kelly in Sad Girl Leisure Attire. "I have to get these feelings under control. I've barely even studied for my multivariable calculus test that got pushed to after the break. Earlier today I cried at the words *divergence theorem*."

Carmen and I glance at each other, not getting it.

"You know . . . because Lizzy and I *diverged*?" After a pause, Hen giggles. To her credit, she's always been able to laugh at herself.

"Well, Gretch." Carmen gestures to the neater half of the room. "You can sit on Sabrina's bed if you want. Kick her stuff around. Maybe fart into her pillows."

"Ew, Carmen!" says Hen.

"Still mad, huh?" I say, settling onto the traitorous girl's unsuspecting comforter.

"Of course I'm still mad!" says Carmen. "Is this something I'm just supposed to move on from? My roommate kissed my boyfriend!" She closes her wing-tipped eyes, sort of . . . power meditating. "Tell me. Truly. What kind of person does that?"

"A monster," sighs Hen, giving her nose a loud honk.

I open my mouth, but think better of it. "What?" demands Carmen.

"Just . . ." I shrug. "I thought you weren't even that into the guy."

"Huh," says Hen. "I kind of thought that, too. Also, hadn't you only been hanging out for a few weeks?"

"Okay, yes," says Carmen. "I actually got the vibe he was kind of a bullshit artist. Super vague if you asked him about himself. And cute, but too . . ." She searches for the words. "Like, hardy-har jokey all the time."

"What's his last name again?" asks Hen. "I want to do some Google stalking."

"You know what? Don't," says Carmen. "I'm done talking about him. This is about the girl code. You just don't go around kissing your friend's new boo."

Hen's breath hitches. *"I miss kissing my boo!"*

"Crap," says Carmen, climbing onto the bed to put an arm around her. "Come on. Let's really try it. No more Lizzy talk." Hen tucks herself into the crook of Carmen's neck, letting her breathing slow.

For a second I feel left out, watching them—like I'm five again, and they're seven. We feel like our own little girl gang now, but growing up, Hen and Carmen were always a unit—practically another set of twins, just like Mom and Aunt Viv. One white, one half Filipina, the resemblance is still striking, with their heart-shaped faces and button noses, Pantene Pro-V hair, and lanky extremities. They clearly took the bulk of our mothers' identical DNA.

By contrast, I'm basically my dad without the mustache: thick brown waves; round face; the low-to-the-ground, sturdy build of a reliable farmhand. There are advantages. If the zombie apocalypse ever strikes, I'd bet on me.

Hen swipes her eyes. "Stupid Stanford. Why'd she have to go so far away?"

At the words *far away*, I picture Sam in New York next year, and wonder where we'll have left things by then. Will we be friends? More than friends? Deceased from sheer awkwardness?

"At least you've been in love," Carmen is saying.

"Hey, um . . ." I really got sidetracked here.

"I don't know," sighs Hen. "I'm starting to think love isn't worth it."

I clear my throat. "You guys?"

"You know what really pisses me off?" says Carmen. "Sabrina told me she didn't *mean to*. How could you not *mean* to kiss someone?"

"Guys," I say, more adamant now. I need them to be talking about *my thing*. Why is it never about *my thing*?

"Oh God," says Hen. "Do you think Lizzy's going to kiss someone else?"

"You guys!" My voice rings out, and I freeze.

"Whoa," says Hen, as she and Carmen stare at me. The room has gone quiet, apart from my own heavy breaths. I feel abruptly sheepish. They're just chattering like they always do. But it's somehow more irritating today.

"So . . ." says Carmen. "What crawled up your butt?"

I laugh, though the question kind of makes me mad. For the record, *so many things* have crawled up *both* these girls' butts for basically our entire lives.

Hen sniffs and dabs her tears with a tissue, before making a face like, *well*? I open my mouth, unsure of where to start. It's funny. I thought I hadn't told them about the Sam stuff because I didn't feel like getting into it. Now I wonder if it's more that they never asked. Anyway, the energy is weird all of a sudden.

I breathe out, letting it go. "Shouldn't we get over to the house? You know. Start the festivities?"

"Oh," says Carmen. "Actually, we were thinking of going out."

Hen looks herself over. "The only problem is I'm all sloppy."

"So?" says Carmen. "Go raid my dresser."

"Wait," I say, as Hen gets up and starts pawing through Carmen's drawers. "What do you mean, *out*? What about our movie night? Rice Krispies treats? It's New Year's Eve-Eve tradition."

"Everything is a tradition with you," sighs Carmen.

I feel stung. "I thought we liked this tradition."

"Of course we do," says Hen diplomatically as she considers a corduroy skirt.

"But in light of recent heartbreaks and betrayals," says Carmen, walking over to her makeup bag, "we thought we could mix it up. Maybe go find a bar or something."

"A bar," I say. That literally could not sound any worse, even if it weren't illegal. "Carmen. We're underage."

"Yeah, about that," she says, dabbing on lip gloss. "We've actually both had fake IDs since Thanksgiving."

I gape at Hen. "You don't even drink!"

"Conformity seemed like the best practice for making friends in college," she says. "Slap on a toga, maybe play some flip cup . . ." She holds up a sparkly shirt to measure against herself. "I think I was tired of being known around school as the chick who cried in the bathroom."

"Well, did it work?" I ask, feeling strangely uneasy. "Did conformity solve your problems?"

"Kind of," says Hen. "Though now I mostly just cry in the toga party bathrooms."

I laugh, still at a loss. "All right . . . I guess you can go without me."

"Please," says Carmen. "I obviously have a plan." She tosses something onto the bed beside me. It's an ID. "Sabrina forgot to take hers home, I guess. We got ours done at the same time. We'll use it to get you in."

I hold up the phony license. "Yeah . . . I am very clearly not this person."

"Details," says Carmen, walking off again.

I study the girl in the corner of the ID, her dark brown hair pinned up into two messy little buns like mouse ears. Aside from being brunettes, Sabrina and I look nothing alike. She's wearing a hostile expression, with red-framed glasses, fierce makeup, and black clothing. "This is quite a photo," I say. "She looks like some kind of . . . angry graphic designer."

Carmen sighs. "She wants to come off all tough, but really she's the kind of person who, like, rewatches *Friends* every year and drinks pumpkin spice lattes."

"What's wrong with pumpkin spice lattes?" asks Hen, still testing outfits.

"They're just so basic," says Carmen, back to rummaging through Sabrina's stuff. "Though I'll admit, they are kind of delicious. But you don't want to be that person."

"That person who likes things other people like?" I say, eliciting a smirk from Hen. "What's your drink order? Borscht flavored? Dill pickle?"

"Aha!" cries Carmen. "These might help." She tosses me a pair of red-framed glasses. "They're fake because she's like that. But at least they won't hurt your eyes."

I climb off the bed and go to the full-length mirror, studying myself with the stylish glasses on. "You're right," I say. "This is foolproof. I am utterly transformed."

"Oh, come on," says Carmen. "Don't you think some of us could use a little fun?" She tilts her head toward Hen, who's now twisting back to admire her own butt in a pair of acid-washed mom jeans. She does seem to have brightened at the idea of going out.

I glance at the ID again. "According to this, Sabrina Martin is five six."

"So you'll wear heels." Carmen bites her lip, her eyes darting around the room. "Just . . . give me twenty minutes."

THREE

Makeover(!) | The process after which the whole world goes, "Aw man, she could have looked like that the whole time!"

As kids, Hen, Carmen, and I went through a *Grease* phase. We probably saw it a hundred times. And every time, Mom or Aunt Viv would pop in with side commentary to ensure we didn't wind up brainwashed by the story and all its patriarchal nonsense.

Mom: "Please don't go reinventing yourselves for anyone, okay, girls?"

Aunt Viv: "And, girls? Reformed bad boys are not a thing. Repeat after me: once a dirtbag, always a dirtbag."

Mom: "Also, girls? Leather pants are not a personality trait. They're just not!"

Standing before the mirror now, though, I have to admit the effects of Sabrina's leather pants aren't lost on me. By some sorcery of pencils, brushes, and gels, Carmen has seriously transformed my features—eyes smoldering behind glasses, lips almost seductive from a bright red stain. The two buns in my hair look sleek but loose, and Sabrina's sleeveless black top is hugging my figure nicely. Carmen even snagged a pair of the girl's high-heeled black booties from the closet, along with a cropped suede black jacket. It all miraculously fits.

"I don't know," I say, feeling a nip of pride at how weirdly attractive I feel. This is a real-life Sandra Dee, Cinderella, Mia Thermopolis situation—just with a dash of *I will cut you*. "This stuff looks expensive. What if I mess something up?"

"You could incinerate the whole outfit and she wouldn't notice," says Carmen. "She's at her vacation home in Aspen right now. And her dad owns, like, all the windmills in Virginia or . . . something."

I twist from side to side, checking myself out. "Are you sure about this?"

"You look hot," says Carmen, holding up the ID to compare. "And pretty convincing."

Hen grins. "I'd be afraid of you if I hired you to make my website."

The suede jacket is useless against the cold. We park and head for the booming music of a bar, snow coming down in sheets.

My teeth are still chattering by the time we find a table, Hen and Carmen hurrying off and returning with tequila shots. If I'm being honest, I feel a little skeeved out as they shoot the liquid back, sucking on limes and smacking the table. It's like they held a board meeting without me, and decided our childhood was over.

After another round of limes and squealing, a pop song I vaguely recognize comes on—something about love and forever. And suddenly, Hen's eyes fill with tears.

"Come on, boo-boo!" Carmen calls over the music. "You were supposed to be getting your mind *off* Lizzy."

"She's right!" I shout. "If I have to be out, in pants this tight, I at least want to see you having fun. Remember fun? I want to see you laugh!"

Carmen looks inspired now. "Gretchen, you're a goddamn *genius*."

"What?" I say as she hands me my coat.

"Come on," she says, linking arms with us to pull us toward the door. "Let's go."

In a way, I guess it was me who landed us here—Carmen latching onto my words with the overzealous determination unique to the heavily inebriated. Over the years, driving by, this comedy club has always been a mild curiosity of ours—brick, with very few windows, a crooked blinking sign that reads *The Chuckle Parlor.*

Carmen was certain as she shepherded us back to my car: with a name like that, this place *had* to be the antidote.

I puff warm air into my hands, switching my weight from foot to foot, these absurd lady-stilts spiked dangerously into ice and sidewalk salt. "You got this, lil' cuz," hiccups Carmen, patting me affectionately as we take a step forward in the slow-moving line.

"Toootally," says Hen. I think they can tell I'm nervous. The last place only carded if you ordered. Here, it happens at the door. *Oh God.* I never should have agreed to this. I'm no miscreant. I get stressed when people lie in *movies*, let alone when it's me.

"Hey, what's your sign?" asks Carmen, elbowing me.

"My what?"

"Know your astrology," she snaps. "You're a Libra. Mellow, thoughtful. Ultimately driven by the desire to be loved."

"Well, that's easy. I actually am a Libra. But doesn't everyone want that?"

"Such a Libra thing to say," she sighs. "Thinkin' you have all the answers . . ."

Henrietta starts humming a happy little tune to herself, and the group ahead of us glances back, looking charmed. My sister tends to have that effect. Carmen too. I think there's something about me and shiny people. Like it's my preordained position in life: shiny-person adjacent.

Carmen sways and I have to steady her, then Hen, who keeps drifting off to look up at the stars. I feel like a babysitter. A very cold babysitter. I picture myself from above for a second. What would Sam think if he could see me now? In these clothes? Packing a fake ID?

The thought comes down like a hammer: *He's moving.* And then I remember: *He put his hand on my cheek.* I squeeze my eyes shut, feeling a strange sort of dissonance, these competing facts like clashing cords clomped down on a piano.

Enough, I tell myself. *For now, just put Samuel out of your—*

"Hi there."

I've reached the entrance, where a door guy is waiting on a stool. I swallow hard and thrust the ID out, my arm unnaturally straight. "How we doing tonight?" he asks, grinning in a gray beanie, no jacket on. Just a T-shirt. Like it's not effing freezing out here. He's pretty cute, though, and the voice inside my head says, *Well, aren't you a dashing cold-resistant fella?*

The boy gives me a strange look, and I freeze, mentally rewinding the tape to ensure I didn't somehow say that aloud. "Uh . . . good," I say. "And you?"

For a moment, he frowns. "Sabrina, huh?"

And now I'm crumpling. The ID is clearly fake. But I hold my head up. "Yep. My friends call me—" God, what's a nickname for Sabrina? "Well, they just call me Sabrina."

He chuckles, glancing over to where Hen and Carmen have wandered off. It's messy, but it looks like they're trying for a two-woman conga line. "Sorry about them," I say, already calling it. We should leave before we get in trouble.

"You know what? It's fine," he says, clearing his throat. "All three of you can head in." I stare at him, surprised to have gotten off so easily. "Maybe go easy on the drinks," he adds.

I nod, grateful, and hurry over to round them up. *"Hey!"* I hiss at my disobedient charges. The boy smirks when I turn to steal one last glance. Then he ducks down to check a new ID as Hen and Carmen dance on in.

The club is mostly full, with tables and chairs set up in tight clusters. "There's space toward the front," the hostess whispers, coming over to us. Onstage under a spotlight, a woman is talking into a microphone. "We don't do table service on weeknights, so just grab drinks from the bar."

"Okay, thanks," I say.

She nods to the stage. "Any of you here for the Comithon? It's the first night. Comics can sign up with the bartender."

I shake my head. "Nope, not the people you're looking for."

We find seats, and Carmen makes a drink run before I can stop her, Hen already absorbed by the redhead in the spotlight. I think she said she was a preschool teacher. She's pretty with a kind look about her, full-figured and rosy-cheeked.

"You know what kind of children parents never expect?" asks the woman.

A pause.

"Pervert kids." The audience lets out a burst of laughter, and the woman brightens, a contained, satisfied look on her face. "I think there must be a window where it comes innately to them, like how newborns can swim if you toss them in water. Every day during story time, it's just a sea of three-year-olds humping the carpet. To be clear, they're still very invested in what's happening with the Berenstain Bears. . . ." She gestures to a man up front. "Don't give me that look, sir. Do you know how many Barbie doll sex scenes I've walked in on in my lifetime? One minute, Lucy and Antonio are playing nicely at the toy kitchen. Next thing, I look over and they've got Ken stripped down, tea-bagging Ms. Piggy."

Carmen returns with drinks as another big laugh tears through the room. Hen blinks up at the stage. *"Tea-bagging?"* Carmen grins and whispers in her ear. Hen's face falls. "I'm so glad I like girls," she says, shuddering.

Carmen holds up her glass. "Wanna try it?"

"Fine," I say, taking a quick sip. My throat immediately catches fire. "Holy shit, what is this?"

"Long Island iced tea?" she says with a shrug. Her laugh is an actual *tee-hee* as she nudges Hen. "Speaking of tea . . ."

I sigh. "I'm getting us water."

I'm learning a lot tonight. Like, here's what I've learned about Long Island iced tea: don't drink it. It's not even tea. Just some gross, semilethal agent of destruction. Also confidence.

A few minutes ago, Carmen set down her empty glass and announced she was signing up for an open mic slot. Hen and I looked at each other, stunned, as she weaved her way toward the cute young bartender I got our waters from earlier. The guy nodded as she spoke, writing something on a clipboard. And then, in a leap from A to B I couldn't possibly explain, they started making out across the bar.

They're still going at it now. This has to be a health code violation.

Onstage, the club owner, who introduced herself as Dolores, is bringing up a new comic. I feel a flurry of excitement as he takes the mic. Even the bad sets have been good tonight, in a *please kill me this is awkward* sort of way. It's something about this show of bravery—all these people who don't seem *entirely* ready just . . . going for it anyway.

It's sort of charming how shabby it is in here. Behind the microphone, a faded velvet curtain hangs crooked against a brick wall. The tables are chipped and wobbly, bits of foam exposed on every chair. It's a far cry from the flashy theaters I'm used to seeing my favorite comedians tape their specials in. But those gold-leafed playhouses must be the end result. This place feels like a beginning.

I check on Carmen and the bartender—still going at it. And from the way she's mussing up his hair, you'd think he was a sailor shipping off to sea. I have to hand it to her, though. If she wants something, she goes for it. There's no way, in my shoes, she would have left so much unsaid with Sam today.

I feel another pang at the thought. *What the hell am I going to do?*

Beside me, Hen laughs breathlessly at a joke I missed. I've been distracted, but I heard pieces of the latest comic's opening, all about life as a Black guy in Maine. He seemed to be having fun with this mostly white audience, stoking a bit of discomfort before deftly dispelling it.

Now he's talking about Tinder.

"So after this amazing date, she comes back to my place for a drink and asks to use the bathroom." He paces the stage in his bomber jacket and jeans. "I fix us some cocktails, a few minutes go by. A few *more* minutes . . . After a while, I'm like . . ." He mimes knocking gently. "'Hey . . . you okay?' Finally, I creak open the door, and—" He lets out a shrill scream, lurching back from the imaginary horror. "The girl is gone," he says, dropping his voice low. "She must have snuck out the open window. And . . ." He sighs. "There's a poop." The audience starts to laugh. "Floating in my toilet. I try the handle: nothing. I see my plunger: wet. I check her Tinder profile: *blocked.* And suddenly, it's like I'm the detective cracking the case, the whole sequence of the crime finally coming together. Me and this girl had a *connection.* We could have built a *life* together. But then the bobble thing in my toilet broke and she decided it was easier to just never see me again."

A few older women in front of us are crying from laughter, and I make a mental note that sex and poop remain foolproof comedy gold among all demographics. Meanwhile Hen keeps *literally* slapping her knee. She's still hammered, but it seems once she crosses the weepy drunk threshold, she enters some cartoon dimension, emerging like a cheerful Disney princess talking to all the squirrels.

"All right!" rasps Dolores when she takes the stage again. "Isaiah Lewis, everybody! I knew there was a reason I didn't use that Tindah. Coming up we have a first-timer. Always exciting . . ." She looks down her glasses at the clipboard on her hip. "Let's put our hands together for *Carmen Aquino*!" Henrietta claps excitedly, bugging her eyes at me. I crane to look behind us, but Carmen and the bartender have vanished.

"Where'd she go?" hiccups Hen, right as the hostess from earlier rushes to the side of the stage, hissing, *"Dolores!"* The audience goes quiet as the two women share a hushed conversation, then hurry off together.

"We should go find her," I say, getting to my feet. The audience begins to clap and I frown, looking around at everyone. "Oh. Ha! No, I'm not . . ."

Hen jumps up. "I'll get her," she says, leaving me standing there.

People in the audience are still cheering, nodding and whistling their encouragement. "Look, you're all very nice, but . . ." I can barely hear myself over the noise. "I'm not . . ." I don't like that Carmen's left these people waiting. I feel weirdly responsible for their good time. I weave through tables and step onto the squat stage, tapping the microphone. "Yeah, hi."

I squint away the spotlight. "Sorry for the mix-up. I'm not Carmen Aquino." My voice sounds funny amplified like this. Sharp and fizzy somehow. "I'm . . ."

My eyes adjust, right as the boy who took my ID earlier steps inside.

". . . Sabrina Martin." The name feels strange on my lips, but when I look down at myself—teetering in tall boots, the shiny pants glowing in the light—I have to suppress a laugh. I sure as hell don't feel like Gretchen Wilder.

I scan the room for Carmen again before my gaze falls on the crowd. Everyone looks so eager to listen. It's actually really nice. "Whoa, this is weird," I say, my voice the only sound in the room now.

I take in the silence—a waiting void. It's strangely enticing.

"I mean, I can . . . keep you guys company for a minute, if you want." I hear a *woo!* ring out from somewhere and grin. "Oh, um. Thank you?" The quiet stretches on again and I shake my head. "Sorry. Guess the old . . . cat got my tongue?"

I wince at how cheesy I sound, but then I think of Sam. I tug the mic out from the stand, smirking a little as I walk to the lip of the stage. "So, um . . ." I clear my throat. "Where do you guys think that expression came from? *Cat's got your tongue?*" I'm already picturing it. "Do you think, like, during the Roman Empire, a cat took out his little paws and just—*rrraire!* Grabbed hold of someone's tongue? And then some guy walking by with those leaf thingies in his hair was like, 'Hey, check it out, he can't speak! The cat's got his tongue!' And then everybody else was like, 'Oh whoa, that has a nice ring to it.' And then someone else was like, 'Hey, we should make that a thing.'"

I stop for a gulp of air, abruptly startled by this moment. *What am I doing?*

But I hear a little laughter from the audience, and my body begins to thrum. I shake my head, looking out plainly at everyone. "Anyway, I'm not a historian. But it seems like that's probably what happened."

The crowd quiets down again, and I shrug. "That's a game my friend Sam and I play." Even saying his name out loud like this makes my heart hurt a little. But it also feels . . . good. "***Drunk etymology***, I guess you could call it? Sam's really funny. And smart, and nice. And freaking *hot* now, which for me is sort of terrible . . ." I look up, almost sheepish. "I'm pretty into him, if you all can't tell. Not that any of you need to know this." A few people in the front row look up at me with curiosity, and I bite my lip. "Maybe this is weird, but . . . Do you all mind if I get this out? I'm kind of working through a thing here."

I interpret a few smiles up front as a yes.

"Okay, so . . ." I sigh. "Can I just say, falling for a friend is not as fun or adorable as it is in the movies?" Another small laugh gives me a strange, heady feeling. I'm oddly detached from myself, but also *right freaking here*. "I feel like such a cliché. I seriously keep imagining that I'm trapped inside a rom-com.

Every morning I wake up, like, 'Did it happen? Do I work at a women's magazine in New York now? Has the lonely-at-Christmas montage started?'"

Another happy murmur.

Another head rush.

"Except so far, nothing is quite following the rules. He's my oldest friend, yes. In theory, we could be a total Harry-and-Sally situation. But when I look back, I'm not sure this was always meant to be our story. One day he got, like, annoyingly good-looking. And a little more distant, maybe. And apparently *that* is what's doing it for me now." I laugh, baffled. "Am I the kind of person who likes *unattainable*? Is this a reflection of my own crappy self-esteem?" I pause, looking out again. "Can you guys tell my mom is a women's studies professor?"

"Hey, tha's my cousin!"

I look toward the back, hearing giggling, and wave Carmen over. "Carmen! This is your slot!" She and Hen keep stumbling, their arms around each other. With a shriek, they fall back into the ladies' room, the door swinging behind them.

I hear muttering: "This night is just one disaster after the next. . . ." Dolores hops up on the stage, taking the mic from me and clipping it into the stand. "Sorry I left you on for so long," she whispers, leaning in. "Someone slipped on our walkway, but I don't think they're gonna sue. Fuckin' snow. I swear I never stop shoveling."

She looks at me, and I realize that's my cue. "Well, um . . ."

I start to leave, then double back to lean into the microphone. "Thank you, Portland!"

My blood is hot with adrenaline as I round the corner of the building. I stop to press my back into the cold brick, barely even noticing the snow as I catch my breath. Is this what it feels like to come down off a roller coaster? One summer when we were little, Mom, Aunt Viv, and Gabriela took us all to Palace Playland, an amusement park in Old Orchard Beach. Planted firmly on the ground where I belonged, I watched Sam line up for his first-ever ride. When he found me after, I remember he had this dazed look on his face, like he'd just glimpsed the lifetime of thrills awaiting him. He looked a little woozy, actually, and yet somehow, all he said was "I wanna go again."

I think I get that now.

"Hey, it's you."

I startle and look over. The cute door guy has come out through a side exit, holding a big see-through bag of clanging bottles.

"It's me," I say, with a weird little wave. He grins under the streetlight, and I get a better look at him: the beanie over sandy hair, and muscly build under his T-shirt. When he takes a step closer, I can see that his eyes are blue and curious, and there's a bit of stubble on his face. *Works at a bar equals too old*, I tell myself. But wow.

He dumps the bag and walks back to me. "I, uh . . . liked your set."

I scoff. "*Set* might be too strong a word."

"You definitely had something. It was rough but . . . promising."

"Oh, uh . . . thanks?"

"I'm Jeremy, by the way," he says, a bit of snow catching on his beanie.

"Nice to meet you," I say. "I'm—"

"Sabrina," he interrupts. "I remember. Your friends call you Sabrina?" For half a second I falter, fingers flying to the buns in my hair.

"Oh, *haha*," I say, blushing. But I steady myself, letting the eye contact stretch on. He crosses his arms and leans into the wall next to me, just a smidge closer than necessary. It feels almost like a game of chicken—all the looking at each other—but I don't falter. In fact, I'm smiling. *What in the world?* a little voice says. I think Sabrina might be flirting right now.

"So this Sam guy's really got his hooks in you, huh?" he asks.

"Uh . . ." It dawns on me that I just told a room full of people how I feel about Samuel. And now I'm playing eye chicken with this dude. *What the effing eff is happening with me tonight?* I clear my throat. "Yeah, pretty much."

"Well, love life stuff usually makes for good material," he says. "I'd do more of that next week if I were you."

I frown, confused, right as Dolores pops her head out the side door. "Jer, you're on the set after next." She nods at me. "Also, I'm not one to kick people out of my friendly establishment, but I think your little girlies have had enough."

"Crap," I say. "Sorry. I'll go get them." We follow her through the side entrance and down the narrow hall. "So, wait," I whisper to Jeremy. "You're a comic?"

"I consider myself more a student of the universe," he says. "But for now, comedy is my preferred filter through which to observe."

I laugh but stop short—he's being serious. And maybe I'm imagining it, but I think I catch Dolores roll her eyes as she stops at the opening to the main room. She sighs. "Listen to this guy . . ." I tune in to the set just long enough to deduce that the dude is telling cringey jokes about mail-order brides. The audience is silent. "He's lucky voting doesn't start until next week. This was the trial run while I get organized." Dolores shakes her head, turning back to me. "Look, I'm not taking sides, but I'd like to see another girl really kill it up there. We get more than enough of this . . ." She gestures toward the stage. ". . . charming perspective. And I heard from a couple people that you had some good moments. Just prepare more next time."

I blink at her, then Jeremy. "Okay, I think there's been a misunderstanding."

She frowns. "Did you not know you were entering our Comithon?"

"Your what now?"

"It's a new thing we're trying to attract more people on Wednesdays," says Jeremy. "Our slowest night."

"He says *our* though he has no real affiliation with this place," says Dolores, patting his face. "Just some kid who never seems to leave us alone."

"You're very hurtful," he says before meeting my eyes again. "Anyway, Dolores here thought we'd fill more seats if we turned open mic night into a competition. For six weeks, the group of us who showed up tonight will be the gladiators. And starting next Wednesday, we'll be getting ranked by the bloodthirsty plebes. It's all very degrading."

"Please, you love it. And not for nothing, the winner gets a paid Saturday slot," she says to me. "Which is generous considering how broke we are."

"That might be because you haven't updated your drink prices since the nineties," sighs Jeremy. "As a business student, I can tell you the numbers don't add up."

"I thought you were a student of the universe," I say innocently.

"Huh." Jeremy narrows his eyes. "Sabrina's a little feisty."

"Wait," says Dolores. "I thought your name was—"

"No," I say. "See, I'm not Carmen. She's the one who signed up for the slot. And I'm pretty sure even *she* didn't know this was a formal thing."

"Well, whatever your name is, think about it," says Dolores.

"It's a sweet gig. On top of the regular slot, the three comics with the most votes get a chance to open for Marnie James when she comes here on her tour."

"Seriously?" I say. "I love Marnie James."

"We'll film all three sets on the last night," says Dolores, nodding. "Then I'll send the clips to her, and she can take her pick."

"That's so awesome! She went to my high school," I say, as if that's some kind of accomplishment. Marnie James might not be a *celebrity*-celebrity. But she's definitely a Portland celebrity. My freshman year, everyone was buzzing when she got her first Netflix special. As I watched, I remember thinking she had a no-frills cuteness about her, opting to sit up on a stool for most of her set, in a pair of simple jeans and a T-shirt, her plain white Keds swinging, brown hair messy in a ponytail. The humor was honest, and intimate. When it was over, I had the feeling that I knew her.

"It's like you know her," Jeremy says under his breath, and my eyes snap to his. There's a lot going on in those eyes—blue and excitable, a little devious.

"Exactly," I say.

"Well, by some fuckin' miracle she's agreed to come here," says Dolores, the expletive seeming to extinguish whatever spark just flickered between us. "Please no one tell her what a shithole this place is. I'm pretty sure she only said yes because I grew up with her uncle. Anyway, you almost ready, Jer?"

"Uh, yeah," he says, handing me his phone. I'm surprised to see a new contact on the screen: SABRINA with an upside-down smiley face and a microphone emoji. "Give me your number?"

"Wow, Jer," says Dolores as I search for a response. "That was bold, even for you."

"In case she decides to come back!" he says defensively, a little less smooth as he meets my eyes. I wouldn't say he looks embarrassed, though. His expression is self-aware and silly, with an eyebrow quirk that must do wonders with the ladies.

"What?" he says as I continue to study him. "I can give you some stand-up tips."

"That's actually not a bad idea," says Dolores.

"Oh," I say. "I mean . . . wait, what?" I catch a glimmer of my sister's peachy waves by the main door. She and Carmen aren't so giggly now. They look sort of like sad, lost puppies. Hen spots me and waves, while Carmen stares off into space.

"Shit," says Jeremy. "I should go clear my head in the office for a second before my set." He looks at the phone in my hands. I guess it's now or never.

"Oh, what the hell?" I say, typing in my number. He grins as I give it back to him, and walks off without saying goodbye.

"Nice to meet you, too!" I call after him.

"All right, I gotta put this audience out of their misery," says Dolores. "But maybe I'll see ya." She nods her goodbye, heading for the stage, and I frown as I catch a final glimpse of

Jeremy, disappearing into the back.

"What a weird-ass night," I mutter as I weave through the crowd.

"I think I need to hurl," Hen says matter-of-factly when I reach her.

"I, too, need to hurl," says Carmen beside her.

"No, no," I say. "Just take deep breaths."

Out in the street, I buckle Hen and Carmen into the back seat, brushing off fresh snow before slipping inside the car. "Tonight was exactly what I needed," Hen murmurs as I start up the engine.

"Same," sighs Carmen, her eyelids beginning to lower.

"Yeah," I say, driving off. "Me too."

Within minutes, I hear snores. And blessedly, no one hurls.

FOUR

The Morning After | An uncomfortable period of regret or confusion, often following a one-night stand or some other kind of funny business.

I'm disoriented when I wake up. Too much light in my face. I'm on the futon in Hen's window nook, I remember, as I prop onto my elbows. Down in the yard, the snow has settled, reflective in the clear morning. Hen and Carmen are passed out on the bed, breathing with mouths open, limbs draped every which way.

I frown—the carpet is buzzing—and pick up my phone with a swipe. It's almost noon.

On the group text, Aunt Viv has shared a photo of Uncle Arvin twisting back in an apron, their counter covered in ingredients. My husband requires the whole kitchen to make his famous kare kare. Coming to yours to help prep!

We caved and got party horns for the kids again. Please don't kill us, says my brother William.

Look who's ready! says Mom, below a photo of Nacho, our new maniacally happy Pomeranian, dressed in a sparkly jacket.

My God, he's like a doggy Elton John, says Gabriela, adding heart eyes. P.S. Dessert and drinks didn't feel like enough so I'm also bringing feijoada. It's a stew. Samuel's favorite!

I sit up. Think of Sam's hand on my cheek. That *happened.* And now he's coming here for the party tonight. I imagine us watching each other steadily, the whole room counting down from ten. . . .

More texts pop up on my screen, this time from a number I don't recognize.

Thought about it, and you should definitely do the competition with us.

It's Jeremy, by the way.

Seriously, it'll be fun. You'll be a star.

I blink a moment, more events from last night returning. And then I laugh out loud. *"Shhhhhh!"* hisses Carmen before letting out a groan. Ah yes. The demon tea.

"Sorry," I whisper, getting to my feet. I catch a glimpse of my reflection in the mirror and freeze. I still have traces of the Sabrina makeup around my eyes, my hair a little curly from the buns. "Whoa," I say back to myself. Until this moment, last night felt like a wisp of a dream. The kind you tell a reluctant listener about, like, *I was trying to open a door, only I couldn't because my hands were bananas?*

Except right now, I really *do* have banana hands. Metaphorically, that is.

"What is it, Gretch?" croaks Carmen.

"Nothing," I say reflexively.

I highly doubt she and Hen even remember my odd blip onstage last night. I barely thought of it myself after we left, too concerned with getting them inside unnoticed. I knew they had no chance of pulling off sober if intercepted by my parents. Luckily, Mom and Dad were asleep by the time we tiptoed in, Hen tripping on the stairs and Carmen snort-laughing while I shushed them up to bed.

In the mirror, I glimpse Hen stuffing her head under a pillow, her words coming out muffled: "You did this to us, Carmen. I really hate you."

"Understandable," says Carmen, slinging an elbow over her face.

I smile before my reflection pulls me back, a strange, pleasant warmth spreading over me as I return to thoughts of last night. It still doesn't feel possible. I stood in front of a crowd and talked about Sam. I gave my number to a stranger. I had a freaking *alias*.

"Yoo-hoo! Earth to Gretchen!"

"Hm?" I turn around.

"Coffee run?" Carmen murmurs pitifully. "Please?"

"Sure," I say, snapping out of it.

"You're an angel," she sighs. "Will you get me a pumpkin spice latte? They really are good, and I'm too hungover to care about being basic right now."

"Our true colors are really showing here," says Hen, peeking out from her pillow. "Make that two PSLs, please."

I park my car and step out into the crisp sunny air, relieved to see no sign of Sam. Willard Beach Coffee is right next to Keep Calm Yoga, among the short cluster of businesses along the otherwise residential street. I pause on the sidewalk, squinting past all the hanging plants in the window. I *think* I'm relieved. I'm wearing plaid pajamas under this coat. And I haven't brushed my teeth yet. Still, I have this urge. Like I want something to *happen* already.

I keep getting flashes of that spotlight last night, that fizziness in my limbs when my voice first crackled through the mic. I felt like I'd stumbled into some low-gravity free fall up there, calm and exhilarated at once. In a way, it was effortless. Thoughts in my head turned to words said aloud. Until I felt lighter. Freer. *Braver.*

My breath fogs the window as I laugh, baffled. I think some reckless part of me wants that sensation back. The mere possibility gives me a mildly nauseated rush: Would it be the worst thing if I told Sam the truth tonight? (*Yes*, a small voice says.)

But maybe not. Maybe I could do it—just close my eyes and blurt it all out. Maybe this is the part where I bust out the grand gesture, creepy-John-Cusack style!

I hurry the rest of the block and step into the café, surprised to see Ethan Spears on a laptop by the register, the only person here.

"Gretchen, hey," he says, glancing up as the jangly bell rings above my head.

I put on a smile, definitely regretting the pj's all right. "Oh, uh . . . Hi." I know Ethan from yearbook, but he's also Sam's friend, which is apparently enough to make my cheeks go hot, a strange humming sensation picking up from within. I wonder if Ethan knows about that moment we had last night. Can he tell I feel weird right now? Will this get back to Sam? *For the love of God, be normal, Gretchen!*

Ethan appears oblivious to the inferno inside my head. "What can I do ya for?" he asks like some old-fashioned saloon guy. The dorkiness of it oddly settles me. And suddenly, I laugh.

"Ethan, how many jobs do you have? I thought you quit this place."

He shrugs, clasping his hands behind his grown-out mop—mullet-*ish*. But weirdly not in a bad way. Definitely not full mullet. "They were down a barista, so I'm back on weekend shifts for a while. And I hear photojournalism is a dying field. Better save my pennies." I bob my head at this. Beyond doing photography for yearbook, Ethan is known for picking up odd jobs, mowing lawns in summer and shoveling driveways in winter. Plus, I think he helps out at his parents' hardware store year-round. I still don't really understand how he fits the football team into his schedule. But he's only a kicker. Maybe they don't make you practice as much when all you do is kick.

He's looking at me like it's my turn to speak.

"Oh, um." I nod toward his laptop. "Got anything good for us?"

"Just touching up a headshot. Actor found me on Craigslist." He pauses, as if only now making the connection. "So I guess I'm doing two jobs at once today. But in terms of yearbook . . ." He swings open the counter, waving me toward him as he clicks through files. "I shot some stuff last night that might be cool to include. We all ended up at the football field during the storm. Pilsner and Grody figured out how to get the stadium lights on."

"Is that allowed?" I ask, still hanging back a little.

"Oh, definitely not," he says. "But check these out."

I shuffle over and lean in, spotting Sam immediately, along with a few football guys, plus Natalie Hughes-Watanabe, our yearbook editor, and her friends Sasha and Lexi. The pictures are stunning, everyone tackling each other in scarves and hats and jackets, happy and beautiful, with little white orbs blotting out bits of the frame. It's like something out of a catalog: popular high school kids edition.

"Wow, these are great," I say, pushing through the tight feeling in my chest. In one shot, Jake Pilsner and Dick Grody, aka the broiest of bros, are lifting Sam up in the air, smacking the ass of his wet jeans. It's still weird to me that Samuel is part of this world. But maybe it was inevitable. The child of a yogi, he could always meet any physical challenge, whether that meant teaching himself back handsprings in the yard, crushing it at youth soccer, or leading the sword fight choreography for our sixth-grade production of *Peter Pan*. The Carlton football coach figured this out about him our freshman year, and got him to play a few games while their star wide receiver was recovering from an injury. It wasn't long before Gabriela found out and made Sam quit, convinced he'd wind up brain damaged. But as far as my life went, the damage was done.

Sam's stock went way up at school just by gracing that team.

And I never fully got him back after that.

"You have to see the snowman Grody made," says Ethan, returning me to the moment. "Probably won't make the year-book cut. Since it's, um . . ." He hesitates. "Very anatomically specific."

I move closer to the screen. "Wait. Is that a *vein*?"

Ethan chuckles, scrolling some more. "These were fun, too. . . ." He lands on a shot of Sam and Natalie, making snow angels on their backs. There's a whole series like this. Arms up, then down, then up again. Natalie laughs with her whole body, dark curls getting caught in the corner of her mouth. Sam keeps grinning over at her. In one frame, he reaches out for the fuzzy pom-pom dangling from her hat.

"Kinda cute, huh?" says Ethan.

"Oh." I glance up at him. "I didn't . . . Do you . . . ? I mean, you don't think they're . . . ?"

"Oh, I don't know," says Ethan, eyeing me strangely. "She's been hanging out with us a lot. But I haven't heard anything. Why, have you?"

"No," I say immediately, the photo drawing me in again. "At least, I don't think so. . . ." I've always liked Natalie. As editor, she toes the line between friendly and commanding, and she has this way of shrugging off stuff that might go to a lesser person's head—like her early acceptance to Columbia, or the fact that she rarely walks into a room unnoticed. With her expertly put-together outfits, flawless brown skin, and warm, infectious smile, she's undeniably gorgeous. But feminism was the closest thing I had to religion growing up, so while I'm sure it defies some long-ingrained cavewoman instinct, I've always tried not to hold that against her.

"Gretchen?" Ethan ducks down to catch my gaze.

"Sorry." I shake it off. "I think I'm really tired."

"Of course," he says, his face falling. "You came for caffeine and I've been keeping you here."

"Oh please," I say quickly, "it's fine."

"It's been nice to have a customer," he says, sighing at the empty place as I scan the rows of coffee options written out in chalk. "I think I got screwed with these later shifts. Seems like most of our regulars have had their second coffee by like seven a.m. Tips aren't doing much for the photojournalism fund."

"Well, I've got a Washington with your name on it," I say like a total dad. He chuckles, closing the counter, and I tilt my head. "Ethan, what are your thoughts on pumpkin spice lattes?"

"I think they're fucking awesome," he says without hesitation.

I laugh. "Okay, give me three of those."

The house feels more awake now as I step inside with my tray of wafting spices. I start to slip off my coat, but keep it on, silently cursing Dad, aka the Vladimir Putin of thermostats.

I find Hen and Carmen taking feeble bites of toast along the bench seat in the kitchen window. Across the room, Mom and Aunt Viv crowd over a cookbook in matching reading glasses, the countertops covered in diced onions and carrots, herbs and resting pastry dough. It's entirely possible they've been too preoccupied to notice their daughters are mere shells of themselves. Or maybe they're playing dumb as a kindness.

"Morning, Gretch," Aunt Viv says vaguely. She drops a cutting board into the sink, making Hen and Carmen flinch in unison.

"Morning," I say, very quietly.

I pull out cups from their cardboard slots. "Bless you," whispers Hen, taking hers with a shudder. Carmen nods vigorously, downing a big sip with instant relief.

"Ack!" I jump, something wet along my sock line. Despite all my winter-loathing layers, Nacho always manages to find some bare skin to lick. He quivers at my feet, all tiny legs and electrocuted fur, staring up at me with the eyes of someone who just tried meth for the first time and is quite pleased with the decision.

"Nacho, do you love Gretchen?" Mom calls, her voice going full Muppet. "Are you the best little brother in the world?" Let the record show, my mom is a newly tenured professor, published widely in feminist journals. But something happens to her brain around this dog. "Oh, that reminds me," she says, human again. "I picked up the cutest rain jacket yesterday."

"For Nacho," I say. "Tell me you didn't get the little shoes."

"In three colors," she sighs. "I took him with me to my office earlier, and got a few cute pictures." She shows me on her phone—Nacho in fire-engine red, prancing in the snow between collegiate buildings. "So pretty in winter. That'll be you frolicking in that quad in a couple years."

"Uh-huh," I say, remembering to smile.

Dad pops up from the basement then, wearing a big puffy vest and fur-flapped hat, a perfectly reasonable alternative to indoor heating. He goes to the fridge and sets out a massive hunk of meat wrapped in butcher paper. "Let this sit out at room temp for a while." He gives Mom a kiss on the cheek. "Then I'll come back and work my meat magic."

"Mmm," she says happily. "You are very good with meat." I

grimace as Dad walks off. I don't exactly know what that could be innuendo for, but I still don't like it.

I scoot in next to Carmen, who's had her eyes locked on a screen since I got here. I bump her side. "Whatcha doin'?"

"Deleting old Instagram posts."

"Carmen is being hypocritical," says Hen primly. "She literally confiscated my phone earlier for looking at too many old Lizzy posts."

"Because you were being a masochist," says Carmen. "This is different. I am Marie Kondo–ing my past." She passes me her phone with a photo up: a selfie of her and Sabrina on Halloween. My heart flutters a little when I notice Sam and me in the background. We met them at a haunted house that night, both of us dressed as Dwight Schrute from *The Office*—double Dwights. We got the idea over the summer, long before my crush set in. So as much as I might have liked the opportunity to dazzle him, I was stuck wearing a mustard-colored button-down and tie while most of the girls we passed were dressed as some kind of professional with the word *slutty* tacked on to the beginning.

Still, it was nice to feel like us, out together, away from school. With Sabrina and Carmen close behind, we screamed and laughed every time a zombie jumped out at us. Later, the four of us went out for milkshakes. It was fun. That is, until Sabrina suggested we stop by a college party she'd been invited to. Of course, Sam lit up the moment we walked in. It took all of five seconds before he'd struck up a conversation with a sexy cardiologist, or veterinarian, and suddenly Sabrina was grabbing Carmen by the hand to greet a friend of theirs. In a blink, I was alone, feeling radioactive in a swirl of people. I found myself pushing through the crowd, telling myself I was an actress, in the role of Girl Looking for the Bathroom. But then I felt Sam's hand on my shoulder, our best-friend ESP to the rescue, and all I wanted was to grab him by the pocket protector and kiss him.

"Gretchen," says Carmen.

"Hm?" I realize I'm still clutching her phone. Carmen looks adorable as a black cat in this picture, her arm slung around Sabrina in a witch's hat, both of them mid-laugh. It's actually kind of sad.

Carmen sighs, taking back her phone. "More like Sabrina the teenage *bitch*."

"Carmen!" says Aunt Viv, glancing up from her recipe. "We don't talk about other women that way."

Mom tilts her head as she picks a sprig of rosemary. "Is it weird I almost prefer *cunt* to *bitch*?"

Henrietta chokes on her latte. "Mom!"

"What? I'm just saying. At least when people throw the word *cunt* around they feel some pressure to justify it. *Bitch* gets used for everything. If you're serious about your job, or don't feel like being hit on. Or God forbid you have the slightest bit of confidence."

"Fine, Aunt Lulu," says Carmen. "Sabrina the teenage cunt. Better?"

Mom frowns. "I think so."

A shiver runs through me and I roll my eyes. "Okay, did someone forget to tell me we moved to Soviet Russia?"

Mom shoots me a sympathetic pout, looking after Dad to make sure he's really gone. She tiptoes across the room and raises the temperature with a wink.

Thank you, I mouth.

"Do I detect the patriarchy at work?" I say to the TV—half serious, half making fun of our moms. "Ah yes. Another tale of women shitting all over each other."

"Shhhh," says Carmen through a chuckle, still very much hungover.

I sigh and lean back as Kate Hudson and Anne Hathaway continue to sabotage one another, all for a chance at the perfect rich-girl wedding. Tradition has prevailed this afternoon—almost. We're eating marshmallows straight from the bag, our movie night pushed to movie day.

"Also, I see you painting girls as histrionic, Hollywood," I add on, unable to help myself. "And I'm *extremely upset about it*!"

This time the "Shhhh" comes from Hen, who is apparently most comfortable while draped around the arm of the couch like a limp towel. Carmen yawns on my other side, her legs outstretched across both our laps. It's dark out but still early, a couple hours left to go before the party. I've been content enough to put Sam out of my head for long stretches, only occasionally checking the time. When I look now, I have two new texts.

This guy again.

Are you ghosting me?

That's cold, Sabrina.

It's strange to see that name on my screen as I sit here in the living room. I know there's no point in replying. I can't go back to the club. And even if I weren't working up the nerve to bare my soul to another guy tonight, Jeremy is too old for me. And thinks I'm someone else.

Still, it seems my alias can't help herself.

A little waiting is good for you, I type out quickly. That will throw him off his game. And then, because why the hell not, I add a winky face.

"So *Bride Wars* was not a feminist rallying cry," says Carmen when it ends.

"But the wedding dresses were pretty," says Hen. We all nod.

"What next?" asks Carmen, yawning. "*Never Been Kissed*?"

"See, I don't know about that one," I say. "Wouldn't Drew Barrymore have been kissed?"

Hen purses her lips impatiently. "What about *10 Things I Hate About You*?"

"Sorry," I say. "I *just* rewatched it. God, I love that one."

My sister sighs. "When Heath Ledger sings 'Can't Take My Eyes Off of You' . . ."

"It's, like, the best winning-someone-back scene in a movie," says Carmen. "Maybe ever."

"When I was little, I definitely assumed that was a normal high school rite of passage," I say wistfully. "Someone super attractive just . . . casually enlisting a marching band to publicly sing to you."

Carmen lets out a long breath. "Is it so much to ask?"

In the end, we settle on *When Harry Met Sally*, and this time, I don't yell at the screen at all. It's a testament to Nora Ephron, I guess. Her films are, like, the *fine wine* of rom-coms. And sometimes, you really do want to watch two friends fall in love.

People trickle into the house as we near the end. Uncle Arvin waves wordlessly, my brother and his wife and kids passing by like a torrent. But we stay focused on Billy Crystal, running through New York while Meg Ryan waits in her ball gown.

It occurs to me that this movie must be *directly responsible* for every New Year's Eve that's ever felt lackluster. Who are these people going to galas every year? And how does one gain entry to such an event?

"Happy New Year!" I hear from the hall. It's Gabriela, chit-chatting with Mom and Aunt Viv. I hear Sam's voice next as he greets everyone. I sit up, hitting pause.

"Hey," says Sam, stepping into the living room. His lips form a tight smile, eyes finding mine only briefly. I didn't quite catch the expression. Was that a bashful smile? A *pity* smile?

"Hey," I say back, searching for more words as his phone begins to buzz.

"Well, I'll let you guys finish your movie," he says, typing something out. And with that, he drifts off to the kitchen.

From my seat, I watch a mishmash of potluck-style dishes flow down the long table, chairs scraping, napkins unfurling, all while Mom, Aunt Viv, and Gabriela guide and hover like air traffic controllers. Beside my brother, William, and his wife, Zarin, my twin niece and nephew blow on party horns, flailing against the constraints of their highchairs. Nacho's paws scratch the floor as he yips and whines for scraps. It all somehow fades to a hum.

Sam and I haven't talked yet, which can't be a coincidence. When the credits finally rolled, I found him still tapping on his phone at the far end of the crowded kitchen. Then dinner was announced.

When I look up, he's pulling out the chair directly across from me, right by Gabriela, who's now busy passing down cocktails. I fix my gaze on my food, which I realize a second too late was the wrong move.

Because now I have an eye contact problem: super weird to make it, and just as weird not to. The food staring feels especially noticeable with Hen and Carmen drooped on either side of me, Hen stubbornly removing all the peas from Mom's chicken potpie, while Carmen eats Uncle Arvin's oxtail and rice one tiny bite at a time.

Finally, I let myself look at Sam, my body melting with relief. He's smiling as he fills his plate, clearly delighted by the insane conversations already zigzagging around us. We have a term for this Wilder house phenomenon: *The Symphony.*

Zarin: "Could you wipe Mina's face?"

William: "She's a toddler eating spaghetti. She's just going to get sticky again."

Dad: "You should have fed them my pork roast. I don't understand why kids need separate meals these days."

Zarin: "Gus isn't sticky."

William: "Gus doesn't have sauce."

Mom: "William never liked sauce."

Gabriela: "Samuel either. Is it a boy thing?"

Uncle Arvin: "I liked sauce."

I feel a jolt as Sam looks at me, his grin widening. His eyes seem to say, *I know just what you're thinking now, friend from forever.*

And I think, *Almost.*

Dad: "Meals weren't kid-friendly when I was growing up. And it was all from a can!"

Aunt Viv: "Carmen liked pesto. Isn't that right, Car?"

Carmen: "This can't possibly be interesting to you, Mom."

Dad: "Beef stew from a can . . . cream of mushroom from a can . . ."

Sam and I break at the exact same moment, snorting loudly. "What?" says Dad. "We ate every gross bite!" We snort again, dissolving into laughter, and it's clear we won't be able to stop if we keep looking at each other.

"Yes, yes. And you walked to school uphill both ways," says Mom, patting Dad's hand. "You're driving away the children, Harold." She looks over at Henrietta, suddenly worried. "Hey, you okay, Henny-bee?"

"Just tired still," Hen mumbles into her food.

Carmen sighs. "I need more water."

"Me too," says Hen, following her out to the kitchen.

Gabriela leans into Mom as they walk off, her eyes trailing my sister. "When does she go back?"

"Couple days." Mom sighs wistfully. "Can't say I care much for this whole empty-nester thing."

"Right here, Mom," I say, making Dad choke-laugh on his beer.

Mom pauses, chuckling in her spacy way at her own gaffe, as Gabriela reaches out to comb a hand through Sam's hair. "I'm next."

Sam bobs his head slowly as the table grows quiet, before my niece and nephew rescue us with another concerto of party horns. A few years ago, Sam's dad would have been here at the table, telling adventure stories from his youth or discussing the hoppiness of Dad's latest home-brewed beer.

Sam wolfs down the rest of his food and turns to Gabriela. "Mamãe, I should get going."

She gives him a disbelieving look. "Samuel. You've been here barely an hour."

"And we need you for Pictionary," says Mom.

"My buddy Grody is having a few friends over," Sam says politely—*too* politely. Like he's handling her, which weirdly stings. Sam is never phony with my mom.

Gabriela frowns warningly, and his expression shifts from cool to pleading. "Please? Everyone's going to be there."

"Fine," she sighs, before her eyes flit over to me.

Sam clears his throat. "Walk me out, Gretch?"

"Um." My voice fails me a second. "Uh-huh."

In the foyer, I lean into the wall, watching as he slides into his nice wool coat. "Listen," he says. "I would have invited you to come along, but I knew you wouldn't want to."

I shrug, keeping my voice low. "I take it *a few friends over* is code for *massive keg party full of idiots*?"

"I mean, I wouldn't put it that way."

"So that's a yes," I say. "And you're right. I'd rather give Nacho his rectal medication."

Sam frowns, which annoys me. Normally that would have made him laugh. "What's up with you?"

"Nothing. Just . . . you usually stay on New Year's."

"Well, this year I'm going to a party," he says, wrapping his neck up in his stupid preppy scarf. It's a truly infuriating scarf. "I'm making the most of the time I have left."

"Clearly," I say, fighting off the sudden burning behind my eyes. I don't understand what's happening right now. A few hours ago, I was contemplating romantic gestures of John Cusack proportions. Now I'm picking a fight?

A car pulls up outside. "Well, that's me," he says after an odd little pause.

It's freezing out, but I stand in the open doorway as he trudges through the snow. Natalie peers out from the driver's side of her Mini Cooper, the car light on, and gives me a big, friendly wave. I can see Ethan and Jake Pilsner squished in the back seat. "Happy New Year, Gretchen!" Ethan calls across the yard, cracking his window.

"You too," I say, a rough shiver coursing through me.

I squint as Pilsner stirs, his head quite possibly resting on Ethan's shoulder. "He's trying to nap," Ethan explains. "Saving his strength for tonight."

"Ah," I say. I don't think I've ever said two words to Pilsner. Or his counterpart, Grody. They've always reminded me of the clumsy bad guys in movies, the ones always screwing up the crimes.

Sam slides into the passenger seat, saying something to Natalie before smiling easily at her response. The sight makes me ache, senses tingling with alarm. Maybe there's something to that—to *them*.

"Sure you don't want to come with us?" says Ethan.

"I'm sure," I say, hoping my expression reads Not At All Devastated.

Natalie cracks Sam's window, leaning over him. "We'll see you next year, Gretchen!"

"Yep!" I call out as the windows close back up again.

Sam holds my gaze as the car pulls away. And this time, I have no idea what his eyes are saying.

It's two a.m. and I'm still up. Also, this is happening:

What's it going to take to get you back at the club, Sabrina?

Why do you care, JEREMY? I reply, mocking the way he insists on referring to me by name. (Okay, not *my* name, but you know. Details.) Also, it's NYE. Shouldn't you be out doing something cool instead of texting some random girl?

You're not random. And to answer your question, I thought you had something. A spark, you know? Plus, Dolores told me to work on you. She wants more girls for the competition.

Well that's a little reductive.

It's not. Sometimes you have to be heavy-handed to level out the scales. Guys always think they're funny. (Though I really am.) Sometimes you ladies need a nudge.

Hmmm, I say. Thank you? Anyway, I can't.

Why not?

That's where I leave it, the *Why not?* just sitting there.

I put the phone on the charger and pad down the hall.

Carmen went home with her parents about five seconds after the ball dropped on TV. Meanwhile Henrietta was already zonked out in her room before we even counted down from ten.

I wash my face and brush my teeth, a slow dread seeping in. Soon, Hen will be a state away again, and Carmen will be nearby but busy with another grueling semester of architecture school. And I'll be stuck going back to Carlton High, hiding away in shadowy pockets of awkward-girl obscurity, even in the presence of my oldest friend—*especially* in his presence.

I spit, annoyed all of a sudden. I know it's normal to feel weird around a crush. But should I feel *this* weird? It's hard to tell: Is Sam being cruel or oblivious? It's not like him to be either.

Back in my room, I tidy up, lingering on mementos here and there. This space hasn't changed much since middle school, the edges of my mirror lined with yellowing movie stubs, old photos, and postcards from Sam in São Paulo, or Carmen in Manila. I've even kept my dorky old Justin Bieber poster—pre–neck tattoo, the Selena Gomez era. It was a simpler time.

My eyes land on the floor by my closet, where I dumped Sabrina's high-heeled booties after carrying them inside last night. The black outfit is crumpled up beside them, red frames resting on the heap. I guess Carmen wasn't overly concerned with returning them to their owner.

I reach for the glasses, putting them on as I walk over to the mirror. I still can't believe I went out like this.

I pick up a hairbrush from my dresser and hold it to my lips. "You know how people either love cilantro or hate cilantro? I just feel okay about cilantro. Is that something I should be worried about?" I laugh under my breath. "Stupid . . ."

Nacho yips in the doorway and I jump.

"Jesus!" He stares, that tiny face locked in a permanent smile. "You liked that, huh? Little herb humor?" His tail vibrates.

"Okay. Well . . ." I think. Jokes. What even *are* jokes? "Uhhh . . . okay. What's the deal with calling it *the birds and the bees*? Like, did a bird bang a bee or . . . ?" Nacho tilts his head. "Yeah, that wasn't very good." I sigh down at him. "Bet I could write a set about you, huh, little buddy? Talk about how you've usurped me as the baby of the family?" He holds his chin out and I crouch down and give it a scratch. "Did you usurp me, Nacho?" I say in Mom's absurd Muppet voice. "You *did*! Yes, you *did*!"

I sit all the way down, letting Nacho help himself to my lap. "But hey, that's life, right?" I meet his beady eyes and shrug. "Nothing stays the same forever."

FIVE

Shy Overalls Girl | Female high school student, invisible to her peers due to an affinity for overalls. Is actually a supermodel.

I step into the hall after third period, immediately bumped by some kid's huge backpack as he swivels around cluelessly. I inhale, then let it go. Carlton High is never as bad as I think it will be after these long periods of dread. But it's hardly a joy, either.

"Gretchen," calls Annika when I reach her locker. "What a relief. Yours is the least idiotic face I've seen all day."

"Aw. That's nice." I pull up the recording app on my phone. "Hey, before I forget. Can I get a quote from you on your time at wind ensemble this year? Somehow working for the year-book has turned into me having to *talk* to people. It's awful."

"Sure," she says, swapping out folders before locking up. "The experience has been . . ." She sighs as we walk. "Like dragging multiple boulders up a hill all by myself. No one around here understands the concept of practice. The pursuit of excellence doesn't end just because you got accepted early to Middlebury, *Darren*."

I stop recording. "Okay, great."

"Really?" says Annika.

"No, not really. You think we're going to print that for all of posterity? You shitting on Darren and his early onset senioritis?"

She laughs as we find our table in the cafeteria, piling our backpacks, her oboe, and miscellaneous schoolwork onto the free half, blockading ourselves in. I don't think anyone's ever tried to sit with us before, but it's best not to chance it.

Annika rolls up the sleeves of her vintage windbreaker, thematically at odds with today's bushy tulle skirt, not to mention the vaguely *Game of Thrones*–ish braided half updo she's got going on. The girl defies categorization, and it always somehow works, bright colors screaming against her freckled pale skin. She looks abruptly disturbed as she pulls a tray of grocery store sushi from a paper bag. "There's this one section of my audition piece that keeps tripping me up. . . ." She eyes her music folder. "Do you mind?"

"Course not," I mumble through a bite of PB&J.

Within seconds, she's lost in the music, loosely conducting with her wooden chopsticks between pinching at avocado rolls, white-blond hair grazing the table. An outgoing senior, Annika

Baumgartner is hell-bent on getting into Juilliard next year. Most days, you can find her practicing her oboe or daydreaming about the type of life in the fast lane only a professional oboist can expect. I sort of envy her single-mindedness. She knows exactly what she's meant to do with her time on earth.

Anyway, I like our quiet lunches. They give my mind time to wander, with another human sitting right beside me, thereby validating my existence. Looking around the caf, I check on my favorite characters—like Deborah from math team, who somehow managed to convince the school that her pet iguana, Pete, is a service animal. Pete is a real hit among the Mathletes, from what I can tell, and eats a lot of tater tots. There's also Mr. Radcliff, the young biology teacher who always take his lunches out here. It's both cringey and sweet how hard he tries to connect with students. In fact—I squint—did he just *dab* at someone?

I look beyond him, and my breath hitches.

Sam has walked in with a tray, his gaze fixed on the boisterous table waiting for him across the room. I can hear his laugh over the din of chatter when someone calls out an unintelligible inside joke. It doesn't sound like Sam's real laugh—the one he saves for me. I wonder how many people around school even know we're still friends.

You'd never guess from moments like this one.

Sam turns back abruptly, his gaze finding mine. Shit. Was I staring? I cross my eyes and stick out my tongue: a sign of how very okay I am, despite our weird tiff at my house the other night. He nods, warm eyes softening—a silent *It's all good.*

Before I can think, I reach for my phone and text him. Hang soon?

I watch him check it, hesitate, then type back: Little busy this week. My heart sinks. But then the three little dots appear on my screen. Actually how about Wednesday dinner?

I look up, nodding yes across the caf. I'm heady with relief and giddiness as he returns my smile. Sam wants to get dinner. Dinner is good!

With a sigh, I glance back at Annika, only to do a double take. *"Wasabi!"* I blurt out. She freezes, staring down at the chopsticks holding nothing but green goo.

"Whoa, good save," she says. "How long was I under?"

"Maybe five minutes?" I laugh. She was about two seconds away from popping that whole thing in her mouth.

"This audition may actually kill me, Gretchen."

"You have been especially intense," I say, "even for you."

"My dad has agreed to extend my practice window to midnight. On the condition I go out to eat with him once a week. He says he's started to forget my face."

"Aw. I can't tell if that's sad or cute."

"I can't wait to get to New York," she says. "What do you say? Apply to schools near there next year and then come watch all my super-sweet oboe gigs?"

I smile through a prick of sadness at the thought. "Actually,

I'll be stuck here for college. I shouldn't complain. It's free with my mom's job, so it's kind of a no-brainer."

Annika looks confused. "But isn't your sister at Dartmouth?"

"Well, my mom wasn't tenured at her job when she got in, so it would have been cheaper but still not free. Also, I think my sister was more of a worthwhile investment. Since she has one of those *Good Will Hunting*, 'This Wall of Gibberish Just Spoke to Me' brains. There was no way my parents were going to deny her the Ivy League. My big brother was the same story. Not as brilliant as Hen, but he checked all the right boxes. I'm more . . ." I shrug. "Average, I guess."

She frowns. "I wouldn't say that. But hey, free is good." She picks at her ginger, then pushes the tray aside. "Anyway, tell me about your winter break."

I open my mouth, images splicing together. I see Sam's hand on my cheek in the studio. A stage. Bright lights, and demon tea. I see Ethan's photos with the snow angels. Jeremy's last text. And that black bundle of clothes still heaped on my bedroom floor. "Well?" she says. "Anything interesting happen?"

I laugh. "Nah, not really."

By the time the last bell rings, I'm so done, so itchy to leave this place, that I'm bordering on slaphappy.

"I'm just saying, superlatives are so *tired*," I whine to Mr. Owens inside yearbook headquarters. Our adviser often bears the brunt of my obnoxiousness while I'm at school. I'm weirdly less reserved around teachers than I am other students, and I guess all this energy has to go *somewhere.* "At the very least, we could be having more fun with them. What about, like, 'Most likely to one day own a weird amount of cats'? Or 'Most likely to get super rich but still only shop at Marshall's'?"

"'Most likely to become a taxidermist?'" Ethan offers from the doorway.

I startle. "Oh, uh . . ." I turn his way as he drops his stuff on a beanbag chair and starts unzipping his camera bag. "Yeah, see? Ethan gets it. Or what about . . . 'Most likely to be part of a throuple'? 'Most likely to start a cult.' 'Most likely to commit a white-collar crime'!"

Seemingly unamused, Mr. O loosens the tie under his sweater vest. I think of him as a Cool Dork—maybe something for me to strive for in adulthood. "Thank you for that compelling input," he says in his usual deadpan. "But this is Natalie's vision. She's the editor."

"Hey, don't blame me," says Natalie, appearing inside the room. It never stops striking me how annoyingly pretty she is, all eyelashes and shiny curls. *Cavewoman instincts, deactivate!* "Personally, I'd love to see those in print." She frowns, setting her bag on our big communal table. "But the school would probably get sued if we called a student a future cult leader, right?"

"Oh, big-time," says Mr. O.

I puff my cheeks, a bit petulant, and she laughs. "Hey, any progress on collecting those club quotes, Gretchen?"

"Uh . . . getting there," I say quickly, and by that I mean I have a single, unusable quote from Annika. This assignment has really thrown me for a loop. I didn't exactly get into yearbook for the community engagement—or for any reason, really, other than the fact that every kid here is required to do at least one club. For the record, I am cognizant of the irony in documenting all the cool stuff I *don't* do at this school for my only extracurricular. But at least in the past, I worked strictly on layout. This year, we've shrunk to a team of three: one editor, one photographer, and one everything-else person, who is me.

"Okay, well." Natalie regards me strangely for a moment, then goes to study one of her many to-do lists on the dry-erase board. "Just . . . when you get a chance."

I bob my head, happy to make this future-Gretchen's problem. So far, whenever I've started to approach someone in the halls with my recording app open, I've frozen up, hit with the sudden urge to *run*. I think maybe my fight-or-flight instincts just weren't installed correctly—like the task of talking to fellow teenagers is my version of being hunted in the savanna.

I glance back at Mr. O as he exhales. "Was that the end of today's opening statements, Gretchen?"

"Yes," I say, very serious. "Well, almost. In conclusion, let us usher in a new dawn. Really revolutionize what a yearbook can be, you know?"

Mr. O's nostrils twitch. I think he secretly enjoys all the shit I give him. "Actually, that segues nicely into our next order of business." He waves Natalie and Ethan over, and after a moment, we're all standing around him, circled up. "Principal Young has a request for us this issue. She's extending our budget to include a whole bonus section on the history of Carlton High, in celebration of its one hundredth anniversary."

"History," I say flatly. "That's, like, the exact opposite of all the fun, hilarious stuff I was just saying." Ethan chuckles and Natalie holds back a smile.

"I have a list here of notable alumni that you can work off of for inspiration," Mr. O says, moving right along as he reaches back for a stack of papers on the table. "Maybe you can choose a few you'd like to highlight." He hands us each a stapled copy, names and accomplishments listed by year. I guess only men were notable until around the class of 1946. History can be a real bummer sometimes.

"Poet, physicist . . ." I leaf through the printout. "You've got to be kidding me. Former chairman of L.L.Bean?"

"Hey, that's pretty big-time," says Ethan. "Have some Maine pride."

"Oooh," says Natalie. "This guy invented that little plastic circle you pull out when you open milk."

"You know what? I take it back," I say. "This is going to be riveting."

"Huh," says Ethan, coming closer to the page. "Highly decorated president of the Republic of Lithuania. Are we sure about this one?"

We meet eyes and laugh.

"Oooh! Marnie James," says Natalie.

I get a tiny thrill at the name, feeling the warmth of that spotlight again. I've been having these moments a lot today. Right before I remember Jeremy's *Why not?* text still sitting on my phone. I didn't respond in the end, maybe because there were too many answers.

I'm *not* Sabrina Martin.

I'm *not* twenty-one.

And even if you put those pesky details aside, I'm still *not* some big, charismatic performer type. I might have my silly moments in the right company, but in no universe will you ever hear people say, "You know. Gretchen. The funny girl."

"Okay," I sigh, snapping out of it. "So what now?"

"Now I go home," says Mr. O, tossing a set of keys to Natalie. "But Julie from the library very graciously lent us this cart of yearbooks." He gestures to the ancient wheelie thing near the doorway. "This literally contains a hundred years of history, so please don't forget to lock up."

When he goes, the three of us stand over the library cart.

"Well, we're obviously including Marnie, right?" says Natalie, eyes darting between Ethan and me. "Yes, right? Say yes."

"Definitely yes," I say, grinning at her. "I freaking love Marnie James."

"Oh my God, *same*," she says reverently.

"You know, I've never actually seen her stuff," says Ethan.

"Really?" says Natalie, pulling out her phone and typing something. She waves us over and soon, we're all huddled around the screen, where Marnie James paces the stage in her white Keds, jeans, and a T-shirt. Her first special.

"It was a big change, coming from Maine to New York. The sheer number of people you come across on any given day was a shock. Sure, in Maine you might pass another person while you're snowshoeing to the gym." She grins. "Just kidding. People in Maine don't go to the gym."

"Hehe, Maine joke," says Ethan, looking up at me.

"The catcalling here is a little out of control," Marnie goes on when the rumble of the crowd dies. "Though I guess that's not so much a New York problem as it is a man problem." She laughs. "You ever notice the kinds of words men use to describe having sex with women?"

I smile, remembering this bit now. Marnie drops her voice low and gives a masculine tick of the jaw: "'Hey, man. You pound that pussy last night?' 'Oh big time,'" she says, being the other guy. "'Fuckin' shredded it, bruh.'" I can feel Natalie biting back her reaction alongside me as Marnie levels the audience with a look. "Can you imagine if women talked that way about guys?" She leans forward, flopping her wrist like it's time to gossip. "'Hey, girl. You break that dick last night?' 'Oh you know I did,'" she says, being the friend. "'I snapped that dick in *half*.'"

Natalie and I burst out laughing, right as Ethan says, "Um,

ow." The camera cuts to a close-up, and you can tell Marnie is enjoying the mixed reactions to her joke.

Ethan shudders again.

"I guess we shouldn't get sucked in," says Natalie, hitting pause.

"You're right," I say, though I could happily stand here and watch the whole thing. "Ethan, this is your homework. Watch her stuff and tell us what you think. She's actually rarely this crude. I'm pretty sure that's her only joke that'll make your junk hurt."

I freeze, feeling my cheeks go hot. Did I really just mention Ethan's *junk* to him? But he laughs. "She's actually coming to Portland soon," I go on, recovering quickly. "As part of her new tour."

"Very cool," he says. "Are you some kind of comedy buff?"

"Oh, I don't know," I say, shrugging.

Natalie gives me a brief, skeptical look and goes back to reading Mr. O's printout. "Sam says you are. He also told me your Dwight Schrute impression is excellent."

"False," I say immediately. "I do an *okay* Dwight Schrute impression." I hear her on a delay. "Wait. Sam was talking about me?"

"Well, *yeah* . . ." says Natalie, as if I should know what she's implying. It's so awkward when people do this—just assume you'll know exactly how to fill in their very obscure blanks. I try to summon the powers of deduction.

Sam has talked to Natalie about me.

Ergo, Sam and Natalie have been having "talks." *(Booo.)*

But also ergo, the subject matter has been me. *(Yaasss!)*

"I wonder if I'll ever be notable," says Ethan with an unbothered shrug.

"Your odds are better than mine," I tell him, snapping out of it.

Natalie rolls her eyes. "What are we even saying with lists like this? That most human beings aren't . . . *of note*? That doesn't seem right." She frowns down at the cart. "Anyway, I'll look for that milk carton guy."

"I'll take L.L.Bean," says Ethan.

"And I've got Marnie," I say, already crouching down to find her year. I flip to the *J*s, and there she is: teenage Marnie James.

She looks so . . . regular. A ponytail and ill-fitting sweater. The slightest hint of an acne scar on her chin.

I have to read the quote under her picture twice. Then I laugh.

"Who was she again?"—most of you. Just kidding, it's fine. I don't mind being the girl least likely.

"Huh," I say.

"What?" says Ethan, coming over to look.

"Nothing." I peer down at her little smirk. "Just . . . not what I expected."

SIX

The Big Night | The one that everything changes. And so begins the heart-stopping, head-spinning, whimsical adventure.

When I pull into the Hanoi House parking lot, I see no sign of Sam's car. I sigh. "Way to be the early dork, Gretchen."

I lock up, bristling in the cold, and tell myself it doesn't matter. *He* asked *me* here. To *dinner,* which is not a thing we do. The restaurant itself is nothing new. Sam's parents used to bring us here when we were little, until we got old enough to come ourselves with bikes, and later cars. But we came for lunch. Always lunch.

The moment I step inside, I take in the happy smells, struck by how romantic it is in here at night—all dim and cozy, with frosty windows and string lanterns everywhere. It's funny that such a familiar place can give you such a different feeling in the right light. I half wonder if Sam intended this to be some kind of metaphor.

Or maybe he was just craving Vietnamese.

"Oh, hey, we've missed you!" says Linh, the owner, warmly. "Come. Your favorite table is open." She leads me to a booth in the window and I slide in, stomach doing somersaults as she pours two waters and leaves.

I watch the time on my phone. Two minutes, three. Finally, I grow too restless, and slip in earbuds to resume Marnie James's first special—the one Ethan, Natalie, and I started the other day. I've been watching it in pieces, in moments of angsty downtime.

"It seems like men keep having kids later in life these days," she says in my ear. "In New York, they've taken it to a whole new level. Now, when I'm walking down the street, I like to play this game I call: Dad, or Grandpa?"

I smile as the audience murmurs their approval. "I'll spot a dude coming toward me in his Babybjörn. He looks young from far away, trim in his little hoodie and cool sneakers. But as I get closer, I'll realize it's basically Clint Eastwood dressed as a tech bro." She bugs her eyes out, as if startled. "Oh God. Grandpa. Grandpa! Then I get a little closer and—gah!" She squints beyond the camera, tilting her head. "*Great*-grandpa?"

I laugh, feeling myself relax against the booth. It's still weird to me that Marnie James is a real person. She walked the same high school halls that I did, apparently with similarly little fanfare. And here she is in my palm—larger than life now. In a couple months, she'll be headlining at the Chuckle Parlor, and every comic in the place will be kissing her Keds-adorned feet.

It hasn't escaped me that it's Wednesday, as in the next night of the competition. I feel an odd sort of melancholy when I picture it now, all of last week's comedians, psyching themselves up as they walk back into that club.

"Hey," says a muted voice. I look up, pulling out headphones.

Sam's hair looks wet from a shower. I melt, swallow, then remember to speak. "Hi."

"You know what you want to order?" Linh asks as he slides in across from me.

"Uh, yeah." I clear my throat, skimming the menu quickly. "I'll have a small beef . . . pho," I say, stumbling slightly as I decide to pronounce it the correct way.

"And a large one for me," says Sam.

When she goes, I blink a few times, still pondering the interaction. "Are we saying *foe* or *fuh* now? I know technically it's *fuh*, but saying it properly still kind of makes me feel like a douche."

Sam laughs, loud, and my chest swells. "I think it's a balance," he says, pulling off his coat and settling back. "Take my mom's new yoga instructor you met the other day. She loves talking about her teacher training in Spain, and I'm convinced it's just an excuse to lisp out *Barthhh-elona* in the middle of a sentence. To me, that's unacceptable."

"I mean, it does sound kind of awesome," I say. "Who, me?

I just got back from *Barthhh-elona.* If I *ever* manage to leave Maine, I will totally drop stuff like that into sentences."

"No way," he says. "Anyway, it would be different if you said it."

"I see," I say, feeling we've arrived at some larger truth here. "So it's more of a nail-in-the-coffin sort of trait. Like, if the person already irritates you, then overpronouncing foreign words mostly serves as reinforcement?"

"Yeah," he says hesitantly. "But I mean, at the same time, don't just give up and say *foe.* Maybe it's a matter of holding opposing truths in our minds simultaneously?"

I nod wisely. "I think the Dalai Lama said that."

We smile.

"So . . ." Sam strums his fingers along the table, and I imagine filling the drawn-out silence with the freakish chatter inside my head. *(Do you like me??? Tell me what's in your brain!!!)* I nearly crack up from thinking about it. But now Sam has a weird look on his face. "Okay." He breathes out. "Maybe we should clear the air about the other night."

I tense up. "What do you mean?" I highly doubt he'll buy this innocent act. But I have to know what he's thinking before I say any more.

"I'm not totally sure . . ." Sam says carefully. Is it possible *he's* waiting to know what *I'm* thinking? That's the problem with romantic declarations, right? One person always has to go first.

Should I go first???

"It kind of seemed like . . ." He shrugs, eyes locking in with mine. "Maybe you were mad? Because I left the New Year's party?"

"Oh," I say, a strange mix of relief and disappointment flooding me. "No. I was just . . . You know how I am about sticking to traditions. Carmen recently brought it to my attention that I don't like change."

"Well, that is true," he says, with an odd little laugh. "So we're good?"

"Golden," I say, pushing past the rising ache. *Did* I imagine that moment in the yoga studio? *But he touched my cheek! And he was talking to Natalie about me!*

"Hey, speaking of Carmen," he says, pulling me back. "I meant to ask after the party. What was the deal with her and Hen? They were like zombies all through dinner."

"Well, we got a little wild the night before. We went out to some bars."

"*You.* Went to bars?" He looks genuinely shocked, which I kind of like.

"We had fake IDs," I say, holding my chin up.

"Huh," he says. "Carmen, I can see. But you and Henrietta?"

"Hey, Hen's a college girl now. And what are you trying to say about me?" He doesn't have to know I only had water. Just then Linh arrives with the food, and we make space for two piping hot bowls of pho, adding Sriracha and squeezing limes.

"Oh hell yes," says Sam, diving in.

In seconds, my mouth is blessedly full of noodles. *"Ermergod dis is gerd."*

"So ferging gerrrrrd," Sam says, making me choke on a laugh.

"Well, I'm glad you're not mad." He breathes out, breaking for a swig of water. "It's so weird with this move looming over everything now. I want to soak everything up and see as many people as I can. But my mom's right. I should be better about making time for y—"

I gape, and he winces.

"That came out wrong."

"Sam . . ." I frown a minute, leaning forward across the table. "Did you have me over last week because your *mom* told you to? Wait." My heart sinks. "Is that why we're here now?" He looks resigned, and I cough a laugh. *"Oh my God!"*

"Well, I'm sorry, but you don't make it easy," he says. "I get invited to lots of things you could come along for, but you refuse to ever be in a group. It has to be you and me. All the time."

I roll my eyes. "That's because you hang out with douche-bags, Sam."

"That's not true," he says. "Is Ethan a douchebag? Is Nata-lie?" I shake my head no, feeling suddenly small. "I know for a fact they both really like you. And I'm sure other people would too, if you ever, like, tried. At all."

"I'm not a people person," I say, swirling my spoon through red-tinged broth.

"Why?"

"I don't *know*," I say, sounding completely childish. It's something I've never been able to properly explain to him—how when a group grows too big, or I'm talking to someone who doesn't know me well, I start to feel like I'm on display, and suddenly it's as if I can't access my real self. This low-lying fear is always there—like when the moment comes, I'll say the wrong thing. Or, possibly just as bad: not say anything at all. "Anyway, don't change the subject. You're pity-hanging out with me."

"I'm not!" he says.

I sink back into the booth, covering my face. *"God, this is embarrassing."*

"Come on, Gretch. It's me. You should never be embarrassed around me. Yes, I want to do my own thing sometimes but . . . hey." He waits for me to peek out at him, through a slit between my fingers. "You're still my best friend."

The words should be nice. A good thing. But all I want to do is cry.

"You too," I say, picking up my spoon again to let the broth dribble into my bowl.

"I guess I don't get it," he says after a minute. "I know the real you. You're *awesome.* But it's like, the older we get, the more you . . . I don't know. Shrink, almost? It kind of bums me out, honestly."

"Well, this might be hard for you to understand, Sam, but for some of us, high school is something to survive. Not . . . savor every moment of like it's the pinnacle of glory."

"So you're saying I'm gonna peak in high school?" There's an edge to his voice, but he's smiling again. "Jeez, Gretch. Tell me how you really feel."

"Ugh!" I laugh, rolling my eyes. "I didn't say that. Although, you could probably tone it down with the whole high school golden boy act."

"What *act*?" he says.

I drop my spoon to make two finger pistols and point smarmily to invisible hallway people. "Hey, buddy! . . . How's it hangin', bro?"

"Oh, come on. Stop," he says. "I don't do that."

"Uh, except, you totally do."

For a moment we just stare at each other, tense but still joking around, I think. A part of me wants to tell him there were other places I could have been tonight—one in particular he wouldn't *believe*. I wasn't afraid up on that stage last week. And I didn't *shrink*, thank you very much.

I think of Jeremy's text. *Why not?*

And for the first time, instead of a list of *nots*, I hear it a different way: *Why not?!?*

I pull out my wallet, Sabrina's ID still nestled in the clear pocket. Everything else I need is right there at home. "I have to go," I say, not quite believing myself as I throw down cash.

"What?" Sam looks confused as I slide out of the booth. "Wait. Gretchen—"

"We're good," I tell him. "Really. I'll just see you at school."

Three whole minutes. That's how long it takes to wriggle into a pair of tight leather pants behind a steering wheel. Mom and Dad weren't home when I dropped by, but changing under that roof still felt risky to me.

"How did Carmen even do this?" I say into the rearview mirror now, adding eyeliner, some blush, and the super-bright lipstick she let me hold on to for touch-ups. Normally, my makeup regimen stops at concealer over blemishes, and maybe a bit of tinted Burt's Bees if I'm feeling frisky. But I think I've pretty much pulled this off.

I heave a sigh, heartbeat quickening. Across the street, a crooked sign blinks above the door: *The Chuckle Parlor.*

"Okay, okay, okay . . ." I whisper, yanking on Sabrina's boots before sliding into the cropped black jacket. The words cycle through my head as if on a news ticker: *This is so weird. . . . I am so weird. . . .* And yet, I'm pulling hair ties from my wrist to form two little buns before securing them with pins.

At last, I slip on the red-framed glasses. "Yep," I say to my reflection. "Utterly transformed."

Tonight's door guy waits inside this time. Actually, it's the bartender Carmen made out with. "Hey, I remember you," he says as I shiver away the last traces of the cold outdoors. "I'm Ted, by the way. Your cousin never called me."

"Oh. Sorry," I say, a little weirdly. But he just laughs and waves me along.

Onstage, a new set is starting—a scrawny guy playing hipstery musical chords on a ukulele. He tells the crowd his name is Lennon, as in John, but we can call him Lenny.

I drape my jacket on a barstool, searching the room for Jeremy. Lenny's first few jokes all seem to revolve around the perils of capitalism, kept light with all that happy strumming. Now he's talking about his girlfriend's eco-conscious menstrual cup. There's a quirk to him that definitely works.

I sigh, already starting to relax. I like the feel of everyone packed together in this dark space, with that tangy beer smell permeating everything.

"Sabrina!" I hear from behind me. It's Dolores, whispering so loudly she may as well just talk. "You came back! Thank God. My next guy wandered off and I can't find him. What a friggin' banana-head. Remind me your last name so I can introduce you?"

"Uh . . . Martin," I stammer.

"Sandy!" she hisses to the hostess. "Prep her? I'm gonna go."

I'm not entirely sure what's happening right now, but as Lenny says good night to the audience, Dolores hops up to do her in-between bit. Sandy guides me toward the stage, explaining . . . something or other. I suddenly can't remember what it was I planned to say up here tonight. *Was* I planning on saying anything?

Wait a minute. What am I doing?

Shit.

Abort, abort!

". . . Sabrina Martin!" Dolores announces as the crowd claps. She waves, emphatic, until I walk up the steps to take her place.

I hear the room quiet as I stare out past the lights.

The inside of my brain is a big black nothing.

"Hey, sweetheart!" a voice calls after I-don't-know-how-long. "You gonna say something any time soon? I'm missing the Bruins for this!" I squint to see a man up front getting swatted by his wife.

"Is she okay?" a girl says to her friend in back. Across the room, I glimpse Jeremy for the first time. He looks alarmed, if not slightly amused by my predicament. It's a smaller crowd tonight than last week, and I think that might be making this worse. It's as if I'm failing each individual audience member personally.

"Wow," I say finally, as I continue to take in all the stony faces.

Make a joke, the little voice screams. *Any joke!*

"You guys, uh . . ." I clear my throat. "You all look like I just told you I'm here to administer your next prostate exam."

Silence.

"Okay . . ." I say. "No prostate jokes. I could see how that might bring down some of the guys in the room. This is meant to be a place of fun."

I can hear Bruins Guy's wife talking now. "I don't want to leave. They won't all be this bad."

Somehow, this makes me chuckle. I take the mic from the stand to crouch down. "Excuse me. Ma'am? You know I can *hear* you, right?" That gets a solid laugh, and even if it's mostly at my expense, I will totally take that right now.

"Okay," I say, straightening up. "I will admit, this is not going well. Apparently you can't just barge onto a stage and expect astute, hilarious observations about life to flow effortlessly from your mouth."

The crowd murmurs, perhaps warming to me.

"Anyway . . ." I think a minute. Crowd work. That's a thing, right? "Do we have any visiting tourists here in the audience?"

A couple young guys off to the side raise their hands. "Nice," I say. "Although, *why?* Didn't anyone tell you it's cold here?" I touch my two little buns and adjust my glasses, feeling a slight thrill all of a sudden. Because honestly? Who cares how tonight goes? This is Sabrina's problem.

"What's that?" I say, remembering to listen as the tourist guy talks.

"We're here for a snowboarding trip," he repeats, louder.

"Gotcha," I say, chin up, back straight. "See, for me, most winter sports could be more accurately described as . . . recreational falling down?"

A slight murmur from the room has me encouraged. People are smiling now as I pace the stage. "The last time I went skiing, I wound up in one of those only-big-person-on-the-bunny-slope situations. It's so degrading when a child is better at something than you. This one little kid, Enzo, kept showing me up in our lesson. On the outside I was all, 'Awww! Good job, buddy!' But inside I was like, *Fuck off, Enzo!*"

That gets a laugh, which is a relief. The story is even true, though I've embellished some. Enzo and I actually forged a nice friendship on that bunny hill.

I'm trying to think of something more to say when I glimpse Dolores on the far side of the stage, waving her clipboard to catch my attention. She gives me a pointed look and I realize the blinking light I've been seeing for a while was probably the *wrap it up* signal I now vaguely remember the hostess mentioning before I went on.

I must have wasted quite a lot of time staring out into the middle distance.

Oops.

"All right, well," I say, remembering to stick the landing as I return the mic to its place. "I'm Sabrina Martin. Thank you, Portland!" I start to walk off, then double back. "Oh, and sorry for mentioning prostate exams in your safe space, guys. Won't happen again."

SEVEN

The Roguish Bad Boy | All speech somehow feels like innuendo. Very good at raising one eyebrow. Probably not a good life decision.

A few people clap weakly as I speed down the steps, toward Jeremy at the bar. I can tell he's enjoying this, smiling at me like a guy in a gum commercial—the *ding!* practically sparkling off his canine.

"I know," I say, rolling my eyes when I reach him. He's with some other comics—Tinder Guy and Preschool Lady from last week. To them, I say, "Hi. You're both really funny and I'm embarrassed. I should have prepared something."

Tinder Guy smiles. "It's okay. I've been there."

"We all have," says Preschool Lady. "But hey, you *sort of* got yourself out of it. . . ."

Jeremy shakes his head. "For the record, I would have helped you. All you had to do was text me back."

"I know," I say through a sigh. "I really didn't think I'd be coming here again. Hence the verbal diarrhea. Anyway, lesson learned. That audience was scary."

"Yep," says Tinder Guy. "Sometimes they're dicks even when you're good."

Jeremy reaches over the bar to pour a couple waters from the soda gun. He hands me one and I start to sip, blinking quizzically around at them. "To be honest, I still don't fully understand why I went up there and did that. Either time."

"Same reason all of us do," says Preschool Lady. "You're probably deeply fucked up inside."

I laugh. "Maybe."

"Sabrina, right? I'm Paula."

"Isaiah," says Tinder Guy with a little nod.

"Nice to meet you," I say to them before turning to Jeremy. "This is your fault, you know. You said I was funny."

"I said you were promising," he corrects. "But I do think you're funny."

I pretend to swoon. "Really?"

"I mean, not tonight," he says. "Tonight you were mostly terrible."

"She was not," says Paula, teetering a bit as she meets my eyes. "Okay, it wasn't great. But you'll get there. Then again . . ." She smacks her lips. "The odds of an audience voting *two* female comics into the final three are pretty low. So I guess we're mortal enemies now."

"Damn, that's too bad," I say. "You seemed cool." She smiles and drains her beer, just as Dolores calls out, *"Paula Meiselman!"* With that, Isaiah excuses himself to join some friends who came out to support him—an eclectic bunch of twentysomethings who look ready for a nice brunch, or maybe a poetry slam.

When it's just us, Jeremy and I each take a stool to watch, and I can't tell if we're sitting *together-together*, or if this just happened by default.

I can still feel him smirking beside me, so I shoot him a look, like, *What?!* But then I don't really care, because I'm being pulled into Paula's orbit, the same way everyone else is—from the moment she takes out the mic, rests an elbow on the empty stand, and says, "So I'm a preschool teacher. . . ."

"Wait," I whisper, turning to Jeremy. "Is she just repeating the same thing from last week?"

"Probably not word for word," he says, leaning in. "It evolves. My guess is she'll use some of her tried-and-true bits first, then test out some new stuff. The people in the audience don't usually return week to week, so it's fine."

The room is fairly quiet, laughter trickling in and out, but you can feel her casting a spell on everyone. Even Bruins Guy seems happy with the concept of preschoolers humping stuff.

"That makes sense about evolving," I say after a while, keeping my voice low. Paula's doing a great bit from last week, reenacting awkward sit-downs with what she calls U-POPs: Unsuspecting Parents of Pervs. "It feels more manageable, approaching it that way."

"Yeah," says Jeremy. "Then again, if you recycle too much and don't use this time to test out new material, you could end up screwing yourself."

"What do you mean?"

"Just that if you somehow win this thing, the person who opens for Marnie James will need to fill fifteen minutes. So we'd all be smart to use these opportunities to work out a few different chunks."

"Jeez," I say. "I'm still trying to wrap my brain around writing *one* chunk. But fifteen minutes?"

"I've done it before," he says over the roar of the crowd. "At coffee shops, places like that. It's not as bad as it sounds."

Everyone is going bananas for Paula now. It's heartening to see. As she waves good night, I turn to Jeremy. "So when are you going on?"

"I went up before you got here," he says, cracking his knuckles with outstretched arms. "Too bad. Could have been educational for you."

"Does *this* . . ." I draw a circle around him in the air. ". . . ever stop?"

"I would probably just accept it if I were you."

Up next is Isaiah, his material all seemingly new, with the exception of the Mystery Tinder Poop Story, which is somehow even funnier this time around. His friends in the audience are laughing hysterically, and once in a while he smiles over at their table. I'm not sure I could ever pull that off—being so bold and unencumbered in front of friends and strangers alike. Or in any context, honestly. *What am I doing here again?*

"He's probably the one to beat," says Jeremy. I wouldn't discount Paula so quickly, but he could be right. Isaiah has this crowd whipped into a frenzy, some people cracking up at what he's saying now, while others are still catching their breath from jokes he told two minutes ago. When he finally trades places with Dolores, there's a collective joyfulness thrumming through the room.

"He's *really* good," I say, mildly in awe as he descends the steps from the stage. "Paula, too. They both just have that . . . *thing* that makes a person funny."

Jeremy turns to me. "Do you think you have it? That thing?"

"Oh, um . . ." The question feels too blunt, and personal. But I shrug. "Maybe I'm here to find out."

When Isaiah's friends take off early, Jeremy and I claim their empty seats, waving at Paula to come too. "You both were so amazing," I whisper across the rickety table. They practically beam, obviously happy with how the night went.

Onstage now, a medical student named Lakshmi is describing the strange juxtaposition of starting a family with her new husband while also facing death at the hospital every day. It's grim but honest, funny, and sweet. Next, an extremely deadpan sushi chef manages to make a whole set about fish surprisingly compelling. And then it's someone I've seen before—the man I watched last week from the hall with Jeremy and Dolores.

"Not this guy again," mutters Isaiah, the room growing tense as he starts in.

Paula shakes her head. "If he does that mail-order-bride impression again I'm going to lose my fucking mind."

As I look the man over, I decide he's like a thinner, balder Kevin James—if you took away all the qualities that made Kevin James likeable. So far, the set is just him saying *tits* a lot.

"Titties, tits tits, titties . . ." (Okay, not a *direct* quote, but it might as well be.) I feel like I'm going in and out of a Charlie Brown cartoon: blah blah *stupid slut*, blah blah blah *blow job.* Now he's complaining about his marriage, and the voice he does for his wife is so tired—*if* he has a wife, I should say.

"How much you want to bet he's not even married?" asks Jeremy, apparently reading my thoughts.

"I wish someone would tell these guys that nagging wives aren't funny," says Isaiah. "Like . . . cavemen comics were doing this bit."

Two women in the front row stand up abruptly, their chairs scraping loudly against the floor as they turn to go. "Oh, come on!" Bad Kevin James calls after them as they head for the exit, before muttering into the mic, "Whatever. Probably hormonal."

Just then, Bruins Guy from earlier cups his hands around his mouth to shout from the audience. I brace myself for something truly awful. I open one eye. . . .

"Hey, buddy!" he yells. "You can't fuckin' say that! We don't talk about women that way!"

I look around the table, my heart oddly warmed, and all four of us burst out laughing. At least he's an equal-opportunity heckler.

When Dolores finally says good night, people clap and trickle out, the energy having rebounded from one last act—a retired contractor with a thick Maine accent who divulged his love for *The Great British Baking Show*. It was the exact wholesome opposite of what had preceded it, and you could tell the audience was grateful.

In the emptied-out room, now disorientingly bright, Paula, Isaiah, and I have hung back, our table the only one with its chairs not yet flipped upside down by Jeremy or Ted.

We've been going over all the acts, analyzing key moments like sports fans after a game. The med student said a quick hi-and-goodbye to us before she slipped out—right back to the hospital, I think. British Baking Guy, Ukulele Lenny, and Deadpan Sushi Chef all gave friendly waves of acknowledgment as they talked to friends in the crowd. Meanwhile Bad Kevin James just charged past our table without a word. I guess there was one other comic, too, but she left before I got a chance to meet her.

"You missed a spot!" I call out playfully to Jeremy as he walks by with a broom.

Isaiah drains his glass of water and turns to Paula. "Need a ride?"

"Yes, please," she says, and they both get up, waving their goodbyes. I can't help but smile as I watch them go. It's sort of unbelievable that we just met. As the door closes behind them, Ted pulls out the drawer from the cash register and walks off, leaving Jeremy and me alone at opposite ends of the empty room.

"So." Jeremy comes over, and I stand to let him flip our remaining chairs. "Are you going to accept my help this time?"

"I'm thinking about it," I say, following as he starts flipping stools at the bar. I notice the muscles of his arms flickering under his T-shirt and instinctively look away. "Then again, I've never even seen your act," I go on, composing myself. "For all I know, you could be terrible."

"Oh no, I'm very good," he says, and I'm annoyed that I'm charmed by his confidence. *Why does that work on me?*

"I'll admit the stuff I've been doing lately hasn't been my best. But I'm starting on some new material that might be interesting. For now, I'm doing research."

"Out in the universe?" He smirks, holding my stare with knitted brows. "Why are you looking at me like that?" I ask finally. He's making me uneasy.

"Sorry," he says, though the look of curiosity doesn't quite leave him. "I think I'm . . . trying to figure you out."

"Yeah, well, stop being weird," I say, eyeing him skeptically. "Anyway, fine. Impart your wisdom. What do I do now?"

"Well, now comes the part where you write jokes. Setups? Punch lines?"

"Thank you," I say flatly. "For the explanation. My little lady brain almost couldn't handle that."

"Funny," he says. "See? Do that." I narrow my eyes and he gestures to the two stools still standing upright. "Look," he continues as we sit. "People riff and experiment up there all the time. But first, you have to write some stuff. You can't riff off of nothing."

I nod my head, sighing out. "I don't know where I'd even begin."

"The advice I first got was to work from simple facts about myself. I made a list. Likes, dislikes. Things I wished I could change about myself."

I raise an eyebrow. "*You* have things you'd change about yourself?"

"Not really, no. You're right."

"Okay, land the plane, Jeremy," I say, waving him along.

"Just don't overthink it," he says with a grin. "Start with specifics about yourself, then try to make them broad enough for an audience to relate to. Also . . ." He hesitates. "This might just be my philosophy. But if you need inspiration, it never hurts to find a nice, meaty situation once in a while. Walk *toward* the awkward moments, not away. Just to . . . see what will happen."

"Huh," I say. "I kind of like that. Carpe awkward!"

"I mean, why not, right? If you treat life like an experiment, you can almost make the material come to you."

"Hmm," I say. "I'm not sure I *totally* get what you mean."

"It's like this . . ." he says, leaning in. He smells good. Why does he have to smell good? I realize I'm tuning him out.

"Huh?"

"*What would you do?* questions," he says, apparently repeating himself. "I used to ask them all the time as a kid. You know. What would you do if I shaved off my eyebrow? What would you do if I stripped down naked in the middle of this Olive Garden? And instead of a breadstick—"

"Okay, I think I get the concept," I say, stopping him there.

He laughs. "Basically, when I got into stand-up, I started acting on those impulses. The scenarios have evolved—I haven't defiled any Olive Gardens or anything," he clarifies quickly. "But if I get a curious itch, I just kind of . . . scratch it. It's quite liberating with dating. If I put myself out there and wind up humiliated—great. I get a story out of it. And if I find myself in some train wreck of a relationship, I can talk about it in my act. Which means it won't have been a waste, even when I'm forced to self-destruct."

"What does *that* mean?"

He shrugs. "I guess I haven't really mastered the mature breakup yet. I usually find some creative way to expedite the process. Once I got a girl to break up with me by overusing the word *yeppers.*"

"I think any use of the word *yeppers* is an overuse."

"Yeppers, it is," he says. "When it hit me how wrong we were for each other, I just started working it into sentences. She dumped me within a week. And then I got a bit out of it: *Can your love withstand the yeppers test?*"

"So . . ." I frown a moment. "*Before* you self-destruct, do these girlfriends come to your shows and watch you talk about them? Isn't that weird?"

He teeters a bit. "I . . . usually don't mention my comedy at the start of a relationship. Or at all, sometimes. It's just easier to keep those parts of my life separate for when all the crashing and burning starts."

"Yeesh," I say. "You are *cynical.*"

"And you're not?" The corner of his mouth hikes up, eyes twinkling playfully. "Do you believe in the fairy tale?"

"Maybe not the fairy tale," I say. "But I think I believe in the rom-com. Maybe with a few added tweaks for plausibility."

"Yeah, I can't say I've ever really watched those."

"You should give them a try. It could help with all the nihilism. They make you feel . . . good. Hopeful."

"Oh yeah?" he says, still grinning at me. "How so?"

I bite my lip, considering this a moment. "Maybe it's just a nice thought to hold on to, you know? That someday, somehow, another person will choose *you*—just you. Parents divide their attention among siblings. Friends have other friends. But with that kind of love? *Love*-love?" I shrug. "You're it. And that person is it for you. Well . . . unless you've got some kind of polygamy situation worked out." Jeremy smiles, and there's that *ding!* again. It's highly annoying how much it ruffles me. "Anyway," I say, shaking it off. "It's just fun to wish for, I guess."

"So the wishing itself is fun?"

"Yeah, kinda," I say. "I think they call that optimism. You should try it some time."

Jeremy holds my stare for just a moment too long, and I feel a bit of heat start to pool around my jawline. But then he frowns and gets up, going around the bar. "Can I, uh . . ." He clears his throat. "Can I offer you a nightcap on the house?" He doesn't wait for my reply—just pulls two wet glasses from a crate. "You know what? I'll join you for one."

"Up-up-up, no you won't," says Dolores, appearing from the hall with a basket full of papers marked *Votes*. "We don't serve minors in this establishment, thank you."

I flinch at the word *minors*. Does she know?

"Did I hear him telling you the yeppers story?" she asks, tossing the basket onto the bar. "You'll have to forgive my godson. Thinks he's friggin' Daniel Day-Lewis over here. Very method with his comedy."

"He is a student of the universe," I say, and he winks in a way I somehow don't hate.

I feel a spike of dread as Dolores looks over the voting sheets audience members filled out before leaving. I don't particularly want to know what they thought of me. She squints, moving the slips of paper forward and back to click in with her reading glasses, one after the other. "Ha! See?" she says. "The lowest possible points, from . . ." She cycles through a few more. "Yep. Basically the entire audience."

My stomach dips. "Yeah, I get it. . . ."

"What? No, not you," she says, dropping the voting sheets back into the basket. "Somehow you weren't the worst one tonight. I'm talking about that asswipe who's fond of saying *'me so horny'* and complaining about his imaginary wife."

"Oh, Bad Kevin James," I say, somewhat relieved.

"That feels like an affront to the real Kevin James," says Jeremy. "*Mall Cop*, anybody? But I see what you mean. God, that set was excruciating."

"I agree," says Dolores. "Which is why I told him not to come back. I should have done it last week. Or more like years ago, if you think about it. He was not the first Bad Kevin James to walk through this place."

"Wait," says Jeremy. "He's really not coming back?"

"Nope," says Dolores. "He wasn't happy about it. And he seemed to think I owed him a debate on the first amendment. I'm like, sorry, guy, but it's my club, and you weren't pushing any fuckin' boundaries for Christ's sake."

"Ah yes," I say. "A man talking about titties. So brave."

Dolores sighs. "I wrestle with these questions a lot. And it's not an exact science. From what I've seen, if you're funny enough, and you're coming from an okay place, most audiences will stay with you even if you cross a few lines. Or at least do that thing where they laugh but worry they're going to hell. What this guy couldn't understand was that on top of being just a completely out-of-touch prick, he wasn't fuckin' funny!"

"Well, one less person to compete with," says Jeremy. "Works for me."

"We saw him storm off," I say.

"Oh, he was ripshit," says Dolores, shaking her head. "On his way out, he goes, 'What would know you, bitch? Women aren't funny!'" She chuckles to herself. "What a fuckin' baby."

I must look stricken, because Dolores reaches out to cover my hand with hers. "You know that's a load of crap, right? You weren't funny tonight because you're new at this. And because you didn't prepare anything. It had nothing to do with your jiggly parts."

"Aw," Jeremy says to me. "Your first Dolores pep talk."

"Oh, before I forget," she says, ignoring him. "I need a headshot from you, Sabrina. Yours is the only one I'm missing. Bring it to me next week?"

"Um. Okay . . ." I say, frowning. I'll worry about that later. "Also, I just wanted to apologize about my set. I didn't actually plan to—"

"She's taking this seriously now," Jeremy interrupts. "She's even wisely requested my tutelage."

"I'm accepting a few tips," I clarify.

Jeremy looks hopefully at Dolores. "What do you say? Round of beers to celebrate?"

"Uh, *no*," she says. "Though Sabrina, you can help yourself to a pint if you like, since you're one of us now." I blink as she walks off, even more confused than I was before.

"Wait . . ." The realization hits on a delay as I slowly turn to Jeremy. "So . . ." I scoff at him. "You're under twenty-one?"

"Eighteen," he says, a tiny smile pulling at his lips. "What's it to you, Sabrina?"

"I—" His flirty tone catches me off guard. "But if you're a minor, how do you work at a bar?"

"The laws around that are surprisingly chill in Maine," he says. "At eighteen you can even bartend. Though you technically can't taste the drinks." He laughs. "That was actually Ted until about a month ago." I nod slowly, my brain still catching up. "Anyway, I mostly just bus tables and help around here. And I only check IDs when someone needs a break. Honestly, Dolores isn't much of a stickler for rules. I thought she'd have eased up on the beer policy by now," he adds, before raising his volume. "If this were Europe, it'd be legal!"

"Well, we're not in Europe, are we?" she yells back from another room.

"So you're eighteen," I repeat, mostly to myself. Eighteen as in barely older than me. As in completely appropriate . . .

But then I frown. Because wait a minute. *He* thinks *I'm* twenty-one. And yet here he's been acting all superior since we met! I'm actually kind of offended. Even if he does know more about stand-up than I do, shouldn't he be asking for sage life advice or something?

I am his elder!

"So where were we?" he asks, piercing my silent rant.

"Hm?"

"With your set. Maybe you should talk about that Sam guy again next week. That was nice and pitiful."

"Hey," I say, reaching out to swat him. "You're a jerk." I'm smiling though. Because somehow, I've hardly thought of Sam at all tonight.

"For the record, I'm not a jerk," says Jeremy, meeting my eyes. "Well, not all the time."

I nod as a yawn takes over. I'm exhausted. Is it late?

I freeze, reality *whooshing* back. Because it's Wednesday—a school night. And oh yeah, I'm not *actually* a twenty-one-year-old college girl who casually closes down bars. "What time is it?" I say, not waiting for Jeremy's response as I get my jacket and slip my arms through the sleeves. "God dammit. I completely lost track of myself." I pat down my pockets, looking for my phone. What if my parents are freaking out? Maybe I could say I went to Sam's house after dinner and fell asleep?

But when I look down, the spinning in my head comes to a halt. I have no texts, no calls. Jeez, Mom and Dad. You could worry a *little.*

"Everything okay?" asks Jeremy.

"Oh yeah," I say. "My, uh . . . roommate. She doesn't like it when I stay out too late. I should go."

"Well, I'm around if you need any help this week," he calls after me as I head for the exit. "Maybe a writing session one night?"

"Oh," I say, stopping at the door. "Yeah, okay . . ."

"Good," he says. "I'll look forward to it."

I breathe a laugh, nodding vaguely. And with that, I step out into the cold—back to my car and my real life.

EIGHT

The Perfect Cover | I mean really. Who hasn't been an incognito journalist or a fake fiancé at some point? Just make sure you don't fall in love. . . .

"Did we not watch *Love, Actually* this year?" asks Mom, scrolling through movie options. Dad sips a beer between us, his ridiculous hat flaps up, our communal bowl of buttery home-popped popcorn resting on his stomach. He's already got a piece stuck in his mustache.

"We watched it at Carmen's house at the start of break," I say.

"Without me?" Mom looks wounded. "You girls know how much I love complaining about the creepy parts."

"Sorry," I say through a yawn. "But holiday movie season is over."

"Oh, I disagree," she says.

Dad pauses between handfuls. "Please pick something I can at least mildly tolerate."

I grin at Mom. "Dad loves *Love, Actually* you know."

"Do not," he says.

I wedge myself deeper into the corner of the couch, pulling my fleece blanket around me. "Christmas Eve-Eve, two years ago. I saw a *tiny* tear come out of that eye when the little kid was drumming to the Mariah Carey song."

"Well," he concedes. "That part is adorable. I also like the scene where Hugh Grant dances. What can I say? The man has charisma."

I smile through another yawn, eyes glazing as Mom gets swallowed further into the streaming-options sinkhole. It was after one when I got home from the club last night, and even after I crawled under the covers, I was too twitchy with adrenaline to sleep. Looking at my parents now, I still feel like I got off too easily. Mom even left a sticky note on my door: *We went to bed early. Hope you had a good time with Sam!*

It's sort of funny. My parents *definitely* enforced curfews for Hen and William at my age. And none of us would have had the same experience tiptoeing in last night. My brother, once something of a troublemaker, would have come home to a speech: *How could you be so irresponsible?!* While Henrietta probably would have received a hug before anything else: *Thank God you're all right! We were so worried!*

But with me?

I laugh.

They didn't even wait up!

"*While You Were Sleeping*," says Mom like she's taking a gasp of air. "That will satisfy my holiday craving without going full *Christmas Prince* or whatever."

"Fine," sighs Dad, though I know for a fact he thinks Sandra Bullock is hilarious.

"Hey, before I forget," says Mom, sitting back. "We're going up to Viv and Arvin's cabin to ski for the weekend. Gabriela's bringing her new guy."

"Wow," I say. "They're getting kind of serious."

"Sam isn't going, understandably," says Mom. "I take it you don't want to either?"

"Nope. Still hate winter sports . . . and sports . . . and winter."

"Well then, the house is yours," she says with a laugh. "Don't throw any ragers." She and Dad share a look like she's just said something hysterical. So maybe that's why they didn't wait up for me last night. They're too secure in what a huge dork I am.

I level them both with an eye roll as Mom hits play, the snappy opening credits assuring us that *This will be an everlasting love!* It's a classic, and I want to watch, but my lashes are growing heavy, the edges of my vision fading fast.

When I open my eyes again, a lonely Sandra Bullock is struggling to pull a Christmas tree through a window while her cat looks on. *You will find love*, I want to say. *Someone tell her! We all know the end!*

The next time I stir, Bill Pullman is showing her his rocking chair. If I've learned anything from these movies, it's that you always, *always* marry the guy who can make a rocking chair.

I smile, wishing I had a pen and paper to write that down. That feels like a joke, or the start of one. I guess I write jokes now. . . .

My eyes flutter shut again, and I see myself on that stage last night. It's weird I feel this happy, considering how badly my so-called *set* went. I normally embarrass more easily than this, reliving every word, every misstep, regrets like white-hot lumps lodged stubbornly in my throat.

It's actually bizarre.

I *bombed* last night, but the impulse to replay it—to agonize? It's . . . gone.

And I want to keep it gone.

Because with comedy, I think you have to suck—and I mean utterly, *soul-shatteringly* suck—if you ever want to not suck. People say fortune favors the bold. But now I wonder if it just favors those who don't know how bad they suck. In which case, it's more like, *Fortune eludes the self-aware,* or . . . something.

I'm getting all deep now.

And I honestly can't tell if I'm asleep or not.

Hehe, that's weird.

I am an amorphous brain!

And getting weirder . . .

I'm in a dark void now, walking in a slow circle around the girl with the two little buns, the red frames. A sleep-tinged delirium brings clarity, like a tide rolling toward my feet.

I've found a glitch in the system. A hall pass made of black leather and suede. As Sabrina, I can suck to my heart's content.

And Gretchen can go unscathed.

"Gah!" I wake to Nacho catapulting toward me, the throw pillow on my lap saving me from his stabby paws.

"Were you asleep, Gretch?" says Mom, her face falling. "Aw. You okay?"

"Yeah, sorry," I say, rubbing my eyes. "Just tired."

"While we're paused, we need more popcorn," says Dad, getting up.

Mom takes Nacho from my lap and lifts him up. "Hello, my good boy. Did you wake your sister up? Did you not want her to miss the movie? How sweet are you?"

"Yes, he's very considerate," I say, grinning. It's amazing how happy he looks in Mom's arms.

"We should do something special for his birthday next month," she says. "Throw a big bash. And there should be a theme. I've been lamenting our family's lack of religion. This week, one of the other dog moms from the park is throwing her Boston terrier a bark mitzvah."

I snort, and Mom's big goofy smile looks so much like Hen's.

It's another way they're alike: Mom can laugh at herself.

My phone starts buzzing on the coffee table then. "Jeremy," says Mom with a frown as she hands it to me. "Do I know this Jeremy?"

"No," I say, extremely awake now. *Why is he calling me?!* "He's . . . from school. We have a project. But I'll let it go to voice mail."

"Okay," she says, eyeing me strangely. "Well, I need a kombucha."

I watch Mom get up and go as the buzzing continues in my hand, my own words sort of echoing in my head: *I'll let it go to voice mail.* "Omigod, voice mail!" I almost drop the phone as I flinch and hit the button. "Hello?"

"Hey," says Jeremy. I catch my breath, tempted to remind him that we are *not,* in fact, in a 1990s rom-com right now. Who calls people on the phone? "I was just wondering about our writing session this weekend. When's good for you?"

"Oh," I say, peering down the hall to make sure Mom and Dad aren't coming back yet. I guess it's good they're going out of town. I won't have to worry about tripping over backstories. "I'm . . . pretty free."

"Cool, cool . . ."

I strain to listen: Mom and Dad rummaging around, the fridge door opening and closing. "Do we need to decide this now?"

"My bad," says Jeremy, a hint of mischief in his voice. "I just assumed you'd want to pin me down. My weekends fill up fast. Wouldn't want to miss your chance."

"Hmm," I say. "Can we come up with some kind of code word for when you're being the worst?"

He laughs. "How about . . . *Hey, handsome.* Although, no, that won't work. What about all the times you want to say that to me sincerely?"

"Hey, handsome," I say tersely.

I swear I can hear him smiling. "Hey yourself."

Down the hall, Nacho starts prancing this direction like he's the front of a parade, Mom and Dad following. "Jeremy, I have to go."

"Wait," he says. "I didn't actually make you mad, did I? We can come up with a real code word if you want."

"No," I say, softening. "But I can't talk. Just . . . text me like a normal person from our generation."

I hang up right as everyone descends upon the couch.

"Everything okay?" asks Mom. I must look dazed.

"Yeah," I say. "But . . . I have to pee." I jump up and hurry to the bathroom, closing the door and pulling up the voice mail settings on my phone. My stomach flips as I listen: *"Hey, it's Gretchen. Leave a message."*

"That was *way* too close," I whisper, clearing my throat as I hit record.

"Hey, it's . . . me," I say. "Do the thing."

Satisfied, I save the message and return to the living room.

As Mom hits play, I swaddle myself back up. I have a newfound respect for Sandra Bullock pulling off her fake identity as long as she does in this movie.

My phone vibrates during her big coming-clean speech. It's a text from Jeremy. How about we write at the club on Saturday? I can open early and we can stay for the show after. Meet there at 6?

Sure, I type under my blanket.

Three little dots appear, then vanish. I think I might be holding my breath. Finally, the text pops up: It's a date.

NINE

The That-Was-Easy Montage | An agent of acceleration for any process that takes long. Like finding love, or getting good at stand-up comedy. Could someone cue the music?

I woke up cuddling a composition notebook this morning, pencil scribbles and cross-outs imprinted lightly on my cheek. I got a second wind after the movie last night and stayed up late, trying to write that list about myself, like Jeremy suggested. (Defective Mainer, shiny-person adjacent, crushing on my oldest friend, youngest of three, middle child if you count Nacho . . .) It was fun at first. Then really hard. The jumping-off points were all there. But I never really . . . jumped.

I figure today I'll try thinking my thoughts out loud, even if it's mostly nonsense. I talk softly into my phone, the recording app rolling, as I move from class to class.

After PE: "What kind of sociopath invented dodgeball?"

After art history: "Did women spend the whole sixteenth century with one boob out?"

After math: "Okay, but what *is* a sine? Like what *is* it?"

"Hey, Gretchen," says Annika when I reach her locker. She's wearing a lacy white dress with some kind of army coat over it. "Shall we dine?"

"Yes," I say, slipping the phone into my pocket. I look beyond her and flinch: Sam's coming this way. Annika starts to close up but I stop her, pulling the locker back to hide behind.

"Gretchen?"

"Just keep blocking me," I whisper. Sam and I haven't said a peep to each other since the Hanoi House, and I'm way too sleep-deprived to act normal around him right now.

"Hey there," a voice says—Sam's voice. I wince. "You do realize I saw you before, right? Which means I know you're there now?"

"Stupid object permanence," I mutter.

"Well, that," he says. "And the bottom half of your body is showing."

I step out and lift my eyes to his, almost startled to find so much humor and warmth still crackling between us. With all the distractions these past couple days, I kind of hoped my feelings might finally start to fade. But no.

"Look . . ." Sam glances at Annika, who seems quite comfortable staying for this private conversation. "I didn't mean to be a jerk at dinner. I think maybe I'm . . . stressed about moving or something."

"You weren't a jerk," I say. Because he wasn't. Not really.

"Anyway . . ." He runs a hand through his hair. "I'm throwing a party at my house on Saturday, while my mom is up at the cabin. It won't be anything huge, not the sort of thing you hate. You should come." The invitation seems genuine, which in another moment might make me consider subjecting myself to a high school party. But that's also my writing night with Jeremy. And I can't miss that. No way.

Sam turns to Annika, still watching us. "You could . . . come too. Annika, is it?"

"You'll know the name one day," she says, completely serious. "But I'm hosting a jam session with some of the wind ensemble peeps that night."

"Right," he says through a puzzled grin. "Well, what about you, Gretch?"

"Sorry, I have plans."

He levels me with a look. "Come on. Hen's away. Carmen keeps posting about how buried she is at school. And Annika here just told us she's busy. Doesn't that pretty much leave me?"

"Yeah, normally," I say. Then I frown, because—*mean.*

"Sorry," he says, walking backward into the crowded hall. "You know what? Do your thing. But the door's open if you change your mind, okay?"

"Okay," I call after him. "Thank you!"

I hear myself. *Thank you?*

Annika locks up and comes to stand beside me as I watch him disappear. "Was it me or was that weird?"

"It was weird," I say. "Come on. Let's go eat."

"Cool ranch?"

Ethan holds out his open Doritos to me on the beanbag chairs. I take a chip and talk to it. "Oh, ranch. You're so cool." Ethan gives me a look, like, *not your best*, and I chuckle to myself. "Can you tell I'm sleep-deprived? That's two nights in a row."

"What's keeping you up so late?" he asks, taking the class of 1987 from the pile on the floor.

I finish chewing and dust my hands clean. "I . . . can't say."

"Okay . . ." he says, eyes on his page.

"Well, it's just you two for the rest of today," says Natalie, coming over to us with her satchel backpack on, a coat draped over the crook of her arm. "Some guys from the chess team invited me to be a guest at their big banquet tonight. How could I say no to that? It's going to be fit for a king. Or a rook! Get it?"

I smile, having to hand it to her. The girl's got dad jokes.

"I can get some quotes for you while I'm there, Gretchen. Actually, I'll take the film club, too. We've got a screening this weekend. Something French and existential. And I can interview the BSU kids next time we meet—Black student union," she clarifies. "It's a pretty small group, so it won't take very long."

"Thanks," I say, meeting her little smile.

Her eyes narrow. "But you *were* going to send me the ones you've done so far, right?"

"Right," I lie. I've still made zero progress on that assignment. "I just have to . . . type them up."

"Oh, also, before I forget," she says, doubling back. "It's my birthday soon and my dad said I could reserve a table at his restaurant, invite friends for a big dinner—on the house, of course. It's mostly sushi and small plates—it's really good. Can I add you two to the reservation? Say yes."

"Obviously yes," says Ethan, looking at me. "Trust me. You want to go. His food is, like, world-famous."

"Wow. I didn't know that."

"You've probably seen him on food shows and stuff," he says.

"It's actually how he got his start," says Natalie. "He was like, one of the OG chef personalities, before that whole industry blew up."

"So awesome," says Ethan, shaking his head.

"Not to brag, but Bobby Flay *was* at my fifth birthday party," she says, making me chuckle. "It's actually how my parents met before they came up here. My mom was his producer." That seems about right—Natalie *would* have cool parents like that. "Anyway. *Speaking* of my birthday. We'll have so much fun.

Please say you'll come, Gretchen."

"Um . . ." I guess there's no reason not to. "Okay."

She claps her hands, then pulls it together. "Sorry. I'm an only child and was raised to believe my birthday should be a national holiday. It's too late to change my personality, but on the plus side, it will be *super* fun and fancy, and you'll be so well fed, I promise."

"Sounds great," I say.

She tosses Ethan the keys. "Make sure you lock up so Mr. O doesn't freak out?"

"Yep," he says.

"Now, get to work, you two!" she calls over her shoulder.

When the door closes behind her, Ethan and I resume our task in silence, marking images we like with little neon sticky notes. At today's meeting, we all decided we wanted the anniversary issue to be more than a highlight reel. So on top of write-ups on Marnie James and the other Notables, we'll be dedicating a whole spread to *Randos of the Century!* (Okay, Natalie nixed that title suggestion, but that's the basic concept.) Ethan had the idea of splicing together senior photos from different years to make them move through time. An ode to untold stories, as Natalie put it.

Plus, I thought it'd be fun to watch the hairstyles evolve.

I shut the class of 1952, another yawn overtaking me.

"Okay," says Ethan, setting down 1997. "You haven't slept in two days and you won't say why. . . ." His brows shoot up.

"Wait, weren't you with Sam on Wednesday night? Actually, yeah—he totally bailed on us to hang out with you."

I cough a laugh. "Uh, we hung out for like an hour, and all we did was argue. Trust me. He doesn't—" I blush. What am I saying? "It's not like that with us."

Ethan nods, a look of understanding flashing across his face. "But you want it to be?" I stare at him. "Sorry. I shouldn't have . . ."

I'm too stunned to speak for a second. But then my shoulders slump, the words coming out small: "Am I that obvious?"

"No," he says quickly, the beanbag under him crunching as he sits up straighter. "I just . . . saw how you reacted to those snow angel shots I took over break, the ones of him and Natalie? Not that they even mean anything. I have no idea who he likes. He never talks about that stuff."

I try to slow my breath, a heady rush swooping in. Oh my God. Did I really just admit that I like Sam? To his *friend*? This is why people need sleep!

"Hey." He works to catch my gaze, his expression amused but not unkind. "I won't tell him, okay?"

"Thank you." I breathe out, swiftly reaching for a new yearbook.

He frowns and takes a volume, too. "Are *you* gonna tell him?"

"Don't think so," I say, thumbing through 1963. "I briefly considered it over break. But I've mostly returned to my senses.

I'm me, and Sam is . . . *Sam*. He's like . . . Mr. Prom King or whatever."

"Maybe," says Ethan. "But that doesn't mean he wouldn't . . . I mean, people might not notice *right away*, but you're definitely . . ."

"What?" I ask, unable to keep from smiling a little as he trails off.

"I'm just saying, it's not like you're some gross troll."

"Oh, wow." I laugh. "That really means a lot, Ethan."

"Sorry," he says with a wince. "I've been told my pep talks kind of suck sometimes."

"Is *that* what this is?" I grin at him. "Though, I don't know. You are weirdly making me feel better right now."

"Well, then you're welcome," he says as we go back to skimming pages. After a minute, he breaks the silence again. "Hey, are you going to Sam's party tomorrow?"

"Uh, *no*." I place a sticky note on a large bouffant. "I have important plans. And anyway, parties make me feel like I'm going to die of awkward." Ethan glances up from his page, seeming once again amused by my struggle. "What?" I say. "I just hate how blasé everyone is at those things. Like, 'Oh, this? This is just a regular Saturday night for me, over here with my extensive knowledge of casual sex and alternative uses for Adderall.' Aren't we still too young for that? Did you know we don't even have a fully formed prefrontal cortex yet?"

"I . . . think I knew that," he says, blinking back at me. "But you seem to have a very good brain, Gretchen. And I don't think anyone's opting for an Adderall sex party at Sam's house if that's what you're worried about. I could text you and tell you what the vibe's like. In case you want to come by after . . . whatever it is you're doing."

I consider this, turning to a new page. "Oooh, beehive!"

Ethan leans in to look as I add another sticky. "Wow. That is some seriously vertical hair." He holds up 1986. "I stopped flagging the funny ones in here. It's literally all of them." We add both books to the To-Scan pile and grab new ones. "So what are these important plans tomorrow?"

"Um . . ." I look at him, biting my lip. *Oh, what the hell?* "I'm actually meeting a guy—not from school. He's very cute but possibly a douche? He also used the phrase *It's a date* when we were texting, but I don't *think* it's a date." I come a little closer to study Ethan's face, like maybe he has some answer to this Boy Code.

But he just says, "*How* do you know him?"

"That I can't tell you," I say, pulling back again.

He grins. "You're a tough nut, Gretchen. If I guess correctly will you tell me? Maybe . . . you're both really into polka dance. Or no. You're in a lawn gnome–carving club. Yep." He nods himself along. "You just get together and carve gnomes."

"That's a real thing, you know," I say. "It's like a whole sub-genre of YouTube. My dad got weirdly into it one summer."

He laughs. "Anyway, I'll stop harassing you. You are entitled to your secrets, Gretchen." He tosses a yearbook down onto the carpet and stretches his arms overhead. "Should we pack it in?"

"Yeah." With a yawn, I place a sticky note on a Farrah Fawcett, then close the class of '77.

When I get up to my room, I dive into bed and reach for my list, scrawling out, *Parties make me feel like I'm going to die of awkward.*

I shiver and slap the notebook down. "Dad, it's like five degrees in here!"

"It's not that bad!" I hear from somewhere in the house. "Just add a jacket!" I roll my eyes, and scribble, *Daughter of a thermal despot!!!* on the next line.

My phone buzzes in my backpack on the floor and I get up to dig it out.

For a second, I'm confused by the message: Pretty good! It's from Henrietta, a follow-up to the How does it feel to be back? I texted her forever ago.

"Good talk, Hen," I grumble.

A few rows down is the unanswered message I sent to Carmen—a meme of Justin Bieber saying, Hey girl, I belieb in you, since I knew she was swamped with school. Maybe she felt it didn't require a response. Sam's comments about my social life hit hard today. What will next year look like, with him and Annika both gone, too?

I look around my room—all these pictures from growing up. It's all so different now. All going away. I crawl back into bed, and scrawl out, *People keep leaving. And I keep standing still.*

There's a knock, and I stuff the notebook under my pillow.

"We're taking off," says Mom, letting herself in. She pauses in the doorway, a funny look on her face. "You sure you'll be okay by yourself all weekend?"

"I'm sure," I tell her, getting up and following her down the stairs. It takes three trips for Mom and Dad to load the car, and when they finally start backing out of the icy driveway, I wave Nacho's little paw from the front step.

Once the car disappears around a corner, I shut the door and head straight for the thermostat. Then I move to the sound system, pulling up William Onyeabor's "Fantastic Man" and cranking the volume.

I get a rush as the music starts. I have no predictions for this weekend. Only question marks. And that's a good thing, I think.

"Woot, woot, Friday night!" I say to Nacho, setting him down. "You ready for this?" He yips his response as the groove picks up: *Tell me, tell me, please tell me how I look. . . .*

I twirl, my whole body relaxing. And for a while, all around the house, Nacho and I go full Hugh Grant from *Love, Actually.*

TEN

The Classic Love Triangle | He is cute! Oh no, he's also cute! . . . Actually, yeah, that's pretty much it. The plot that launched a thousand rom-coms.

Two buns—check. Glasses—check. High-heeled booties—ow, but check.

I step inside the empty club and catch my breath, having just sprinted from my car through the snow. It's weird to see this place with no people in it. Beneath the harsh overhead lighting, I'm more aware of the rather small, knitted black crop top I have on under this jacket. I bought it two summers ago in the spirit of *I could be this person* and then never removed the tags until tonight.

I shrug it off. Doesn't matter. *I'm Sabrina tonight*, I remind myself.

I went with ripped black jeans to complete the look because

(A) I'm not trying to be a cartoon character who wears the same outfit every day and (B) I still haven't gotten around to googling how to wash leather.

"You made it," says Jeremy, stepping out from the back. It's honestly a little silly how attractive he is, and for a flash, all thoughts of Sam are temporarily suspended.

"I have my notebook," I say, my voice coming out hoarse. "And I started my list. But I don't have many jokes yet."

"That's okay," he says, pulling down two stools from the bar. "Show me what you've got." I sit and hand him the notebook, my place bookmarked with a pencil. "Shiny-person adjacent?" he says, glancing up at me.

"Oh," I say dismissively. I didn't actually give much thought to him reading these. "It just means the people I hang out with tend to attract more attention than I do."

"Wow." He gives me the once-over before returning to my list. "Guess I need to meet these friends of yours."

I blush but lift my chin, feeling I should put some distance between us. "May I remind you that I am three years your elder?"

I know it's a lie, but the boy needs to slow his roll.

He laughs. "My apologies. Now what's this *defective Mainer* line about?"

"Oh," I say. "It's about how I hate being cold. And how I'm convinced I missed out on some kind of gene that makes you rugged and outdoorsy."

"That could be good," he says, scratching at his jaw. "Who's Nacho?"

"My mom's Pomeranian. Or my brother, as I'm supposed to call him. I've been dethroned as the baby of the family."

"That's funny," he says matter-of-factly. "How many siblings are there?"

"Three," I say. "Well, four if you count Nacho."

He laughs. "Okay, well, family's always a good place to start."

"Do you talk about your family a lot in your act?"

"Well, no," he says. "But we're kind of an unfunny family. It's just me and my dad. My mom walked out on us when I was little. She"—he makes quotes—"'*wasn't a kid person.*'"

"Yeesh," I say, feeling the air go out of the room. "I'm so sorry, Jeremy."

"See? Extremely unfunny. But I'm fine, really." Despite his smile, I can still see a flicker of sadness there—which is unnerving for all his unrelenting irony. "I'm *fine,*" he says again. "We all moved on in our weird little way. She's even quasi in touch now. . . . Now that I'm not a kid, I guess. Anyway, tell me about your family story. I want the whole childhood vibe."

"Well," I say, thinking a minute. Talking about my relatively easy life seems borderline inappropriate after that. But he seems to really want to know. "Like I said, I'm the youngest of three. And my cousin was always around too, since our moms are twins and are still totally codependent. So it's sort of like I have two big sisters, though they're both really busy now. Hen lives far away, and Carmen is—"

"Maybe you should start with childhood," he says, stopping me there.

"Okay, yeah," I say. "Basically, there was always a ton going on growing up. And I guess I'd say the vibe was . . . chaotic happy?"

"That sounds nice," he says.

"It was. With all that activity around you all the time, you can almost just stay still and enjoy it. Like listening to the ocean or something."

"And what was your role in all the activity?"

"I'm not sure," I say.

"Were you the troublemaker, the golden child . . . ?"

"Neither," I say. "Though you pretty much just described my brother and sister. I was more the one who floated along. My mom and dad got less strict over time. And basically abandoned all of their parenting standards."

He laughs. "Such as?"

"Like . . . take extracurriculars. My parents made my brother play soccer and learn percussion. They got my sister into dance, and even got a special tutor for her when they found out she was 'gifted' at math. But me? I . . . got the remote."

Jeremy looks up from skimming the list. "You're telling me you never did a single thing outside of school?"

"I mean, I know they put me in karate at some point, but

it didn't take. I just wanted to play and do my own thing. And I really did like TV. It's why I'm so into comedy. Still. They could have pushed me a *little.* I'm headed straight for middle management over here with my total lack of skills. Meanwhile my brother's a lawyer. And my sister's probably going to, like, cure cancer or something someday."

Jeremy bobs his head, tossing the notebook down onto the bar. "Do you feel like there was something about you that made them treat you differently, or was it just that you came last?"

"I don't know," I say. "Can those things even be separated? My siblings were probably more work than me. My brother was this popular athlete, with a bit of a rebellious streak. My parents were so terrified the whole time he was in high school. I swear they'd pelt him with condoms every time he walked out the door. My mom would be all, 'Get consent!' and my dad would be like, 'Wrap that rascal!'"

Jeremy taps the page between us. "You should probably write that down."

I nod, scrawling. *"Wrap . . . that . . . rascal. . . ."*

I sigh and drop the pencil. "And then there's my sister. Who's a total peach but . . . has a lot of feelings? My parents have always been delicate with her, ever since she was little. I remember them getting choked up when she came out, even though they didn't care about that kind of thing. You could tell they were just scared—that the world was going to be that much harder on her. Of course, my dad went out and got a mini rainbow flag for the corkboard of his woodshop. And my mom immediately joined, like, every LGBTQ ally group in the state of Maine."

"They sound sweet," says Jeremy.

"They are," I say. "And it's not like they don't love me or anything. It's more like they assume I'm always fine. Which I guess is fair. I mostly *am* fine."

Jeremy frames the air with his hands: "The girl who was mostly fine."

I smile faintly. "I actually just remembered something that might work for a set. . . ."

"Let's hear it," he says, reaching over the bar now to pour us each a water.

"It's about how we all learned to ride bikes," I say, doing my best to ignore the very nice, boy-scented torso in my face.

He lowers back down onto his stool, handing me a glass and waving me along. I clear my throat. "So my brother learned first," I say. "I remember watching him out there with my dad. We're talking hours of practice—serious technique analysis. Later, it came time for my sister to learn. It was the same thing. Similarly thorough training, but with a lot more padding. And then one day, not long after that . . ." I sip my water, frowning slightly. "I remember getting it in my head that it was my time to learn. So I taught myself." I can see it now—falling down and getting back up again; the scrapes along my knees. "And that's what I did. It was just me. Figuring it out on the street by our house while everyone was busy. If I even had a helmet, I very much doubt it was strapped under my chin."

"Aw," says Jeremy. "That's a little sad. But, like, funny-sad. You'd need to add some jokes."

I roll my eyes, the slight tightness in my throat letting up now. "I know I need jokes, Jeremy."

He grins, reading down the list again. "Still *crushing on your oldest friend*, huh? Any developments there?"

I sigh. "Just more overall confusion."

"Well, what about someone else?" he says. "Any . . . new handsome fella you've got your eye on?"

I hold his gaze a moment to confirm it, and yep—he is absolutely referring to himself right now. What must that be like, walking through the world with so much confidence?

I make a show of thinking it over, taking a drink from my water. "Nope. No one comes to mind."

"Mike Birbiglia," I say.

"Chris Rock," says Jeremy. "Jim Gaffigan, Jerry Seinfeld . . ."

"John Mulaney," I add, counting off. "Ali Wong, Dulcé Sloan . . ."

"Bill Burr, Wanda Sykes . . ."

I snap. "Kumail Nanjiani. Great stand-up *and* he cowrote *The Big Sick*, which is, like, a modern-day Nora Ephron film. Seriously, I've never identified so strongly with a forty-something-year-old man. Oh, also Fortune Feimster . . . and Ronny Chieng . . . and Tig!" I say, clutching my heart.

Jeremy clutches his heart, too. "Oh, Tig."

I think we could go on trading faves like this all night, but the show is starting soon. Leaning forward on my stool, I make the universal gesture for *hit me*, and Ted comes over to fill my ginger ale.

"I think you may have to cut her off soon," says Jeremy.

"I'm just excited," I tell them. "A real Saturday night show!"

"Yep, this is the big time," says Ted, the overhead lights flickering briefly. "Or at least slightly more big-time than Wednesdays." There are waiters taking orders in the audience, drink trays resting on hips. The whole operation feels more professional—like everything's been kicked up a notch.

Abruptly, music starts booming from speakers, and Dolores steps up to greet the big, boisterous crowd.

The first comic hails from New Hampshire, by way of Sweden, and has lots of feedback for stupid Americans. It's pretty much the whole set, and it totally works.

"He has such a clear *thing*," I whisper to Jeremy, leaning in. "Like every joke is pretty much dumbass Americans through the eyes of a Swede."

Jeremy nods. "A thing definitely helps."

"Shoot," I say. "I need a thing!"

The next comic spends most of her time talking about sex. She's graphic, unapologetic. Clever but not exactly inventive. "You don't think she's funny?" whispers Jeremy, noticing my face.

I hesitate. "She's a little . . . vagina-y? It feels too easy. Like talking about vaginas is just automatic comedy."

"It works for Ali Wong."

"Yeah, but Ali Wong is, like, a master of vagina comedy."

"It's true. You never get bored hearing about Ali Wong's vagina."

"Okay, I think we've said *vagina* too many times," I whisper. And I laugh at myself, as this woman onstage works for my approval. Because, *man*, is it easier down here as the critic.

After a while, we get too carried away for commentary.

There's something so dizzyingly great about laughing with other people, strangers mostly, all of us packed together. The comics keeping coming, each one funnier than the last. Topics include recycling, changing tires, aliens, and shitty reality TV. It seems pretty much anything can be a worthwhile subject when approached from the right angle, with some particular voice, or humanity brought into the mix.

The jokes don't always land, but when they do, it's magic. I can tell Jeremy feels the magic, too, from the focused look he has now—watching the stage so fiercely, like he's soaking up every second. Meanwhile, the twitchy feeling in my limbs is back, like I'm craving that mic to my lips again, eyes on me, people listening, feeling connected to the room. Knowing that someone out there might actually know what the hell it is I'm talking about—might even feel delighted by it.

I wonder if this means I'm secretly an egomaniac.

Jeremy too.

Or maybe we're just honest.

Maybe everyone needs a spotlight now and then.

When the house lights come up, Jeremy declares he better go help close. "But that was fun," he says as I hop down from my stool. "You feeling pumped for Wednesday?"

"So pumped," I say teasingly.

"Let me know if you want to brainstorm anymore."

"Yeah, I'll see how far I get." We look at each other a hair too long. Long enough for me to notice that his eyes are ocean blue—not sky.

"Sabrina! You get that headshot for me?"

"Oh shoot," I say, whipping around as Dolores walks over to us. "I completely forgot. But I'll . . . figure something out, I promise."

"Okay," she says, eyeing Jeremy. "You planning on working anytime soon? And shovel the walk, will you? I've done it enough times today. Fuckin' snow's gonna be the death of me."

"Always busting my balls, this one," sighs Jeremy, heading for the back. "I'm going, okay? I'll see you later, Sabrina."

"Okay, yeah. Bye," I say with a feeble wave.

"Really don't forget it this time," Dolores says to me as I push open the door. "And please try to be funny Wednesday!"

"Thank you for that," I call over my shoulder. "No pressure or anything!"

Hey, this is weird, I type out as I slide into my car. But I need a photo of myself. How much would you charge for that sort of thing?

It's a questionable move on my part, but I can't think of another option.

I'd say you qualify for the friends and family rate, Ethan replies after a minute.

Oh yeah? And what would that be?

Dunno, he says. Maybe like a sandwich?

I laugh. I think I can swing that.

Cool. Want to meet me at the café when I'm out of work tmr? We close at 3 on Sundays.

I send a thumbs-up, but see he's typing again. After a beat, a long message comes in: Also, I forgot to update you about the party. I don't think you'd die of awkward. It's not that crowded, and Natalie is literally doing a one-hundred-piece puzzle with some of the football guys at the kitchen table. Sam is easily the tipsiest person here and that's only because he's a lightweight. Just saying, the night is young!

More typing . . .

Anyway putting my phone down now. Gotta get in on this puzzle action!

And some more . . .

P.S. I just told Sam we're texting and he seems to really want you here.

My heart lifts, sort of, and I groan. "Now what am I supposed to do with that?" I toss my phone aside and glance at the clock—not yet midnight. I'm still wide awake, hopped up from the show and seeing Jeremy.

I hear the name like a girlish swoon inside my head: *Jeremy* . . . It's vaguely mortifying. But how else does one respond to a grin like that? And those eyes . . .

I sigh.

Sam *also* has great eyes. Not to mention the cheek dimple. And then there's the matter of how it feels to make him laugh. The swoony voice comes back: *Sam*. . . .

"Ugh!" I say to the empty car, shaking off my ping-ponging thoughts. I feel like I should be in a PSA or something: *This is your brain on boys!*

Clutching the steering wheel with both hands, I breathe in and out, trying to imagine what it would feel like to step into that party tonight.

I don't really want to go home. And what about Jeremy's advice last week, about making the material come to me? *Treat life like an experiment*, he said. *Walk toward the awkward moments, not away.* It's a pretty freeing concept, if you think about it. Maybe tonight is simply . . . research in the field?

"Oh, *fine*," I say, pulling down the mirror. I take the buns out of my hair and shake my waves free, kicking off boots and reaching around for the Chuck Taylors I tossed in back, in case my blisters got too bad. Without the heels, the outfit isn't *that* wild. I remove the glasses and use a tissue to wipe the makeup from my eyes and lips, until it's not quite gone but softer—at least halfway back to Gretchen.

I nod to myself and put the car in drive. "Worse comes to worst, it all goes in the act. . . ."

"Oh, hey, you came," says Natalie when I let myself into Sam's apartment. She's looking bright and cozy in her cashmere cardigan, the same red as the plastic cup in her hand.

"Hi, Natalie," I say, already jolted by the vibe in here as I slip off my jacket and hang it on a hook. I turn around.

"Whoa," she says, stepping back. "Gretchen. *Look* at you!"

I shrug, feeling more exposed now in this tiny shirt than I did twenty minutes ago. "Yeah, I don't know," I say, wrapping my arms around my middle. "I, uh . . ."

Ethan walks up to us and does a double take. "Dang, Gretchen. How was gnome carving?" Natalie's confused frown makes me laugh, but neither of us bothers to explain. "No Sasha and Lexi tonight?" he asks her.

Natalie sighs. "Nah, they bailed."

"Sam's over there, by the way," Ethan says to me, gesturing to what appears to be a Sam-sized lump on the couch. "He was asking for you earlier, but he's not in the best shape anymore. He kind of . . . threw up on our puzzle."

Ethan and Natalie share a somber beat of silence. "We had just lined up all the edge pieces," she says.

Sam's living room feels strange like this, the lights dimmed and furniture rearranged. There are maybe twenty people in here—manageable, I guess. But still a lot.

"I need a refill," says Ethan, pointing back toward the cooler across the room. "I assume you don't want anything, Gretch?"

"I'm good, thanks." He leaves us there and I look at Sam again, still dead asleep. . . . Hopefully not *dead-dead.* "You're sure it's not alcohol poisoning, right?" I say, turning to Natalie. "I paid very close attention to that unit in health class."

"He had four high-percentage beers on an empty stomach," she says reassuringly. "Not the smartest move, but he'll be all right." I bob my head, heart sinking a little as he begins to snore. I don't know why exactly, but I have a feeling this wasn't the fun kind of drinking tonight. Maybe it has something to do with his mom being off on her couples' weekend—a glimmer of next year when he's gone. Sam's already learned from his dad how quickly old lives can be replaced. I'm sure this can't be easy.

"Don't worry," says Natalie gently. "We've been checking on him."

"Okay," I say, looking around. I'm surprised to catch a few senior guys openly staring at us—or maybe just her. She notices, too, rolling her eyes a little, and I cover my middle again, just in case.

Natalie seems amused by how jumpy I am. "Sorry," I say. "I'm not really in the business of standing out."

"Yeah, well," she sighs. "It's never been much of a choice for me."

"Natalie!" Dick Grody yells over several people's heads. He's carrying a plate on upturned fingers like a cater-waiter. "Want a Jell-O shot?"

"I'm good!" she calls back with a laugh, right as a few girls slip into the party, taking off coats and instantly pulling her into a conversation. Somehow, I've positioned myself *just* outside their circle, but it feels too late to take a step closer.

This seems about right: me just standing here like a houseplant.

I'm getting that skin-crawly feeling I hate, and with Sam passed out, there's no real point in being here. Why did I say yes to this again? Jeremy's *carpe awkward* advice seems so patently ridiculous now as my mouth goes dry, gaze drifting longingly to the front door. *How to leave a place when you've only just walked in . . .*

I startle as Natalie appears at my side. "You could try holding a Solo cup," she says under her breath.

"What?"

"You know. Jack and Coke, hold the Jack? That's what this is." She swishes the brown liquid in her hand. "In my case, it's because I have an early morning. I actually do drink, but only as of this year. Before that, I held *a lot* of these cups with soda in them at parties."

"Oh," I say, frowning on a delay. ". . . Why?"

She shrugs. "Got people off my butt, basically. Plus, it's nice to have something to sip on if you're having a weird moment. Or feeling kind of . . . out of place?"

I flinch a little, somehow both appreciative and embarrassed that she's read me so easily. "Well, I'm not sure a plastic cup is any match for my awkwardness."

She looks me over. "I really don't think you're that awkward, Gretchen. Or if you are, it's like . . . a good awkward?"

"I'm going to take that as a compliment," I say, making her laugh. For a moment, we look out at the boisterous room in silence, and just by our proximity, I feel a lot less like a houseplant.

"Ethan!" she calls, waving to him as he scans the crowd. She leans into me as he walks our way. "If you can stand to stick it out a little longer, I highly recommend this side of Ethan. He gets pretty chatty when he's had a couple. And he's got some pretty sweet dance moves."

I turn to her, nodding heartily. "I'd actually *really* like to see that."

I didn't think this night could get much weirder.

But, as the internet once said, *hold my beer.*

Actually, Ethan is holding my beer—a whole sequence of beers—which he's been pounding on my behalf whenever Pilsner or Grody slosh a Ping-Pong ball into a cup on our end. Sidebar, *wow,* this game is unhygienic.

"Look alive, Gretchen!" Natalie calls from her perch atop the couch, like she's out on a bleacher somewhere instead of three feet away from us.

There's only one cup left at the other side of the table, and I'm staring straight ahead with the ball clutched between my fingers. Ethan steps closer and speaks into my ear. "Come on, Gretch. . . . You can do this. You were born to this. Your great-grandmother was born so that you could *do this*."

I glance back at him, holding in a laugh. Then I aim, and—*plunk*.

"Yessssss!" Ethan erupts, pumping his fists victoriously to a mix of cheers and groans.

I look over, wide-eyed, as Pilsner shakes his head at his teammate. "You seriously let her do you like that?"

"What? She made the shot," says Grody. "We left it all on the field, man."

"Whoa," I say, blinking around at everyone. "Does this mean I'm athletic? This has never happened to me before."

Sam stirs below on the couch, poking his head up and meeting my eyes with confusion. It might be my new favorite thing, surprising Sam like this.

"You doing okay there?" Natalie calls down to him, reaching out to give his nose a playful *boop!* "You just missed Gretchen schooling Pils and Grody at beer pong. It was epic."

"Weird," he says, frowning a minute. But then he flops down to resume his nap.

Grody walks around the table to shake my hand, swishing the blond hair from his eyes like a gnarly surfer. "It was an honor, Gretchen." Pilsner follows suit, his bulldog-like face a bit more sullen than I've seen it before.

"You know, boys," I hear myself say. "It's not whether you get knocked down. It's whether you get back up again." They laugh, and I do too, because seriously, *Who am I right now?* When I turn to Ethan, he looks proud . . . also wobbly. He *did* just drink all that beer for me.

"Uh-oh," he says, touching the back of his ear as a Britney Spears song comes up on Natalie's old-school playlist. He drifts out to an open patch of space, head bobbing.

"You like this?" he calls to Pilsner and Grody, who roll their eyes at him. "This is a victory dance. That's right. I did it *again.* Oops! . . . Wait, sorry, Gretchen. *We* did it again."

"Thanks. It is nice to be recognized!" I call over to him as I lean into the couch next to Natalie. "Is he okay?"

"I think so," she says. We watch as he swishes his hips and does a few chest pops. She glances sidelong at me. "He doesn't look as terrible doing that as he should, huh?"

"It's true," I say, a bit mesmerized honestly. It's something about all that goofy confidence, and the fact that he's so clearly enjoying himself—long limbs jerking around, the Not-Mullet going everywhere.

"It helps that he's totally adorable," she says with a laugh. It's a funny word for such a sturdy, good-looking guy, but I get what she means. "You're welcome, by the way. I knew this song would get him going. He's convinced he and Britney are related."

"We totally are!" he says to us, apparently in earshot. "I've got the Spears family rhythm running through my veins!"

"That among other things," I say under my breath.

Just then, Ethan freezes, frowns. He starts to sway a little. "Okay, let's get him a snack," says Natalie, hopping off the couch. "I've seen enough barf for one day."

In the kitchen, she pours him a big glass of water while I dig out cold cuts from Sam's fridge, producing a quick sandwich and wrapping it in a paper towel.

The beers have definitely gone to Ethan's head. "Gretchen is so *mysterious*," he's saying to Natalie now as we make our way through the crowd. "Isn't she so *mysterious*?"

"Just eat your sandwich," I tell him as we claim an open patch of space in the hallway by Sam's room. Natalie darts off to find the bathroom, and we slide down the wall to sit.

"You paid me in advance," he says around a mouthful.

"What?"

"The sandwich. For your photo tomorrow. You paid me in advance."

"Oh, no, no," I say seriously. "I have every intention of getting you a much fancier sandwich than this, Ethan. Something with, like . . . capers on it. Or Gouda."

"I don't think I've ever had Gouda before," he says dreamily. "Is it *Gouda*?" I snort. "Sorry." He forces his eyes open. "I always get a little silly on these nights, but I am *not* used to drinking for two."

I smile at him. "Thanks for that, by the way."

He nods, then frowns. "So. *Why* do you need this photo tomorrow?"

"Oh . . ." I look over my shoulder, unsure of how to put this. "We're becoming friends, right, Ethan?"

"Yes, yes, definitely friends," he says, back to eating.

"Okay, great. So . . ." I clear my throat. "*I believe* that the sign of a *really* good friendship is when one person is willing to do a kind of weird favor for the other person without asking too many questions . . . ?"

"This!" he says. "This is what I'm talking about. So *mysterious*!"

"Shhhh," I say, as Natalie walks back to us.

She pauses to examine a photo on the wall, grinning immediately. It's of Sam and me in his backyard—age seven or so, the two of us showing off matching tie-dye T-shirts and hockey player smiles. It's wild to think those tiny people were *us*. "You two are pretty close, huh?" she says, lowering down to sit. When I shrug, Ethan flashes me a knowing look, and I bug my eyes like, *You better keep your mouth shut, drunky!* He chuckles like he heard me loud and clear. "So, can I ask . . ." Natalie begins tentatively as she glances toward the living room. "What's Sam's deal? Like with girls and stuff?"

For a minute, I just blink. I don't know where this is going, but I don't think I like it. "Well, we're not . . . big on talking about our love lives."

She shakes her head as if talking herself down from something. "I probably shouldn't even be thinking this way right before graduation. But there's something about Sam. . . . Even if he did dash my puzzle dreams tonight." I laugh lightly, glimpsing down the hall to the couch, where he's still snoring through his own party. "He has this sweet side that's such a nice surprise." When I look back at her, her smile is growing. "I mean, right now we're just friends, but I feel like when we talk, he really sees me, you know? Like, all of me. And I can just . . . relax. Does that make sense?"

"Uh . . ." My eyes flit to Ethan, then back to her before I remember to nod my head.

"Anyway." She breathes out, appearing giddy despite herself. "If I *were* to complicate my life right now, I'd want to be sure it was for somebody worthwhile. And I figured, you would know, Gretchen. I mean . . ." She holds my gaze meaningfully. "Sam's a good guy, right?"

Ethan catches my gaze again and gives a sympathetic smile.

"Yeah," I sigh, looking back at her. "Yeah, Sam's a great guy."

ELEVEN

The Other Girl | A temporary obstacle. Obviously the worst. Under no circumstances do we like her. Be gone, woman!

"I'll be right out!" I call to Ethan Sunday afternoon inside Willard Beach Coffee. Duffel bag on my shoulder, I stuff myself into the tight bathroom, quickly putting on makeup and doing my best to snap out of my mood.

I spent the morning sheepishly scrolling through Natalie's Instagram, hoping to find something hateable to latch on to.

But alas, nada. Which is impressive, honestly. Most people are at least *a little* hateable on Instagram.

Anyway, I feel like a hypocrite—or, I don't know. Greedy? It's been, what, fifteen hours since I was drinking in the blue of Jeremy's eyes inside the Chuckle Parlor? And here I am wanting Sam for myself, too, at least while I figure this out. I suppose what I want is irrelevant. It's not like I can put a hold on either of them. They're not library books.

"Okay, let's do this," I sigh, stepping out into the empty café in my Sabrina getup. From the way Ethan is gaping at me, I realize I probably should have eased him into this moment a bit more. *"Friends do weird favors!"* I remind him as his gaze darts between the glasses, the little buns, the gleam of my skintight pants—which are clean now, by the way. I finally got around to that.

"Wow," says Ethan. I guess it was naive to hope he wouldn't have *any* questions for me today. But actually, he recovers quite quickly. "Okay then . . ." He smacks his lips, hooking a strap around his neck before he attaches a lens. "Let's try having you against the brick wall." He drags a table out of the way. "The light here is pretty decent, from the windows and the skylight. . . ."

I strike a pose, hoping to project some Sabrina badassery, and Ethan starts, only to lower the camera to his chest, brows knitted together. "Just tell me this isn't for some weird sex thing."

I straighten up. *"What?!"*

"I don't know. All the leather? I'm just saying, be safe out there."

"Ethan." I level him with a look. "This is not for a weird sex thing. I haven't even done *not*-weird sex things yet." As the words fly from my mouth, I feel my cheeks heat up. Immediately, I start looking around for my duffel bag. "All right, well.

Mind if we pick this up later? I think I need to go die now."

His lips twitch, amused. "It's nothing to be embarrassed about. I mean, I haven't . . . well, I guess I've done sex-*ish* stuff, but . . ."

"Sex-*ish*?" For some reason, this makes my cheeks heat up even more. "Oh God. What does *that* mean?"

"I . . . don't know," he says, going a little pink himself. "I'm regretting everything I'm saying as I'm saying it."

I let out an odd laugh, meeting his eyes. Then we both clear our throats at the same time.

"Okay then," I say.

He nods. "Back to taking pictures?"

"Yep," I say, returning to my spot against the wall. I try a hand on my hip, angling my face one way or another as he clicks and clicks. But then I frown. "I'm sort of surprised by that, honestly. That it's only been . . . ish." I'm not sure sure why I've led us down this road again. "I just mean . . . A friendly, popular athlete like you. I feel like you'd have had plenty of opportunities."

"Yeah, I guess," he says, adjusting the lens with one eye closed. "I've had a couple girlfriends who were really nice and cool, but . . . I don't know. Can I tell you something kind of weird?"

I smile. "Always."

"I think one of my big deterrents has been that I'd have to tell my parents."

I snort. "Seriously?"

"What? We're a very communicative family! And so far, it

just . . . hasn't felt worth that level of supreme awkwardness. I think it's going to take someone special." He notices my face then. "Gretchen, are you *laughing* at me? I thought this was a safe space!"

I bite back a grin. "I'm laughing *with* you. Definitely *with.* And it's not like I'd have a leg to stand on. I've never even been on a date."

"Really," he says.

I shrug. "It's what happens when you're not outgoing, I guess. And I don't think I make a very good first impression. I have worse than resting bitch face. I have, like . . . resting bitch *whole personality.*"

"You do not," he says.

"No, I think I do! But it's only because I feel weird."

"Well, for what it's worth, I don't remember thinking that when we started at yearbook together."

"Thanks," I say, feeling almost squirmy now. It's oddly disarming how unironically nice Ethan can be sometimes. "Anyway, it's just . . . hard to date people when you never really *meet* people. Unless you want to date your existing friends, which . . . well, we both know how that's going for me."

"Yeah," he says, frowning. "That whole Natalie conversation last night must have kinda sucked, huh?"

"Yeah it did," I sigh. "I also find it weirdly unnerving to feel competitive with another girl. Like it goes against my feminist training or something."

"Huh," he says.

"I'm hoping I can at least partially blame the patriarchy? Like, whatever I'm feeling now probably traces back to a long legacy of beauty pageants and, like, televised sexy Jell-O wrestling or whatever."

He laughs. "Your brain never stops going, does it?"

"Guess not," I say with a shrug.

"Well, at the risk of employing my male gaze here, I think I got some good shots of you. Well, *you*, or . . . whatever *this* is," he says, gesturing vaguely at my whole deal.

I ignore the comment, leaning in to look. "Oooh, these are great, Ethan. We definitely got it. Done and done. Thank you." I pick up my bag. "I'm going to go change."

"Oh? You don't want to go out like that?" he calls after me.

"Can't risk running into Sam!" I close the bathroom door. "He, unlike you, would not relent with the questions."

"So, what, I'm some kind of wimp?"

"Not a wimp. Zen!" I wriggle out of the pants and slide on leggings, trading the jacket for a frumpy sweater. "It's why I can trust you with all the secret details of my sordid love triangle."

"Huh?" I hear him say. "Oh, right. Your gnome-carver guy."

Leaning into the sink, I wipe off my lipstick before chucking the glasses into the duffel bag and freeing my hair. "Yeah, he's been really flirty lately, which is fun. It's hard to know how I feel sometimes, but we have a lot in common. Since we're both so into"—I frown—"gnome carving. Anyway, it's harmless."

When I step out, Ethan is back at the espresso machine. "Pumpkin spice latte for the road?"

"Wow. You read my mind, Ethan."

He hands me the cup and I sip happily. "Mmmmmm, basic."

"Hey . . ." He grabs his camera again. "Do you mind if I try one more?"

"Oh . . ." I blink down at myself.

"In case you want it someday. Just real quick."

I feel silly, but I humor him, wiping the foam off my upper lip as I walk back to the wall. I look into the lens, stiffer now, and he takes a few shots. They aren't going to be good *at all*. I can feel it.

"Try letting out a big breath," he says as he checks the last few frames with a wince, confirming my suspicions.

I do as I'm told, then force a smile—which I guess does the trick.

He bobs his head. "Okay, great."

"Cool," I say, glancing at the clock. Mom and Dad should be home from their trip soon. I should go. "Well, thanks for doing this. And just so you know, weird unexplained friend favors go both ways."

"Excellent," he says. "I'll have to start thinking some up."

"Hey, sky's the limit," I tell him. "We're in this together now."

"The *this* being the thing you refuse to explain to me," he says, peering through the viewfinder again.

"Yes," I say, seriously.

I laugh, and the shutter clicks.

TWELVE

Big, Fat, Snowballing Lies | One leads to another leads to another. But it's all very quirky and understandable. What could possibly go wrong?

"What's that?" Mom asks as we're cleaning up dinner. I pause from slotting plates into the dishwasher. I've been practicing tonight's set all day—in the shower, at school, and apparently right now.

Whoops.

"I figured it out, by the way," she says to my back.

I freeze, slowly turning around. "Figured out what?"

"The theme for Nacho's birthday party. I'm thinking: *Gatsby*!" She traces a hand across the sky like a Broadway star, and I laugh with relief. "Can't you picture it?"

"Oh definitely," I say, making a mental note that she and Nacho should probably make their way into my act.

My act—listen to me.

I get a flutter in my stomach just thinking about it.

The last few days have been hectic—writing jokes and texting with Jeremy. I picked out my official headshot from Ethan, had it printed, then hand-delivered it to Dolores last night, which meant *another* round of car changing, before and after. I don't know how Clark Kent managed with just a phone booth. And then of course there has still been the utter inconvenience that is *school*, plus all the time spent at yearbook. Natalie has been fishing for more Sam info the past few days, in a series of conversations vaguely akin to medieval torture. Ethan's been in my corner, at least, smoothly changing the subject whenever Sam comes up.

All that is to say, you wouldn't think I'd feel this good right now. But the truth is, I am bursting.

I can't wait to get back to that club.

"Hey, do you have a lot of homework?" asks Mom. "We could watch another movie tonight. . . ."

"Oh, um." I dry my hands on a towel. I need to get out of here soon, but I still haven't landed on a solid-sounding excuse. "I'm . . . going to Sam's," I blurt out, immediately wishing I'd gone with something else. It's hardly believable, with him so absent lately.

But Mom just smiles fondly. "Aw. Tell him to come to our house next time. I miss him."

An hour or so later, I'm back to changing in my car, laughing and cursing my tight pants before giddily sprinting through the cold. Once inside, I peel off the suede jacket and drape it on a barstool. As I hop up to sit, Ted starts pouring a ginger ale from the soda gun without even having to be asked. I search for a quip about how I've finally found my *Cheers*. But then I stop, because actually at this bar, *nobody* knows my name.

"Did you see your picture out front?" says Dolores, coming up from behind me. "Lookin' feisty, huh? By the way, I have you on first tonight."

I almost choke on my soda. "Wow. First is soon."

"You'll be fine," she says, already off to check in with the rest of the comics. Jeremy walks in, and she rushes up to him, saying something in his ear. He nods, his eyes landing on me, prompting a weird little squirm. Good *lord* he's attractive.

"You ready?" he asks a minute later, taking the stool next to mine.

"Yeah," I say, clearing my throat. "Although . . . Dolores just said I'm going first."

"Ah," he says. "It can be tough breaking in the audience. But on the plus side, you'll have less time to be nervous, right?"

I nod, telling myself to stay calm. "When do you go on?"

"Second to last. Which means the crowd will either be nice and warmed up or super bored and ready to leave." I laugh, glancing at my phone as it lights up.

Huh.

Sam's calling me. That's weird. He usually texts. I should probably ignore it. . . .

Jeremy starts to say something, but I put one finger up, unable to help myself. "Hello?"

"Hey," says Sam, though it's hard to hear.

I plug my ear, trying to block out the chatter. "Uh . . . one second." I lean in to Jeremy, and whisper, "Be right back." Throwing my jacket on, I hurry for the door, immediately blasted by cold. I round the corner into the alley, rubbing one arm for warmth. "Hey! I only have a minute. What's up?"

"You tell me," says Sam, a smile in his voice. "I hear we're hanging out tonight."

"Aw, crap," I say, making him laugh.

"Are we having a good time at least?"

"I'm sorry. I didn't think it would . . ."

"Don't worry, I covered for you," he says. "If the moms are comparing stories, I said we were both going over to Natalie's. Since that's where I'm headed now. Figured keep it simple."

"Oh! So you're hanging out with Natalie tonight?"

"Yeah, she invited me over to her house to play video games. I think it's just us. Should be fun."

"*Super* fun," I spit back like a total weirdo.

"So . . ." he says after an odd beat. "What's got *you* sneaking around? Do you have like a secret boyfriend or something?"

"No, nothing like that," I say, a bit bothered by how *un*bothered he seems by this possibility. Does he really not remember that moment in the yoga studio? Could I have made the whole thing up?

"By the way," he says, "and then I'll let you go. . . . I heard you were the life of the party the other night. Sorry I was so indisposed. I think I wanted to take my mind off everything, but I learned my lesson."

"Huh. I was wondering about that. Was it the mom-boyfriend trip thing?"

"Please don't make me barf . . . again. But yeah, kinda."

"Okay," I say. "Just promise from now on you won't drink your feelings like that? It's, like, literally the textbook thing you're not supposed to do."

"I remember," he sighs. "You paid very close attention to that unit in health class."

I laugh, sort of. "I'm just *saying.* I know the past few years have been hard for you. And . . . I don't know. I guess I used to assume when you got all party-hardy like that, you were doing your whole fakey, cool-guy thing. But that night, for the first time I thought, what if he's just sad?"

The other end goes quiet for a second. "Okay, back up, Gretchen. What's with you calling me fake? I don't know why you're so stuck on this idea. We've been over this. I like parties. I like *people.* I'm a social guy."

"I guess I don't remember you needing this much validation when we were growing up. Sorry . . . I have to go."

"Wait, no. What does this have to do with *validation*?"

"I mean, I'm just spitballing here. But think about it . . . Your dad moves out in eighth grade, then we start high school, and it's like, all of a sudden, you need everyone in the world to like you. I am merely *positing* that those two things could be related. Because you didn't need a million friends before."

"Okay, but you're forgetting that people *change*, Gretch. They have to. Or they'll fucking suffocate."

Now I'm the one who goes quiet.

"And, even if you are right—even if I *was* pretending, or . . . wanted a fresh start. So what? Haven't you ever wanted to reinvent yourself a little?"

"Yes," I say, looking down at myself. Obviously yes.

"You know what, yeah. This is interesting to me, Gretchen. Tell me your plan. Are you going to stay exactly the same for the rest of your life? Do you really want to be that boring?"

I'm winded for a second.

". . . I didn't mean that," he says. There's a hint of remorse in his voice, but I can hear a coldness too. "I just really regret calling you, to be honest."

I swallow, hard. "Well, then I'll hang up, Sam."

I click the button.

And burst into tears.

"There you are!" I whip around to see Paula poking her head out from the side door. I swipe at the makeup under my glasses and her face falls. "We were all looking for you. You're supposed to be on right now."

I scrunch my eyes shut. *Fuck fuck fuckity fuck.* This is really not my night.

"It's okay," she says quickly. "Dolores made Jeremy switch places with you. Between you and me, you're getting a way better slot now. I hate opening. Just tell me you have something good planned."

I shrug, sniffing. "Just some stuff about my life and . . ." I laugh. "Unrequited love."

"That have anything to do with the call you were just on?"

"What gave it away?" She smiles gently as I let out a big breath. "You all right?"

"Yeah, fine," I say, shaking it off. "Although, I don't know. Maybe I'm too much of a mess tonight. I probably shouldn't go onstage like this."

"Are you kidding me?" Paula walks over to take me by the shoulders. *"Use it."*

I nod, meeting her eyes.

"It's the beauty of comedy," she says. "We turn our pain into joy. Not that I should be helping you. We are still mortal enemies, after all." I laugh as she slings an arm around me. "Come on. Let's get you inside. I'm freezing my vag off out here."

Dolores's voice sounds far away from my place offstage. The moment is almost here. I close my eyes, clench my fists and unclench them. I hear hushed conversations, smell beer-soaked wood.

"Give it up for *Sabrina Martin*!"

For half a second, I think, *Who?* But then I snap to attention, tapping my two little buns and pushing the glasses up my nose. I rush the short flight of steps and adjust the mic. It's a fun, boisterous crowd, energized by the feel-good acts that came before me.

"Hey, everybody." The boom of my voice is just as shocking as it was that first night. "Thank you . . ." I say, looking out at the cheering crowd. "Wow. Really. Thank you. You're seriously cheering me up right now. I just had a fight with my friend Sam, who I think I'm in love with? And he's *definitely* not in love with me back. . . ."

Someone in the crowd lets out an *Aww*.

"I know," I say, deadpan. "How dare he, right? It's ironic because I've always hated that one nice guy in the rom coms who's all, 'No fair, you friend-zoned me!' And the girl is like, 'Because you're my friend?'"

I laugh lightly as the room goes quiet—not bad quiet, though. It's weird, but I can tell the difference now. "Speaking of rom-coms, I've been feeling lied to lately. I watched so many growing up that I always assumed heartbreak would be this . . . almost charming rite of passage? I figured when the day came, I'd just sort of . . . cry adorably into some ice cream, maybe sing 'All By Myself' into a hairbrush. But soon after that, the pain would be gone and my love life would be all worked out—*forever*."

I hold back a smile—this seems to work if I play it a little grouchy. I can feel the audience warming up, the laughter trickling in.

"I guess *love life* is sort of a big phrase for whatever it is I've experienced so far. One thing you should know is: I'm a *lurker.* I lurk." That gets a laugh. "Before Sam, if I liked someone, I pretty much just . . . watched them. Not in, like, a binoculars-outside-your-window kind of way. But if we were in the same room, I would be on the *other side* of that room. Talking to the person? *Interacting* with them?" I shake my head. "Yeah, that never occurred to me."

I think muscle memory must be kicking in from all my practicing, time skipping forward, my consciousness almost fading to black before I'm spit out into the present again, with all its sharp edges, my mouth still running somehow.

"It's funny that we dwell so much on ourselves when it's not like we get to choose our personalities. Like, I obviously wouldn't have *chosen* to be the lurker girl." I hunch over and put a fist to my hip. "'What attributes are you looking for, little lady?'" This is my higher-power impression, apparently.

"'I guess . . .'" I pretend to think about this. "'Can you give me stress sweats, verbal diarrhea, and maybe like a really strange, unnerving stare for when I'm standing in the corner at social events?'"

For a second, I look down at the mic in my hand, hit with the sensation of free fall. *Holy shit, I am doing this. This is happening*. . . . But then I remember: I'm protected. I'm *Sabrina*.

"Think about it," I hear myself say. "Like, if someone goes, 'Aw, you're such a cool person!' should you really thank them for that? Or is it more like, 'Yeah, man, pretty sweet. Luck of the draw, am I right?'"

Another happy murmur gives me a rush.

"So the way I see it, there are only two possible explanations for why I am the way I am. One, I got some rare awkward gene that no one else I'm related to has. Or two, it's . . . all my family's fault." That gets a laugh.

"I'm the runt of the pack, youngest of three kids. We always had extended family around. Which was all very fun and wonderful—truly—but . . . everyone was *a lot*. So when I came out last, I sort of feel like all my relatives just collectively went, 'Can you be *less*?'"

Another rumble makes me smile.

"It has to be pretty common among third children. Parents are so precious with their firstborns. Everything is a miracle. With second kids, parents have the benefit of experience—maybe they're a bit wiser, a bit more patient. . . . And then the third kid comes and they're like, 'Wait, we have *another* one of these?'"

A married couple in the front row laughs a bit too hard at this. "You two totally have a bunch of kids, don't you?" I say, drifting over to them. The wife nods, still cracking up. "Okay, I'll be curious to see how your negligence compares.

Let's discuss how me and my siblings all learned to ride bikes, shall we?"

I quickly explain the breakdown of our bicycle education—same as I did for Jeremy. "But I get it," I say, pacing the stage. "My parents were *tired*. And they already had two whole children who were turning out fine. There was nothing more I could do to get their attention. *'Mom! Dad!'*" I say, switching my voice to kid me, waving a hand overhead. "'I'm gonna test my bike out on this *enormous* hill. . . . It has a highway at the bottom.'" I pretend to squint, checking for a reaction. "'And a shark tank!'"

The rumble of the crowd is growing. It feels amazing.

Then I notice the blinking light.

"Oh, dangit, they want me out of here." I wedge the mic into the stand, eyeing the married couple in front. "Anyway, I'm sure your youngest children will be fine. Just make sure you help them out with their therapy bills." I give a quick wave. "Thank you, Portland, you've been great!"

As Dolores and I trade places on the stage, she makes a muscle with one arm and Paula practically has to catch me at the base of the steps. I just did that—a real, solid set. "You were great, Ms. Mortal Enemy!" I hear, in a daze. "Isaiah and I are taking off now but we'll see you next week!" I glide over to the bar as Dolores introduces the last act. I think Isaiah waved from the crowd as Paula hugged me goodbye. I don't entirely know; I'm still floating. A new voice starts up as I sit, and a ginger ale appears in front of me, breaking through the fog. "Nicely done."

"Thanks, Ted," I say, blinking up at him. "You know, my cousin really should have called you."

Grinning, he leaves me to my soda, and I half listen to the voice at my back.

"A lot of people think I'm one of these bizarro Gwyneth Paltrow Goop ladies. And . . . okay, I'll admit, I *have* bought a few of her products. What? They have vitamin packs that return you to your high school metabolism!" I smile to myself. She's walking the line between self-aware and ditzy in a way that really works. "Seriously, *nothing* brings you back to that level of fitness. I didn't even get there when I was doing my teacher training in *Barthhhelona*."

I sit up straighter. Why does that sound familiar?

"Anyway . . . shoot. I really was going somewhere with this. My brain, you guys. Laugh all you want. Mercury really *is* in retrograde!"

I turn around to look. *"No. Way,"* I whisper. It's Amber from Keep Calm Yoga, now in jeans instead of spandex.

Jeremy walks up to me as I watch her, my mouth agape. "She's a funny one, huh?" he says. "Although, wait, were you here for her set last week?"

"Uh . . . nope," I say, too stunned to string words together. "So. She's . . ." I clear my throat. "She's in the Comithon? She'll be . . . here? Every week?"

"Yes," he says strangely.

I wonder if she watched my set just now. Could she have recognized me from the day we met at the yoga studio?

"Easy, girl," says Jeremy. "Don't get jealous. You're both very cute in different ways."

"Can you shush?" I say. If I weren't so flustered I'd be more focused on how obnoxious that was.

"I'm just saying you can take her. . . ."

I swat at him like a fly in my ear. Why why *why* did I have to talk about Sam again tonight?

I tell myself to breathe as the audience laughs.

"Look, a part of me realizes it's ridiculous," Amber is saying. "But that's what it is to be human, right? We see Gwyneth chopping vegetables on the cover of a cookbook, and we think, 'Maybe making smoothies with chia seeds really *will* bring out my inner earth goddess.'" She lets out a long sigh, looking deep in thought. "Oh right!" She snaps her fingers. "I remember the thing now. So when I was really in my Goop phase, my boyfriend would get so mad whenever he saw my credit card bill. To be fair, I was the *tiniest* bit behind on rent, but I kept telling him I was doing it for us! Like, Goop sells these pyrite crystals that are good for money stuff? All you have to do is close your eyes, hug it to your chest, and say, 'I program this pyrite crystal for financial success.'" She shrugs. "Anyway, when I got a job it totally started working."

Jeremy and I both laugh out loud in unison.

"Okay, that's my time," she says to the audience.

"I should go," I say immediately.

"Wait," says Jeremy. "Don't you want to stay for the voting results?"

"Eh, it's fine. I have an early morning and . . ." I realize Amber is walking straight toward us. Oh God. It's like my feet have been glued to the floor.

"Jeremy, right?" she says as she comes over. "I don't think we've properly met. Nice job tonight!"

"Thanks. And you . . ." He rests a hand on her arm. "You were terrific."

"Thank you." She pats the hand touching her before smoothly removing it. "I'm Amber, by the way," she says, turning to me. "Amber Bernhardt. You were great."

"Thanks," I say plastering on a smile as I reach out to shake her hand. "You too. I'm Sabrina."

For a moment we lock eyes and she tilts her head. "Have we met?"

"I don't think so," I say, hoping to communicate mild, unconcerned confusion.

She pulls back to look at me. "You're giving off a familiar aura. I like your vibe. Are you a Libra?"

"Um." I frown. "Yeah, actually." She nods like that explains it.

"Well, this has been a fun night," I say, gearing up for a graceful exit as the lights above us go from bright to brighter. People are filing out, leaving marked ballots in a basket by the door.

Amber sighs contentedly. "Wasn't it? That Isaiah guy is *hilarious.* And what's her name—Paula? Also, I hear the icky dude is gone now. Oh, hold up." She looks past Jeremy, calling out, "Haru, right? You're so funny!"

The deadpan sushi chef joins our cluster. "Thanks. You too. All of you."

"Have you been doing stand-up long?" asks Jeremy once we've exchanged proper introductions.

"I did the circuit in San Fran for a while," he says. "But then I got the offer to come to Portland. It was sort of a dream job, so I took it. I was happy to find this club."

"I have to ask," says Amber. "Is all your stand-up about fish?"

Haru shrugs. "Pretty much."

"Huh," I say, smiling at him. "I kind of love that."

The med student, Lakshmi, pops into our circle then, with the British Baking guy at her heels. "Just wanted to say great job, everyone. I wish I could stay, but I have to be back at the hospital in like—" She checks her watch with a wince. "Eight hours."

"It's past my bedtime, too," says the British Baking guy with a kindly smile. "I'm Bill, by the way."

"And I'm Lenny," says Lenny, walking up with the ukulele case on his back. "Anyway, sorry, dudes. My lady waits, so I'd better scoot."

Dolores comes over then. "So you all know, I've added your pictures to the website and Jeremy suggested I also get your social media name thingies. . . . What do you call them?" She snaps her fingers. "Handles! Send them to me?"

The others nod at her as I freeze in place. How did I not prepare for this? "Actually . . ." The words tumble out: "I don't . . . *do* social media?" It's hardly a lie, considering how little I've touched my accounts lately. "I try to stay off the grid," I go on. "To get in touch with myself and just . . . really be present, you know?"

"Oh my God *yasss*," says Amber, throwing back her head. "It's so important to disconnect. I talk about it *all the time* on my Instagram." I laugh, then stop short. It's extremely hard to tell if she's in on her own jokes.

"Well, it doesn't matter to me," says Dolores. "This technology stuff is not my area. I *just* figured out emojis, and now people keep saying I'm using them wrong."

"You texted me *peach eggplant eggplant* the other day," says Jeremy teasingly. "With a question mark."

"I heard you were bringing takeout from that Middle Eastern fusion place," she says. "I like their grilled peach baba ganoush!"

I think they're still talking now, people cracking up. But I'm barely listening, the gravitational pull of my phone growing stronger as my heart begins to thrum.

"I'll be right back," I blurt out before slipping away.

In the hall by the exit, I check over my shoulder, quickly pulling up Instagram and then searching the name *Amber*

Bernhardt. Her account is among the first to pop up. Apparently there's a huge demand for her sexy, bendy poses, with captions like *Self love, y'all.* I sigh with relief when I check—Sam doesn't follow her, which is lucky because he tends to follow everyone. But even if he did, there's been no mention of the comedy club in her posts. Must not fit the brand.

I bite my lip, thinking. I'm not worried about my own account. It's private, and not the kind of thing someone might randomly stumble upon. But what about Sabrina's? *How did I never think to check?*

I pull it up—public but modest. It's a little sad, actually. She hasn't posted lately, her grid still peppered with glimpses of Carmen. She's even got a group shot with me and Sam in it, twinning as Dwight Schrutes at that haunted house on Halloween.

Guess she hasn't Marie Kondo–ed yet.

"Okay . . ." With a wince, I type her name into the search bar, then exhale, just scrolling through Sabrina Martins now. There must be hundreds, meaning even if someone *were* to go searching for me, they'd have to weed through a lot of profiles before coming across this girl with the two little buns. "Wow," I mutter. "Thank God her last name wasn't, like, *Dusseldorf* or something."

"What's that?" says Jeremy, making me jump. "Sorry." He slows his approach. "You okay?"

"Yeah," I say, catching my breath. "Guess I'm still jittery from being onstage."

"How'd you feel about tonight? I thought you were pretty decent up there."

I narrow my eyes at the word *decent*. I think he's being self-aware, doubling down on that ironic douche persona he's got going on. Still, it's a bit much. "Yeah, yeah," I say, leaning into the wall to look him over. "Meanwhile I *still* haven't seen your act. How do I even know you're a comic? This could all be a ruse."

He grins. "A ruse, huh?"

"Yes," I say, lifting my chin without breaking eye contact. "I've seen no evidence. Prove to me that you're a comedian, Jeremy. Tell me a joke!"

"Okay . . ." He thinks. "What's the difference between a musician and a large cheese pizza?" I blink. "A large cheese pizza can feed a family of four." I pout at the tragic nature of the punch line, then laugh. "It's not mine," he adds quickly—honorably, I suppose. "I heard it somewhere."

"Well, you still pass the test," I say. "Although, I don't know. You want to be a comedian, right? Isn't telling that joke sort of a glass house situation?"

"Not if I make it big," he says, the coy smile returning.

"I see. And do you think tonight's set got you any closer to fame and fortune?"

"Maybe. I just talked about an ex. It's possible I came off like an ass."

"You do that sometimes," I say, making him laugh. "Then

again, I mocked my mostly functional, very nice family for a lot of tonight. But I'm telling myself all's fair in love and comedy."

His knits his brows, one corner of his lips hiking up. "I agree."

I glance at my phone, noticing the time. "I really do need to go."

"Wait," he says, sidestepping me. Now we're standing close. "How about another writing session this weekend? Saturday?"

"Sure," I say, feeling a surprise nip of excitement.

"Maybe a café in the afternoon? Do you know that place Willard Beach Coffee?"

"No, not there!" I blurt out, smooth as always.

"Okay . . ." he says strangely.

I try to appear casual as I consider an alternative. The café is obviously a no-go. But I don't love the idea of going to *any* public place in my Sabrina getup. And I can't exactly invite him over to my house. . . .

"How about your dorm?" I say suddenly. When his eyebrows shoot up, I realize that may have come off as suggestive. It wasn't my intention, but the thought actually gives me a slight thrill. I think I like being the forward one, even if it *was* sort of an accident this time. My mind flits to Sam, but I remind myself that he's off with Natalie tonight. And if he's not a library book, neither am I. Also, Jeremy really is just unnervingly good-looking—and has a very nice mouth, I'm noticing.

It's actually slightly open right now, like he's not quite sure how to respond.

"Uh . . . sure," he says finally. He clears his throat. "My roommate's usually out, so we'd probably have the space to ourselves. To *work*," he adds, respectfully. Which I do appreciate.

"Okay, cool," I say, a flush coming over me. We look at each other, an unspoken question crackling between us: Is *this* a date? It's sort of fun not knowing the answer. So I just smile and brush past him, calling out, "Good night, Jeremy!"

THIRTEEN

The Is-This-Love? Sequence | Head in the clouds. Heart singing. Magic in the air.

The first to the lunch table, I plop down and start eating a PB&J, my mind quickly conjuring up the dank interior of the Chuckle Parlor, the spotlight, the applause, even the gut-wrenching silences. I thrill at all of it, trying to recall the moments that worked last night. I should venture out more with my material next week. And talk less about Sam. I'm sick of him.

Across the cafeteria, he's gone so far as to trade seats with Ethan, his back to me now. What a butthead. As my eyes begin to narrow, Ethan looks over, smiling faintly. I wonder if Sam told him about our fight.

With a sigh, I do a sweep around the caf. At the Mathletes' table, Deb is feeding Pete the Service Iguana some kind of leafy green instead of his usual tater tot. Maybe he's on a diet. Meanwhile, the ever-thirsty Mr. Radcliff is talking the ears off a bunch of lax girls in the hot bar line. Sitting alone, I don't feel as inconspicuous as usual. Abruptly, the skin-crawly feeling sets in. *Where is Annika?*

I imagine the spotlight returning—this time shining down on me from the cafeteria ceiling. Of course, no one is actually looking at me. I'm inconsequential enough around here that no one bothers to judge. Still, to be safe, I put in my earbuds, hitting play on Marnie James.

"You can start to develop a very Hobbesian view of people in New York," she's saying, "with everyone jammed into tight spaces and honking their horns. At first, I worried I was growing numb to people. But then one night . . ."

I mirror her smile as I gobble up my last few bites. I like this part. "I was walking home when I crossed paths with this woman carrying a pizza box. And as she passed, I realized I felt so . . . *happy* for her." The camera cuts to the audience, looking amused, if a bit puzzled. "It dawned on me that it wasn't the first time I'd felt this way. This was a pattern. Every time I saw someone carrying a pizza box at night, this little voice in my head would start saying, 'Yeah! You go eat that pizza!'"

I laugh under my breath as she touches her heart. "And then I'd picture it. Maybe the person was bringing the pizza home to someone they loved. Or maybe they were going to get inside and devour the whole thing by themselves, which: also awesome. I was honestly thrilled to know this about myself—that I could feel such unbridled joy for someone I would never know. And then I thought—wow. Are there strangers out there, feeling happy for *me* whenever *I'm* about to eat pizza?"

"My life is over," I hear faintly.

"So I guess pizza is my love language. . . ."

"Gretchen!"

I hit pause and take my headphones out, looking up at Annika's horror-struck face. "Wait, what?"

"My life is over!" she repeats, piling her backpack and oboe onto the table before plopping down in a huff. "It's the Juilliard audition. My dad's work is making him travel the same weekend as my slot. I asked why he can't just tell them no, but he says if he gets fired for insubordination then I *definitely* can't go to Juilliard. So, I'm like, 'Can't I just go alone?' And he's all, 'I don't know how I feel about that,' even though the whole point is that I would be living there alone in like eight months anyway."

"Okay . . ." I say, shaking my head. "Let's slow down. Can't you reschedule?"

"I tried, but I just got an email back saying they're all booked. It's this or wait another year. Or I go somewhere else. Which my dad actually seemed kind of cool with on the phone just now! Can you believe that? I'm not trying to be dramatic here, but if I don't at least take a shot at living out my dreams, I *will* die."

From the look on her face, I know better than to laugh at that. "All right, deep breaths. What can we do?"

She sighs. "Well, my dad already booked the train tickets and the hotel, so I can keep trying to convince him that I'm responsible enough to go on my own. *Or* . . ." She looks at me, a glint of excitement in her eyes. "I could suggest bringing a friend?" It takes me a second to realize she's talking about me. "You're always complaining about how you never leave Maine. And this would be a free trip. Completely paid for already. And I think it would at least partially assuage my dad's fears. Like, if we got lost, or needed to quickly mace some creeper following us, at least we'd have each other, right?"

"Maybe don't bring up the mace or the creeper to him, but I see your point," I say, my heart racing all of a sudden. This feels like a sign after watching Marnie—I want to go to the place where strangers feel happy for each other over pizza. And all the rom-coms have obviously added to my New York curiosity. Sometimes, I imagine living there as an adult, high-powered and chic in Manhattan, or funky and free-spirited in Brooklyn. Either way, a handsome architect would be just around the corner.

"So are you in?"

"Yes!" I say immediately. "So incredibly in. I mean, I'll have to ask. But my parents aren't exactly strict these days, so I'm sure I can convince them."

Annika lunges across the table to hug me and I let out a

startled laugh, my arms squished weirdly at my sides. Annika is not a practiced hugger, and it shows.

"Okay," she says, pulling back and looking around. "I'm too excited to eat. I'm gonna go practice. You're the best, Gretchen!"

In a flash, she swipes up her things and goes.

"Have you talked to Sam today?" Natalie asks me, breaking our working silence and prompting Ethan to glance my way.

We each have laptops open, three points of a beanbag triangle. "Nope," I say, pausing from my Marnie write-up. I brace myself. ". . . Why?"

"I invited him over last night," she says, telling me what I already know. "But he seemed . . . off. We played video games for like an hour, didn't talk much. And then he left." She crinkles up her nose. "It kind of sucked."

"Oh," I say, unsure if I should feel happy or guilty or what. I am genuinely disturbed by the disappointment on her face, though. *What the hell, Sam? Are you just making* everyone *miserable now?*

"Did he say anything to you?" she asks Ethan.

"Sorry, no," he says, looking up from typing.

"I'm sure it's not you," I tell her, frowning now. "He gets kind of moody once in a while. Especially with family stuff. I'm guessing it's a weird time for him, getting ready to move away and everything."

"Of course," says Natalie, abruptly sympathetic. "That totally makes sense. And I probably got ahead of myself. I realized the other day that his dad's new place is right by Columbia. Meaning we wouldn't necessarily have an expiration date if something started between us . . ." She laughs weakly. "Maybe he's not even interested."

I open my mouth, then close it, *almost* wanting to help her. It's like Sam is two people to me right now—*my* Sam, and the guy my friend likes. "I . . . really couldn't tell you," I say finally. "We're not actually super close anymore."

"Oh." She seems sincerely sad to hear that. "I'm sorry."

I shrug, cheerful as I can manage.

"So what's on the agenda for today?" says Mr. O, popping back in from the teachers' lounge, his mug of tea refilled. "In other words, show me you're on track so I can feel good about leaving?"

Natalie smiles, pulling out her checklist. "Well, we should probably discuss how we want to present the Notables. And if we *are* going to do the usual superlatives . . ." She smirks my way. "Then I guess we should put out the call for nominations pretty soon."

"Actually, I had another idea," I say, prompting Mr. O's nostrils to twitch, lips pursed at the ready. "Just hear me out!"

"I reaaaally wanted to go home, Gretchen," he says, dragging a rolling chair to the edge of the carpet to sit up above us.

"Okay," I say, setting my laptop aside. "*What if* . . . we made a superlatives page that read more like a Mad Lib? Then people could fill in the blanks and assign themselves and their *own* friend groups to the categories, rather than having the same five most popular kids get voted in for everything—no offense, Natalie."

"None taken," she says happily.

"It's just that democracy can get a little boring. And why not leave it open-ended? I keep thinking about that line under Marnie's senior picture. Where she calls herself *the girl least likely*? Now she's this total surprise, right? And it's a nice thought. Like, I bet *most* of the people on our Notables list had no idea what was coming."

"Except for the milk carton guy," says Ethan. "That guy knew he was headed for greatness."

I laugh. "Anyway, it just kind of stuck with me. Wouldn't it be nice to tell people: 'When you get out of this place, when you go start your real life, you're most likely to be . . . whoever the hell you want to be'?"

"You just got deep on us," says Natalie, bobbing her head. "I like it. And there's something really nice about that—having that chance to define ourselves. I mean, who in high school is actually *quite* what they seem?"

Ethan smirks a little. "Got any weird surprises for us, Natalie?"

She thinks. "I mean, I have a couple death metal songs on my phone—for when I need to really let out my rage in the car."

She heaves a sigh and I crack up at her. "Right in there between Drake and Ethan's long lost cousin, Britney . . . What?" she says as I abruptly frown.

"Oh, well, it's occurring to me . . . if we try the whole Mad Lib format, there's a serious possibility people will just write *butthole* for every blank space. *Best butthole . . . Most likely to butthole . . .*"

Mr. O chokes on his tea, and I brighten. I *knew* he thought I was funny.

"The *butthole* issue aside, it's a cool idea," says Ethan.

"I agree," says Natalie. "Let's definitely play with it."

"Look at you all cooperating as a team," says Mr. O, getting up. "I think this means I can leave."

"Yes, be free!" says Natalie, waving him away. When he goes, she perks up again. "Hey, speaking of Marnie, I meant to tell you guys. I was talking to one of the chefs from my dad's restaurant the other night and he said he's in some competition to open for her when she comes to Portland. Cool, right?" For a moment, I just freeze. "Anyway, I was thinking, we should go see her when she's here. Maybe we could even try to get an interview with her for the retrospective."

"Oooh, good idea," says Ethan. "I wonder if she'd let me take her picture. How sweet would that be for my portfolio?"

I gape at them, my brain scrambling to catch up.

Natalie knows someone from the show?

But then it clicks: Haru. I almost have to laugh. Because of all the high-end Japanese restaurants in Portland, *of course* he works for the one owned by her dad. It's not enough that I just narrowly avoided a catastrophe with Amber. I know we live in a small city, but *come on*.

Also, six degrees of separation my butthole.

"I wonder if we can buy our tickets yet . . ." I hear Natalie say faintly.

"No!" I shout. *Real smooth, Gretchen*. I clear my throat. "I mean. I doubt we can . . . I'm sure you have to be twenty-one to get into a place like that."

Natalie frowns. "I think Haru said something about different-colored wristbands that night? Since she has such a big teen following?"

"Sweet," says Ethan. "I'll look it up. What's the comedy club?"

"The Chuckle Parlor," she says, grinning. "Quite the name, huh?"

I feel like I'm watching the world's most banal car crash as I crawl over from my beanbag and Ethan types out *c-h-u* . . . on his computer.

I can't seem to say anything. Can't seem to stop him. The homepage loads, and there we are: three rows of headshots, with me right in the center.

It's the photo Ethan took.

And someone else's name . . .

"Hmm." He closes the laptop. "Looks like maybe you do have to be twenty-one."

"Oh. Damn," says Natalie, already focused on her screen again, back to work.

Ethan holds my stare meaningfully. "Can you help me with something in the hall?" With a single nod, I get up and follow him out, shutting the door behind us. We walk several paces before he says, "Now's the part where you give in and tell me what's going on, right?"

Groaning, I lean into a locker, then slide down to sit on the cold floor. "Okay, okay . . . Ever since winter break, I've sort of been . . . doing stand-up comedy under an alias. Happy now?"

"Kind of, actually," he says, looking pleasantly intrigued. "But . . . why the alias?"

"Well, I didn't plan it," I say. "One night my sister and cousin dressed me up to match this fake ID they had. . . . We all went out, ended up at a comedy club. And basically, I got onstage and weirdly liked it. The next thing I knew, I was going back every week to compete."

He nods, thoughtful, then takes a seat against the row of lockers across from me. "So, you're *also* competing to open for Marnie James?"

"Yep. Pretty nuts, right? The three top-rated comics get their clips sent to her. Then she'll watch and take her pick for the big night."

"Huh," he says. "Well then, I guess you better win."

"Uh, I have no delusions here," I say, rolling my eyes. "It's just been fun to try this out—while being shielded from any major humiliation. The whole alias thing is pretty perfect in that way. The girl I am up there . . ." I shrug. "She's freakin' cool, man. And it's, like, one night a week, I'm not stuck being . . ." I gesture to myself. *"This."*

Ethan frowns, but seems to let go of whatever it is he's thinking. I wince at him across the empty corridor. "So . . . what do you say? Can you keep one more weird friend secret for me?"

"Yeah, put it on my tab," he says with a wave. He laughs lightly, leaning his head back and hiking up one knee. "I can see it, you know."

"What?"

"You on a stage. It makes sense. You're funny. I've always thought that."

"Oh." I don't know why this makes me blush. "Thank you." I shrug it off. "I was really just venting at first. It's sort of ridiculous, but I think this whole thing only started because I needed someone to *listen* to me."

He chuckles. "I would have listened."

"Yeah, well, I didn't know that then. You could have saved me a lot of trouble, Ethan. And discomfort. Those leather pants are *tight*."

"I remember," he says wryly.

"Anyway, it's definitely not just about venting anymore," I say, still a bit baffled by this. "I *really like* stand-up. I mean, when I'm about to go on, it feels completely insane, like I've just signed myself up to go skydiving or something. But then you get up there and everything slows down. . . . When it works, it's like you're floating in time or something. Happens when I'm writing too."

"It's the best feeling, right?" he says. "Sometimes, I'll get a shot lined up and completely lose myself. Time jumps, and suddenly, here's this cool thing I apparently did. It's like . . ."

"Magic," we say together, only to laugh.

"That feeling has actually gotten me in trouble before," he says. "I'll take my camera up on a hike, and get obsessed with, like, *a tree* or something, only to realize *way* too late that the sun is already going down."

"Yeesh, that's my nightmare," I say with a shudder. "I'm not an outdoorsy girl. Defective Mainer here."

"Oh, come on, that can't be true," he says. "Maine's the best."

I sigh. "I don't know what to tell you. I was born this way."

He frowns, dubious. "Well, do you at least like skiing?"

"Nope."

"Snowboarding?"

"I'm gonna stop you right there," I say. "It's a no to anything that could lead to frostbite or a potential tailbone injury."

"Okay . . . Well, what about Maine summers?" He smiles enticingly. "The beach? Fried clams?"

"That's probably where I exhibit the most regional pride," I say, conceding. "Give me rocky coastlines and your goopiest fried things any time."

"Question," he says, serious now. "What's your stance on bacon in clam chowder?"

"Oh, it's an abomination."

"Okay then," he says, laughing. "Strong seafood stances. That sounds like a Mainer to me. Thoughts on wall antlers?"

I suck my teeth. "Yeah, not big on severed heads as decoration . . ."

"Fair," he says. "What about plaid shirts?"

"I have no objection to them," I say, noting the green one he has on over his white tee. "Are you fishing for compliments, Ethan? Actually, I'll admit it. The shirt does bring out the olive tone in your eyes."

"Stop it," he says, pretending to be bashful. I frown and he looks up. "What?"

"Oh, I was just wondering if I should put some Maine jokes in my next set. The severed head thing was kinda good. I wish I'd recorded that."

I glance down the hall, jolting suddenly. Natalie has crept up on us. "What are *you two* whispering about out here?" I quickly press myself up off the locker, wondering how much she heard. "Is this about my birthday?"

I laugh with relief, just as Ethan gets up and says, "Yessss?"

Judging from her barely suppressed glee, it's obvious that was the right answer. "Well, no gifts necessary," she says, tamping down her smile. "Just bring your wonderful selves. And don't be late! I want to make sure you get to taste all my dad's food before Pils and Grody gobble everything up. Those guys are like garbage disposals."

My heart sinks as I put it together: she's hosting her birthday at her dad's restaurant—as in Haru's place of work. When Ethan sees the look on my face, I think he must make the connection. "Oh, uh . . . Gretchen, didn't you . . . say you had that *thing*, Saturday night?"

My nod is a silent, *You are a goddamn angel, Ethan.*

"Oh no no," says Natalie, linking her arm through mine and leading us back to HQ. "I reserved you well in advance. Plus, I need a Sam buffer, because I think he's still coming and it's probably going to be weird now. Ethan, back me up. You want her there too, right? Can't you move your plans, Gretchen? Say yes."

I look helplessly at Ethan. Natalie is a very difficult person to say no to.

"Please?"

"Okay," I say, laughing. "I'll . . . see what I can do."

"Gretchen, did you remember the tortilla chips?"

"Yep!" I yell to Mom from the dining room. I've been tasked with setting out chili toppings tonight. At a table set for three, I line up ramekins of scallions and sour cream, cheese, avocado slices, and chips. Also cilantro, which I still feel just okay about.

With Mom and Dad still clanking around in the kitchen, I pull out my phone and speak softly into the recording app:

"Is my cilantro bit too niche? I guess I just like the idea of a polarizing herb. Also, maybe I should play around with other things you're only supposed to love or hate? Like camping, or . . . Taylor Swift . . ."

My phone buzzes in my hand then.

It's a text from Jeremy: At another open mic in town and guess who turned up! I look closer at the photo he's attached: Bad Kevin James, speaking into a microphone.

"I got that sparkling lemonade you like!" calls Mom from the kitchen. "Do you want some?"

"Sure!" I say.

"I really upped the meat-to-bean ratio," Dad announces, carrying out the whole Crock-Pot to the table.

"Just how I like it," I say.

He points. "That's m'girl."

Mom walks in then, holding a beer for Dad and the tall glass bottle of fizzy pink lemonade for the two us. "Amazing," she says, admiring our bounty.

As Mom and Dad pull out chairs, I think of last night's set, a surprising pang of guilt swooping in. All glaring intersibling discrepancies aside, I was only joking around. They're obviously good parents.

"Everything okay?" asks Mom. She's looking at my phone, I realize, now buzzing away. I swipe to open more texts from Jeremy.

He's even worse tonight.

Hellllppp!!!

Oh shit I think he recognizes us.

Yep, he looks mad . . .

"Sorry," I say, quickly crafting a response. Are you cheating on the Chuckle Parlor?!

He writes back immediately. Hey, we were never exclusive. Also, Isaiah and Paula are here so I guess they're cheating too. Sorry, I guess I should have invited you. It was kind of last-minute . . .

Oh that's okay. But I have to go now.

Okay, see you Saturday?

Yep! I bite my lip, setting the phone on the table, screen-side down.

"What are *you* smiling about?" asks Mom as she ladles.

"Nothing," I say, abruptly shivering. Dad has the thermostat set to full-on *Siberia* today, but I suppose some warm meat mush will do the trick. I take my bowl and start adding toppings. Then the buzzing starts up again.

"Popular today," says Dad.

"I'll silence this," I say with a wince, taking one quick peek. But then I smile. The messages are from Annika.

Ahhhhhhhh!

Gretchen!!!!

I proposed the buddy system idea to my dad and he went for it, as long your parents are cool with it too.

Have you asked yet?

My dreams are hanging in the balance here, but you know, no biggie!

Please tell them we'll be safe.

And that I am very good with maps and will be able to deftly navigate their daughter through the city.

And that I will hook them up with all the hot oboe concert tix their hearts could desire if I get into Juilliard.

Are you asking???

"What is it?" says Mom.

I laugh, looking up at them. "It's my friend Annika. . . ." I guess now's as good a time as any. In one long breath, I explain the situation, delivering promises of hot oboe tix as instructed. I really didn't think this would be a hard sell, but as I continue to talk, and their expressions continue to harden, I fear I may have given Annika false hope.

"We would be so safe," I add when they've yet to offer up a clear, resounding *yes*. "And I'd update you constantly. Plus, I'd be helping my friend achieve her dreams, and women are supposed to help other women. Isn't that what you always say, Mom?"

"Well, sure, honey, but . . ." Mom looks at Dad, who still appears to be mulling it over as he sips his beer.

"I'll walk Nacho for a month!" I say, scrambling now. "And . . . I'll even get professional glamour shots taken with him like you've always wanted." Dad chuckles into his glass. "I bet I could even convince Hen and William to go along with it."

For a suspended moment, Mom grows very still, and I can tell I've struck a chord with the vision of an all-four-sibling photo shoot, Nacho posing windswept like a fashion model. I'm encouraged by the appreciative smirk on Dad's face. He's always taken pride in his children's negotiation skills. But then Mom shakes it off, as if coming to her senses. "I don't know, Gretch. . . ."

"Please?" I say. "This is a huge deal for Annika. But it's a cool opportunity for me, too. I've never been to New York—or really anywhere. And we all just sort of *decided* that I'm stuck here for college. Which, whatever, that's fine. But I would like to leave the state at some point before I die."

"Hey," says Mom, frowning now. "You've left Maine. Remember that trip we all took to Canada?"

"I was like three, Mom. That doesn't count. And don't say we sometimes go to New Hampshire because that's basically just Maine with more Harley-Davidsons."

Dad laughs. "What?" he says when Mom stops him with a look. "That was funny."

"Anyway, what do you mean you're *stuck* here?" says Mom, returning her gaze to me. "I thought you were excited about staying local. It's *free*, Gretchen. Do you realize how life-changing that could be for you? Do you know how many kids can barely get their lives off the ground because they're so saddled with debt?"

In retrospect, I should not have brought up the college thing.

I've completely derailed the conversation, and am quite possibly being a brat. Still, I can't seem to quell the sour feelings rising up. "You weren't worried about that with Hen or William," I say. "They both went out of state. To some of the most prestigious schools in the country."

"True, but I wasn't tenured back then. *Free* wasn't on the table for them. And anyway, your siblings were always more . . ."

"Worth it?" I say, the words flying out.

Mom looks stricken. "Gretchen!"

I realize Dad has gone all quiet and serious. The shades of emotion are always hard to distinguish behind the mustache, but I think I'm seeing worry.

Now I feel bad.

"Hon," says Mom after a beat. "Hey . . . you know that's not . . ." She shakes her head. "Hen and William were just totally different kids. They literally wanted to be *doctors and lawyers*, so we didn't feel like bad parents letting them take out all those loans. But you . . ." She shrugs. "Who knows where you're headed? You've always been so independent, and creative, and observant. When you were little, you and Sam just wanted to be left alone to play. We'd hear you two laughing, making up whole worlds together. You never took to the kind of structure your brother and sister liked, and that was fine by us. We knew you'd forge your own path." She looks at Dad, then back at me. "We don't want you to be stuck. We want you to be *free*."

I nod through the quiet, something tight in my chest going slack now.

"Did you really think that, Gretch?" Dad asks after a moment. "That we thought you were less—"

"No," I say, too forcefully. To my horror, tears have sprung to my eyes but I try to laugh it off. "I'm sorry. I think I'm just tired."

When I get up the nerve to peek at their faces again, I can tell Mom and Dad are having one of their silent parent conversations.

"You really want this New York trip, huh?" says Mom finally.

"I really do."

"And you promise us you'll be careful," says Dad. "No dark alleyways. No subways late at night. Updates every few hours."

"Yes, yes, all of it," I say, sniffing, smiling.

"And we'll want to talk to Annika's dad," says Mom. "Just to make sure we're really on the same page."

"Sure. Anything you want."

"When is it again?" asks Dad.

"Not for a couple weeks. I'd have to miss school that Friday but I'd make up all my work, and we'd be back before dinner that Sunday."

They share one last glance; then Mom says, "Okay."

"Oh, thank you thank you thank you!" I jump up to give them each a hug, Mom stroking my hair and Dad giving my back a few hearty pats. For a moment, I feel warm and snug, if a bit silly for getting so emotional.

We start to eat, a silence coming over us. Mom sighs contentedly, then abruptly frowns. She reaches across the table, covering Dad's hand in hers. "Harold, I love you. But it's fucking freezing in here."

FOURTEEN

The Rom-Com Kiss | A smooch worthy of orbiting cameras, a swell of music, maybe a fountain going off somewhere. Rain is preferred. Mouths stay extremely open. Oh, and no breathing breaks. This is serious business, people.

The rain is a nice change from the snow today. I watch from the kitchen window, eating Cheerios standing up, still in my cozy plaid pajamas. I spent the late hours of the morning hovering between stages of consciousness, enjoying the pitter-patter on my windowsill. By the time I got up, I'd decided. It's time I got kissed already.

Even the weather seems to agree.

This afternoon, I will be "writing" with Jeremy in his dorm. The implications of the meeting place are obvious. And he's been finding little ways to stay in touch all week.

Now, I'm thinking logistically. I have mints in the car. And maybe I'll go easy on the lipstick. Mom and Dad are out running errands at the moment, but I think they'll likely be home before I go. Maybe I could wear a more casual black outfit, to avoid the car change?

"It *is* the weekend," I say to Nacho at my feet. "Who wears skin-tight leather pants on a Saturday afternoon?" He tilts his head, like he's really considering this. "Also, it'll be daylight. And I'd rather not flash anyone."

A loud thump from the basement almost makes me spill my cereal, and Nacho starts jumping and yipping hysterically. *"Hello?"* I call, just as the door from downstairs swings open. ". . . Carmen?" My cousin whizzes past me with an armful of two-by-fours, cut down to about her height.

"Hi," she grunts as she heads for the front of the house.

I leave my bowl on the counter to follow as she adds her lumber to the pile in the foyer I somehow didn't notice earlier. "I can't believe you're here," I say, smiling as she turns around. God, I've missed her.

"Only briefly," she says as she reaches for her raincoat on the hook. She looks a bit haggard but still stylish this morning, in her ripped jeans and dirty white tee, neon pink hoops dangling from her earlobes. "There was a long waiting list for the table saw in our woodshop. Your dad said I could cut a few pieces here. I'm the genius who elected to do a quarter-scale model for my project because I thought I could keep it as a fun clubhouse after. There's a chance I won't sleep for five straight days."

"Dang," I say, lowering down onto a step and leaning into the banister. "So I take it there's no way you'd want to stay and hang out, then?" Carmen might be a good person to talk to right about now. I could probably use some advice. I really don't know the first thing about kissing.

Maybe I should practice on, like, an apple.

"I wish," she says, her expression softening as she looks me over. "But I should get back to work."

I nod—easy breezy—though inside I'm racking my brain for ways to trap her here a little longer. It comes to me as she eyes the woodpile, winding up to leave. "How's the roommate drama going?"

Carmen pauses, her momentum thrown off. "It's . . . oh God, it's been so weird, Gretch." She collapses down onto the step beside me—*hook, line, and sinker!* "Especially for our mutual friends. I don't know how this got so dramatic. I feel like I'm in one of the Koreanovelas my lola's always emailing me about." She laughs, almost. "It's just so cowardly, you know? She *still* hasn't had the guts to talk to me about what happened yet. Then again, I basically live at the architecture studio now, so there haven't been many opportunities."

"Is Sabrina still seeing your ex?" I ask. It's odd saying the name like that: *Sabrina,* in the third person.

"No, I heard from a friend that she hasn't seen him since they kissed. That part does make me happy—that he lost both of us." Carmen sighs wistfully to the ceiling. "Is it summer vacation yet? I just want to drag our huge donut-mermaid-unicorn floaties out to the beach, lie on our backs, and do nothing."

"That sounds divine," I say, heart warmed. I think that might be Carmen-speak for *I miss you, too.*

Her phone starts to go off then, and when she digs it out from her jacket pocket, I see a flash of Henrietta, calling on FaceTime. "Eh. I'll hit her back later."

"Wait." I blink a moment. "Hen still calls you?"

She shrugs. "Sometimes."

"Well . . . how often?" I ask, unable to disguise the hurt in my voice.

"I don't know. We'll check in while I'm drafting, or while she's at the gym. It's not some conspiracy to leave you out. We've just both had a lot going on lately."

"Oh, well, that's just wonderful," I say, grabbing the phone to answer it.

"Gretchen?" Hen looks surprised there on the screen, in her little workout top, ponytail swinging side to side like she's on a stationary bike.

"Yes. It is I," I say. "Your sister. You may remember me from various moments of your childhood?"

She laughs. "That does sound familiar. . . . Guess it's been awhile?"

"Uh, *yeah,*" I say, not even trying to hide how annoyed I am. "Ya think?"

"Sorry!" she says defensively. "It's been kind of a whirlwind over here, okay? I have friends! I joined an a capella group! I'm even leading the curve in my organic chemistry class. Take that, nucleophilic aromatic substitution!" Carmen and I share a puzzled glance. "Plus, you'll never believe it, Gretch. I've gone twelve straight days without crying."

"Huh," I say, admittedly impressed. "Does that mean you're over Lizzy?"

"Oh God no," she says, breathlessly. "But I realized after I got back from break, whatever happens with her, none of it can work unless I'm okay here, on my own. If we try this again, no matter how head over heels I get, I can't turn her into a crutch, you know? Also, I've figured out exercise is good for my moods."

I nod, vaguely hating how wise my sister sounds right now, not to mention the fact that she arrived at all of these epiphanies without *me*. Meanwhile, Carmen doesn't seem the least bit surprised by any of this—which weirdly hurts.

I know I sometimes resent being the one they dump their drama on, but now that they've stopped, I guess I don't want to be ignored, either? Maybe I'm just a truly impossible person.

"You okay, Gretch?" Hen asks.

"Yeah," I say, shaking it off.

"Oh crap." She stops moving in the frame and wipes her face with a towel. "I forgot I'm supposed to meet my friends soon. I should go shower."

"No worries," says Carmen. "I need to get back to work anyway."

She and Carmen blow fish-lipped kisses and I wave.

When the call ends, Carmen eyes the woodpile again, letting out a small, exhausted groan.

"I'll help," I say, getting up with her.

Each carrying umbrellas, we lug the wood out to her car, back and forth in tandem, until we're sliding the last of it in and she's pushing down the hatchback.

"I'm actually meeting someone near you later," I tell her, as she walks around to the driver's side. I bite my lip. Maybe I can give her half the story.

"Oh, nice," she says distractedly, fiddling with her umbrella before sliding in behind the wheel. I wait a moment, but she doesn't press for details. Doesn't think to ask if there might be a super-hunk awaiting my arrival—to ask me anything, really.

"I've had a lot going on too, lately," I add, a slight edge to my voice now. "And I'm . . . going to New York. On a trip with my friend."

"That's cool," she says, peeling off her wet jacket with the door still open. But there's no *when?* No *why?*

"Carmen!" I say.

"Huh?" She looks up, and I let out a huffy laugh. Maybe I'm not impossible when it comes to her and Henrietta. Maybe their complete disinterest in my life is actually just kind of shitty. "You know what? You're welcome," I say, gesturing to the pile of wood in back. I think I catch a quick, confused glance from her as I turn to go.

But I just stomp up the steps, ditch my wet umbrella on the porch, and close the door behind me.

In the hallway outside Jeremy's door, I take a moment to collect myself, my bad mood tucked away in a box. I'm not thinking about my tiff with Carmen. And definitely not about Sam. Not at all.

As discussed (with Nacho) I did give Sabrina a casual day, and it's a bit like the two of us have merged: my grubby leggings, black oversize sweater, and Converse sneakers; her red glasses, eye makeup, and messy buns, which I quickly fixed up in the car a few minutes ago.

I'm a little damp from the jog up to the building.

Overall, I think I'm ready. Or as ready as I'll ever be.

"Hi," he says, the door swinging open mere seconds after I knock.

"Hey," I say, feeling a prick of excitement as I peer up at him and glance past the threshold. It's basically the same layout as Carmen and Sabrina's room, just sort of . . . *Gross Boy Edition.*

As if seeing the place through my eyes now, Jeremy spins around himself, stepping in to tidy up some random papers before throwing a single brown apple core into the trash. The little voice pops in, as if to loosen me up: *Maybe Jeremy was practice-kissing, too?*

"I had no idea you went to this school," I say from the doorway when the silence grows too long. "Same as my cousin." For a moment, I feel a pang of regret. I shouldn't have been so pissy with her earlier. *Back in the box*, I tell myself.

Today is about getting my ass kissed.

Well, not my *ass*.

I almost giggle, shooing the mental image away. What a strange first kiss that would be. *Focus, Gretchen!*

Jeremy is back to cleaning, his nervous energy vaguely disappointing. Maybe it's shallow of me, but I didn't sign up for nervous. Jeremy was supposed to bring the confidence—enough swagger to get us through all the kissing. Where is that gum-commercial smile?

"She's in the architecture program," I add, the silence growing too weird.

"Oh, word?" he says, chucking one last rumpled can of Bud into the recycling bin. Similar to the comedy club, the whole room smells vaguely of beer, but not in a way I like as much.

I frown on a delay, pretty certain *word* is not a word Jeremy uses in the slang sense very often. Something is definitely off with him. Though I suppose I can hardly blame him. There's a palpable, unspoken awareness as to where this afternoon could go. It's not actually all that sexy.

It's more like . . . excruciatingly awkward.

"Can I get you anything?" he asks. "I've got some La Croix in the mini fridge." He says it the French way, though I'm not sure that's correct. I briefly think of Sam and his theories on overpronunciation. But actually, no. *He goes in a box, too.*

"Seltzer would be great," I say finally, walking in and lowering myself down onto his standard-variety dorm room couch. I get out my notebook from my tote bag before he hands me the drink. And I have to say, Natalie was right: it really does help, having something to sip on.

"So did you come up with anything new?" he asks, eyeing the notebook.

I feel a swell of relief—talking comedy is something I can do right now. "Okay, so, I've been playing around with some material about the whole dog-sibling thing. I have this one bit in my head where my mom is all, *Why can't you be more like your brother?* Only . . . he's a dog." Jeremy chuckles lightly as he takes the other side of the couch, but he leaves enough room for multiple holy spirits. I watch his Adam's apple bob up and down. I can't take it anymore. "Are you okay?"

He teeters a moment, just as someone bursts into the room.

"Dave!" says Jeremy, his voice almost high-pitched as the guy strides past us toward the beds.

"Sorry," says the guy, turning to me. "Oh, hey!" Abruptly, he frowns. "Wait. Sorry, I thought you were . . ." He looks at Jeremy. "Dude. You have a type."

"Please ignore my roommate," says Jeremy pointedly. "You know—the roommate who was supposed to be *busy* all day?"

Dave winces. "Right. My bad."

But I'm just smiling now, sort of enjoying the flush of Jeremy's cheeks. "I'm your type, huh?"

The roommate swipes a few books from a bed and turns right back around. "Carry on. I was never here. . . ."

"He seems nice," I say when the door closes, returning us to quiet.

"Yeah," says Jeremy, picking up his own notebook and tapping it with a pencil. "But, uh . . . don't listen to him. I mean, not that you're *not* my type." He pauses, seeming confused by the double negative. "I mean, of course you are. You're pretty and funny and smart. But, um . . . You know what, I'm making this worse."

I grin as he scrunches his eyes closed, then scoot over, closing the gap between us on the couch. "Be honest," I say as he turns to me, his eyebrows shooting up. "Are we really just here to write?"

He lets out a laugh of surprise and my smile widens. I kind of can't believe *I'm* being the brave one. But it feels kind of amazing, to just . . . *say the thing!* The enormously obvious thing that might have crushed us if left unsaid. I wish I could do this all the time. Instead of letting all of life's question marks fester, and fracture, and mutate into a million possible *what-ifs*.

My intentions are clear now. I want to kiss Jeremy.

And from the way he's looking at my lips, I think he *really* wants to kiss me too.

He doesn't move, though. Just stares. And as I peer back into the blue of his eyes, tiny prickles cascading down my limbs, it strikes me how tired I am of watching, waiting, vaguely hoping something interesting might happen *to* me. Eventually.

There is no in-between here—I either jump or I don't. So

like toes peeling off a diving board, I let myself lean forward. He leans too.

And then it happens: our lips meet, tentative at first, until something clicks, each of us softening as we breathe each other in. I'm enjoying the sensation enough to keep my internal monologue at bay for a good fifteen seconds, before the little voice inside starts shouting, *Holy shit, I am kissing a boy! I'm kissing an actual, human boy. Is that a tongue? We've got a tongue, folks!!!*

I suppress a giggle as his fingers brush my cheeks. I wouldn't say this is worthy of any swirling cameras, necessarily. And if we were to go outdoors in this rain, I think it would only hinder the experience. But it does feel *good.* Like, *in my body* good. Then again, that heart swell I feel for Sam? That part's not quite there. Is that bad? It doesn't *feel* bad.

The door swings open again and we spring apart.

"Sorry, sorry . . ." Dave is rushing back into the room, a hand blocking his profile out of respect. "I forgot one of my books. *So* sorry . . ."

When the door closes again, Jeremy's devilish grin has returned—a sign that all is right with the world.

I bump him with my side and reach for my notebook. "Should we get back to work? These jokes aren't going to write themselves."

We don't kiss again after that.

Though there is some tentative doorway leaning a couple

hours later. I'm sort of smile-frowning up at him now. There seems to be no natural way of saying goodbye after a day like this, so I just start walking backward into the hallway, snapping finger guns at him like a total freak.

"Hey." He catches my wrist before I'm out of reach.

I hold his stare, our faces close again. "Yes . . . ?"

"Don't think I'm going to go easy on you now because of this. I still want that Marnie James slot."

I laugh, relieved things haven't changed *too* much between us. "Jeremy, it is so on."

In the car, I free my hair and chuck the glasses onto the passenger seat. I feel too buzzy to go home, the early hour feeling disjointed from the night sky up above. For a little while, I poke along bumpy cobblestone roads, windshield wipers sloshing as I peer out at streetlamps still decorated with holiday wreaths and bare trees all strung up in lights.

As I head back over the bridge into SoPo, I'm still thinking about that kiss, feeling excited, and strange, and maybe other things I can't quite name. Without a thought, I pass the turnoff to my street, and soon enough I'm rolling up to the row of storefronts below Sam's apartment.

I wonder if he's home right now, what he's doing.

I wonder if he's rewatched *The Office* lately, alone, or with someone else.

The moment the engine goes silent, the thought lands with a

thud: I kissed someone else today. Whatever happens next, Sam will never be my first.

"Enough," I say, kicking open the door and making a shield of my umbrella. Sneakers already growing soaked, I race past the hanging plants of Keep Calm Yoga until I'm setting off the jangly doorway bells of Willard Beach Coffee.

Ethan looks up from wiping the counter with a rag. "Oh, hello."

"Hi," I say, snapping my umbrella shut and leaving it by the door. "I'm glad you're working. I just had the weirdest afternoon." I pull a squat chair up to the counter, which puts us at a strange height differential, but whatever. Selfishly, I'm glad it's empty in here, though I know it's not great for the tips.

"You want anything?" he asks. "I'm closing soon but I haven't cleaned the espresso maker yet."

"Sure, I'll take a PSL," I sigh. "Apparently it's a habit now."

I watch as he gets to work, feeling as if I'm just now catching my breath—not so much from my sprint here, but from this whole weird-ass day.

"So . . . what's up?" he says.

I laugh, baffled. "Well, long story short, we kissed and now . . . it's, like, I'm excited but I'm also . . ." I groan. "I don't know. I guess Sam's still in my head."

"Wait," he says. "So you *didn't* kiss Sam."

"No, no," I say. "We're not even speaking to each other.

This is my gnome-carving guy—well, my stand-up guy. Jeremy."

"Gotcha," says Ethan, some kind of milk apparatus steaming now. "So you kissed Jeremy and . . . ?"

"And then I came here," I say. "What do you mean?"

"I don't know," he says. "I guess . . . How was it?"

"Oh." I consider this. "It was fine—good."

His face falls. "That bad, huh? Did he lick your teeth?"

"What?" I start to laugh. "No, Ethan, he did not lick my teeth. That's not a thing."

"Oh, it's a thing," he says with a shudder. "Art camp. Summer after eighth grade. It was *not* a pleasant first kiss."

"Well, this was a perfectly fine first kiss. Better than fine," I say quickly. "It was . . . fun. Although . . ." I blink a moment. "Is it weird the guy didn't know my actual name? I guess I should feel guilty about that."

"Look at you," says Ethan. "The duplicity. The scandal!"

"Something tells me this guy can handle it. He's . . . very suave," I say, frowning. "Like, maybe too suave? Although today he actually seemed pretty nervous."

Ethan shrugs, lips forming a line. "Well, maybe he just really likes you."

"Eh," I say. "I think he keeps it pretty casual."

"And is that what you want? Casual?"

I roll my eyes, throwing my hands up. "Do I look like someone who knows what she wants, Ethan?"

He laughs under his breath, then pours my drink into a for-here mug on a saucer, a little heart forming in the foam. "Well, here's to you figuring it out, Gretch." He glances at the clock on the wall. "Hey, did you decide if you're going to Natalie's birthday thing tonight?"

I puff my cheeks. "No. I guess I should come up with an excuse. . . . I really can't risk running into that chef from the competition."

"I mean, the restaurant will probably be pretty packed. And dark."

"Yeah, but what if we bumped into each other with everyone from school there? What if he mentioned the show, or called me Sabrina? It could blow up pretty fast."

"He might not even be working," says Ethan. "And it's gonna be fun. If you want, I could help. Show me his picture. I'll . . . run interference."

"Maybe . . ." I say, sipping, thinking. "I actually *do* want to go. . . . And I definitely *don't* feel like sitting at home all night with my obsessive thoughts."

"So let's do it," he says. "Come on, Gretchen. Don't you want to live dangerously?"

I laugh. "I mean, it is kind of my style now."

"I really don't think this is necessary," Ethan says outside the restaurant. The rain has stopped, and it's actually half pleasant to be outside on this quiet, swanky corner off the harbor. "You look like you're trying to escape the paparazzi."

I adjust the aviators and ball cap we found in his car before riding over, then sigh like a beleaguered celebrity. *"I just want a normal life!"*

"God, you're weird," he says, grinning as he opens the door for me. When we step inside, the muffled nightclub beat kicks up a notch, just barely tolerable. I think the lighting must already be dim in here, because I can't see well through the shades.

"You're seriously being absurd," says Ethan, right before I trip, not noticing the extra step up to the hostess stand. But he catches me in time. "I told you, the coast is clear. This whole backstory is completely unnecessary."

"I got my eyes *dilated*," I say tersely. "Optometrist's orders. It'll make me feel better if you somehow missed him on your recon mission."

"I didn't miss him," says Ethan, sounding annoyed now. "Didn't you notice how long I left you standing out there? If you took off the sunglasses, you'd be able to see that it's an open-air kitchen. Meaning there's nowhere to hide." Through the shades, I actually *can* make out some of the interior—the custom woodwork and funky chandeliers. There's a sushi bar, a *bar*-bar, and one of those bathroom setups where the sinks are outside and everyone washes their hands together, which I guess makes it fancier. "I'm just saying, you can relax. Haru clearly isn't working tonight."

"*Shhhhh*, don't say his name," I hiss, spotting Natalie's big party in back. As we weave through solo diners and couples on dates, I keep hold of Ethan's arm, not that it stops me from tripping again. Twice, actually—the second time resulting in a woman's nigiri flopping straight back down onto her plate. "*So* sorry," Ethan says to her, before guiding me away with a whisper: "This is ridiculous."

"Maybe," I say, "but why not err on the side of caution?"

"At least lose the hat," says Ethan. "It doesn't fit with the optometrist story. And I don't think I've ever seen you wear a hat. That doesn't strike you as suspicious?"

"Maybe I just really like the Red Sox. *Go Sox, kid!*" I say in a Boston accent.

"Name one player."

"Okay, I'll lose the hat." I toss it into my bag as we come upon the rustic wooden table, its gnarled, winding surface like one long slice of a tree. Most of the guests already seem to be here, sitting shoulder to shoulder along bench seats, around candles in mason jars, dried wildflowers in vases, and place settings marked by chopsticks resting on blocks. Down at the other end, I recognize a couple kids from the film club, along with a few of Natalie's BSU friends and some other seniors I don't really know. I'm sure I'll make an extremely normal impression on all these people tonight between my paranoid glances and celebrity disguise.

Sasha and Lexi are here, too, chatting excitedly from their seats across from Natalie, who is standing up, talking to a forty-something couple I realize must be her parents. I can see where she gets her sense of style—her dad in a tailored blue sport coat and nice watch; her mom in a chic black romper, tight curls swept back on one side.

Natalie spots us then and comes over, looking like the belle of the ball in her cream sweater dress and expensive-looking riding boots. I'd probably feel too sloppy for this night if it weren't for Pilsner and Grody over on this end—both of them in schlubby athletic wear, their heads bowed over a shared screen playing some kind of sports highlight.

"Happy birthday!" I say when Natalie reaches us. She smiles, a bit puzzled, and I blurt out, "Eye doctor."

"Ah," she says, apparently satisfied by this explanation as she looks past me. "Oh, hi, Sam."

I stay where I am, suddenly stiff.

"Hi," I hear at my back. There's a sweetness to his voice that I forget is there sometimes—less obvious when coupled with his striking good looks and cool-guy hallway saunter. When I finally turn to face him, I can see he's carrying a gift bag. "It's just a little thing," he says, handing it to Natalie.

Pausing warily, she pushes the tissue paper aside and bursts out laughing. "Oh my God, a narwhal!" She hugs the stuffed animal to her chest, then explains, "Sam didn't know they were real. We had a whole debate one day." She looks at him.

"Thank you." He shrugs, a bit bashful, before flashing me an odd glance. At first, I think it's because of our fight—and the fact that we haven't spoken since. Then I remember the shades.

"Eye doctor," I say.

"Huh," he says. "Didn't you just go this summer?"

Crap. I did not expect him to remember that. "No . . . ?"

"Yeah, you did. I came over after your appointment and you made me hang out in the dark."

I smile faintly—that was actually kind of a funny day. "Well, I . . . went again. Eyes are . . . so important." Beside me, I can feel Ethan holding back a laugh. It's enough to make me do one last sweep for Haru, then give in. "I think I'm good now actually. The allotted time has, uh . . . passed."

I pull off the aviators, the world going brighter, and Ethan touches my arm. "Should we sit?"

"Yes," I say gratefully. We walk around to the open spots on the end across from Pilsner and Grody, who both reach over the table to dap up Ethan.

As we settle in, Grody tips an invisible hat my way. "Gretchen."

"We meet again," I say, deadpan as I can manage.

"I will try to keep this bitter rivalry under control," says Pilsner with a playful glower.

"You sure you're okay over there?" I hear Natalie say. She's wandered back to this side, talking to her parents again. She waves to Sam as she talks, pointing to the one space left, right between her and me.

"I think we'll be just fine at the bar," says her dad, glancing happily at his wife.

"Yeah, you guys do your thing," says her mom, smiling fondly at Sam as he stiffly lowers himself into the seat next to me. From his friendly, almost-deferential nod up at her, I get the sense he wants to maintain her good opinion of him. "Though we do have to embarrass you a *little*," Natalie's mom continues, lifting her wineglass to address the table, her voice now competing with the din. "Hey, everyone! We just wanted to thank you for helping us celebrate our baby's big night." She smiles down at her daughter. "I'm Ayanna, by the way," she adds, waving to some of us.

"And I'm Daniel," says Natalie's dad.

Grody looks up at them from his seat on the end. "This was so nice of you guys. Seriously, thank you so much for having me." I nod my agreement, surprised to be taking my politeness cues from a football bro.

"Oh, you're very welcome," says Natalie's dad, appearing charmed. He raises his voice to call down the table again: "And so you all know, we already have food coming, but feel free to add what you like to the order. Really. Don't be shy."

A waitress appears behind him—a tatted-up girl in a black canvas apron, a pen tucked into her pixie cut. "Hey, Chef."

"Oh good," he says. "You want to get them drinks?" He

turns back to us, giving the whole table Robert De Niro eyes. "Mocktails only, okay?"

"Dad!" says Natalie, sounding more kiddish than I've heard her before. "Okay, you two can go back to the bar now." Her mom chuckles, dragging her husband away, as Natalie looks up at the waitress. "You know, I *will* do a virgin cocktail. Surprise me, Yumi. Something girly."

"Oooh, I want that," says Grody, looking up hopefully. "And could it possibly be pink?"

The waitress laughs. "I'll pass that on to our mixologist."

The chatter starts up again once the drinks have been put in, everyone pausing briefly when Natalie does that thing where the hostess asks if we've all officially met, and we're forced to clumsily announce our names over the music. Even after introductions, though, with Sam at my side, it's like half the table has been walled off. We both seem to be making it our mission not to acknowledge the other. He's deep in conversation with Natalie now, and every time he brushes against me by mistake, I scoot a little closer to Ethan.

It's getting a bit silly, actually. I'm so tightly pressed up against him, I can feel the warmth of his skin through his jeans and plaid shirt. He glances at our touching sides. "Sorry," I whisper. "Is this weird? It's just . . ." I tilt my head in Sam's direction.

"Nah, I don't think it's that weird," he whispers back.

"Oh hell yes," says Pilsner, rubbing his hands together as the small plates start to arrive—a mouthwatering parade of miso scallops and pork buns and blistered green peppers dusted in limey salt.

No one really speaks for a few minutes, except to say things like "Wow." The sushi comes next, laid out in pretty arrangements of pearly white and pink and red. We try salmon, tuna, eel—all of it so fresh you barely have to chew. And then there are Natalie's dad's more playful creations, like the avocado rolls topped with heaps of lobster, and another kind filled with ceviche. It's all delicious, and nothing like the grocery-store stuff Annika brings to school.

With his cheeks stuffed full, Grody extends a big thumbs-up toward the bar, prompting Natalie's parents to grin and raise their wineglasses. "Okay, seriously, he's like parent catnip," says Natalie, making me laugh into my drink.

I lean forward, looking right past Sam to talk to her. "This food is amazing. Do you get to eat like this at home?"

She shrugs. "My dad is usually so tired of food when he isn't working that he'll just make, like, sticky rice, or a scrambled egg. But if I give him the puppy dog eyes, yes. He can pretty much whip up whatever I'm craving."

"That is the frickin' dream," says Pilsner, shaking his head wistfully.

I startle as Ethan leans into me, speaking low in my ear. "Okay, so . . . don't freak out, but we have a problem. . . ." I follow his eyes across the room and flinch.

Haru has walked in, plain-clothed, with a messenger bag.

He's chatting with the hostess now.

"Shit," I say under my breath. "Oh my God. What do I do?"

"Stay calm . . . maybe he's only passing through."

I watch Haru laugh with the woman for another minute before she hands him an envelope, and I sigh with relief. "I bet he's just picking up a check."

As if sensing eyes on him, he looks this way—*right* this way. And without another thought, I'm going down, my body slinking toward the floor like an invertebrate species as I scrape against the bench. From under the table, I take a moment to stare at Ethan's flat sneakers next to me. And then I look down at the long line of other feet.

Uh-oh.

I did not think this through.

"Gretchen?" Ethan's face pops into view. "What uh . . . Whatcha doin' there?"

I cringe up at him. "Any chance that looked super normal?"

"Sorry," he says. "But if it's any consolation, I don't think Haru saw you. He just left."

"Cool," I say, frowning.

Sam's head pops under now. "Okay, what the hell is going on, Gretch?"

"I'm fine," I say quickly. "I just . . . I, uh . . ."

"She dropped something," says Ethan, turning to him at an odd angle.

"Yes," I say. "I did drop something."

Grody's head pops under too now. "What are we doin' down here, guys?" he says, smiling around at us. "You okay, Gretchen?"

"Fine," I say, laughing despite myself.

When they all disappear from view, I hear Ethan announce, "She's fine!"

Slowly, I climb back up, and a couple people from the other end of the table look on curiously.

"Whoops!" I call over the music. "I, uh. . . I dropped my earr—" *Nope, not wearing earrings.* "Hair tie!" I hold my wrist up triumphantly. "I'm always losing these things! It's one of life's great mysteries, isn't it? Like, where *do* all the hair ties go?" Sam's just frowning strangely at me, while Ethan works to keep a straight face. I stare down the long table, feeling myself start to crumple.

Natalie flashes me an odd look, but she laughs. "I know, right?" She starts pointing around at all the empty plates. "Okay, help me stack these up, everybody. Who wants dessert?"

FIFTEEN

Comic Relief | The fun stuff between swoons and kisses. Quite possibly the best part.

"I feel like every girl group needs a listener," I tell the audience Wednesday night. "I've been thinking about this with my sister and cousin. The three of us are really close, but there's a major imbalance there. When we get together, I mean, *they just*—" I move my hand like a talking puppet. "No matter *what's* going on with me. I feel like my hair could be on fire, and they'd be like, 'Okay, we'll *get* to that, but first, let's talk about *my* thing.'"

I shrug as people chuckle. "More of that third-child plight, I guess . . . Also, now, even a dog is surpassing me in the family hierarchy." I quickly catch the room up on Nacho's upcoming

Gatsby party—which, yes, is actually happening. And I can tell from the reactions that these people *love* my mom.

"Do any of you have that person in your life?" I say. "Who just . . . takes dog parenthood *so* extremely seriously? I'm pretty sure she wants to start an Instagram for him, which might have factored into this party idea. The woman loves a photo op, and Nacho always rises to the occasion. He literally perks up whenever he sees her phone. And the weird thing is, the photos come out *flattering*. I'm telling you. That dog really knows his angles."

It feels like my time should be up by now, but the light isn't blinking. And tonight's easy-to-please audience has me feeling like a kid desperate for five more minutes.

"Anyway," I say through a sigh, grinning out at them. "The other day I caught her taking a personality quiz for him. He's ENFP."

After my set, I tiptoe over to Isaiah and Paula in back, exchanging exaggerated high fives before pulling up a chair. Jeremy is helping Ted out with some grunt work behind the bar, but he catches my eye across the room, his grin like a salute.

I did good. We both know it. And that fact may honestly be more thrilling than the memory of our kiss over the weekend—which is saying something.

It's sort of unbelievable, but I missed his set *again* tonight, while trapped in the world's slowest bathroom line. I snuck out for a pee break while Lakshmi was talking about family planning ("I used to very calmly explain to pregnant women that they were going to be *just fine*. Now I'm looking back over my textbooks, like, *Wait, I'm supposed to do what now?*") The crowd was still laughing along when I stepped in and sighed—six girls crowded around tiny sinks. By the time I got out, Jeremy was already waving good night to the audience.

The weird part was, I felt relieved about it. Maybe because I wanted us to stay on equal footing a little longer.

I don't think I'm quite ready for him to be better than me.

The moment the lights come up after the last act, Paula and Isaiah start begging to be invited to Nacho's birthday party.

"Please?" says Paula. "You got us so invested."

"I *have* to see Nacho in a flapper dress," says Isaiah.

"Well, Nacho is no stranger to sequins and feathers," I say. "My mother makes sure of that."

The three of us share a smile, and for a second, I really wish they *could* come meet Nacho, and the rest of my family. I'm not sure what to say, actually, but I'm saved by Isaiah's ringtone.

"I should take this," he says, pushing back in his chair.

"Actually, I need to catch Amber before she goes," says Paula, getting up, too. "She's doing my chart. But I'll be right back!"

I look around vaguely for Jeremy, but he must be off helping Dolores with the ballots now. Is it weird that I feel so relaxed about our kiss? I suppose neither of us is planning the wedding or anything.

But this could be fun, casual.

I guess I do *fun and casual*—between stand-up sets.

This is my life now, apparently.

Across the room, I see Paula wave goodbye to Amber before she and Isaiah converge. Now they're talking. Isaiah is smiling. Paula is squealing and Dolores is rushing over to them. Everyone is hugging now, and suddenly they're all headed this way.

"You'll never believe it!" Dolores calls out to me.

"Isaiah booked a *national* commercial," says Paula, dropping into her chair.

"First one of my life," says Isaiah, lowering down too with a dazed look on his face. "Oh wow . . . I'm going to get my SAG card! I have this long list of goals for this year. That was a big one."

"This is so awesome!" I say. "What's the commercial for? Wait, let me guess. You're the face of a new body spray. Spritz it under your pits and you'll have fifteen girlfriends."

Grinning, he shakes his head no. "You're . . ." I think. "One of those smug, contented drivers in a car commercial?" He laughs and I pound on the table, losing my patience. "Tell me, Isaiah!"

"Two words for you," he says, lips twitching with a smile. *"Light. Beer."*

"Not just any light beer," Dolores calls, walking off again.

"Budweiser," says Paula. "Aka the mother lode."

Jeremy comes up to our table now. "What's going on?"

"He got the commercial," says Paula, reaching out to tap Isaiah's arm excitedly.

Jeremy sits, clearly stunned. "Hey, man, congrats. That's huge."

"Thanks," says Isaiah.

"Is it going to be in the Super Bowl?" I say. "Are you going to make a million dollars?"

"I don't know about that," he says, laughing. "But it'll certainly help finance some of my plans. I came up here from DC to go to college, then stayed for the cheaper rent. I've been driving down to Boston and New York for auditions, but it's probably time to try LA soon. I really want a manager next. Or an agent. If I get to open for Marnie James, that could probably lead to something good."

"Plus, you'd get a regular Saturday slot," Paula says, gesturing to the empty stage.

He shrugs. "Yeah, that, too. For however long I stay, at least." Something in Paula's expression shifts then, like his words have stung her, ever so slightly. "Come on, Paul. This was always meant to be temporary," he says gently. "The material I do in Maine is *very different* from the stuff I do when I'm back home."

"I know," she says quickly. "I'll just miss you is all."

Jeremy and I catch each other's eye, like maybe we shouldn't be here for this private moment. But they seem to shake it off.

"Hey, speaking of Marnie," says Jeremy, clearing his throat. "I meant to tell you guys. Dolores showed me the latest voting data. Isaiah, you're still in first place, with Paula *barely* trailing behind. . . ." He turns to me, an eyebrow lifted. "And then, if you have another night like tonight, it's looking like we'll be duking it out for the third slot, Sabrina."

I stare, unable to fully process this. If I got into the top three, Marnie would see my set. With her *actual eyes*. "Let's not get ahead of ourselves," I say after a brief but very real blackout. "There are a lot of good comics in this competition."

"From where I'm sitting, your biggest threat is Haru," says Isaiah. "I don't get it, but the dude knows how to make fish funny."

"And don't sleep on Amber," says Paula. "For all we know she has a crystal that magically makes you win comedy competitions." Everyone laughs. "I'm kidding. I actually *really* like her."

"This is starting to feel so official," I say through a rush of excitement.

"Right?" says Jeremy. "Oh, I *also* meant to tell you . . ." He pulls out his phone and starts to scroll. "I helped Dolores write her first-ever tweet on the new Chuckle Parlor account today. We're all in it. It's just a little graphic about the show." His face falls. "Whoa, you guys." He looks up. "We're being *trolled*."

"What?" says Paula.

"Bad Kevin James," says Jeremy, gaping down at the screen. "Well, his name is Mike, apparently, but this is definitely him. Jesus, he's, like, losing his mind."

Isaiah pulls out his phone to look it up. "Hashtag boycott the Chuckle Parlor?"

"What did I just hear?" calls a gravelly voice from somewhere. "Boycott *what now*?"

Paula pulls the thread up too as Dolores rushes over, Jeremy reading aloud: "'No one in this show would have survived the glory days. You know, back when stand-up was actually funny? Sorry, snowflakes. Also, Marnie James is your big celebrity? Honestly? No thanks!'"

Paula scoffs. "He did *not* just go after Marnie. Like he's in any position to judge!"

Isaiah's eyes go wide. "Look at that . . . a few of us got a private shout-out."

Paula scrolls through the thread until she finds it: the show graphic with a circle drawn around the row with Isaiah, me, and Paula in alphabetical order—Lewis next to Martin next to Meiselman. Below our names, he's scrawled out, *Not funny!* like some kind of deranged toddler.

Dolores shakes her head. "What a sad little man . . ."

"I bet he's pissed because he caught us making fun of him at that other open mic last week," says Paula. "What's that statistic? Men are more afraid of getting laughed at than being murdered? Anyway, I don't know why he had to drag you into it, Sabrina. Jeremy was our third, not you."

"Yeah, well," says Jeremy, frowning now. "Something tells me he doesn't go after white guys very often."

"That's probably a fair assessment," says Isaiah, somehow looking both bothered and completely unsurprised.

"I'm gonna respond," says Jeremy.

"Eh." Paula shrugs. "Just make a joke about his micropenis and call it a day."

"No!" says Dolores. "Don't stoop to his level. And definitely don't respond from the club account. What you write as yourself is up to you, but I still say keep it classy."

"Fine," sighs Jeremy, typing now.

After a minute, he shows us the draft: *First of all, Marnie's achievements speak for themselves. You would be delusional to think you possessed even an ounce of her talent. And as for the rest of us, that's for the audience to decide. There have been no complaints since you left.*

"There we go," says Dolores, winking. "Just the right amount of salty."

"Still not as fun as Paula's thing," says Isaiah, smiling over at her. "But dignified works."

"All right," sighs Dolores. "Let's not give this another second of our time or energy. Tonight we celebrate Isaiah. And shitty American beer."

I wake to a glowing phone on the nightstand. It must be late—still pitch-black out—but I reach for it anyway, yawning, squinting. The messages are from Hen, sent late to the long-abandoned group thread with Carmen.

I just got so nostalgic you guys. Me and some of the girls on my floor did an old school rom-com double feature.

First up was The Wedding Planner (All hail J-Lo!)

Then Hitch

Do you remember how after the part where Will Smith's face balloons up from anaphylactic shock, the two of you fell off Carmen's bed you were laughing so hard?

P.S. It's just hitting me now that Eva Mendes may have been responsible for my sexual awakening???

I also realized while we were watching that Lizzy looks a little like her

And then I got sad

But also a little happy because we've been texting . . .

(But I really am standing on my own two feet!)

Anyway, just wanted to say miss youuuuuu

I let out a breath of relief when I see Carmen's response below, sent a while later:

Bahahahaha I forgot about falling off my bed

Gretchen, you were definitely crying from laughing too

I love it when you get in that mood

It always gets me and then I can't stop

I smile and adjust the covers. I guess this means she's moved on from our little spat the other day—if she's even aware it *occurred*. I suppose she's never been as weird about conflict as I am. She and Hen go at it all the time, just like Mom and Aunt Viv, briefly unleashing their inner feline beasts, only to let it go, harmony restored. I sort of wish I could pull that off. It's probably a lot healthier than declaring everything *fine* and then randomly exploding every few years.

I laugh. Maybe I should put *that* in a set?

I'm about to write back when a bubble appears—Carmen typing again, hours after her last text. So tonight was weird . . .

I got in super late from the studio and Sabrina was waiting up for me

All of a sudden she wanted to talk about what happened

Saying how it's sad we let a guy come between us and blah blah blahhhh

And then she starts talking about these rumors she's been hearing about him. As if I'd want to sit around analyzing the guy who had his tongue down both our throats???

And I was just so exhausted from building my model all day

So I told her I didn't feel like talking, and she cried and ran out

Am I an asshole?

I know you're probably both asleep

A bubble pops up right as I finish reading—Hen this time.

No I'm up!

And you're not an asshole! You were betrayed and she owes you a proper apology!

Sorry, wait

Lizzy wants to know if we can Facetime tomorrow

What should I say???

Am I an idiot for wanting to try to make this work?

I jump in with a response then: You're not an idiot. And Carmen, you're not an asshole.

Carmen replies: Well that's a relief. Hehe. When did life get so complicated?

Seriously, writes Hen. So much hot goss all the time!

As I scroll back over our chain, it occurs to me that neither one of them ever really waits to be asked about their lives—they just charge right ahead with whatever it is they need to unload. Is it possible this has been an option for me too? Is it really just a matter of piping the hell up?

I bite my lip, then decide to test my theory.

Speaking of hot goss . . .

I have gone the way of Drew Barrymore, girls

Hen sends a question mark.

Then Carmen writes, Wait. You've been kissed???!

I respond with a thumbs-up, at which point Hen replies, WHAAAAAAAAT?

I laugh, typing, Yep! He's a guy from this—I think a moment—club I'm in.

Carmen responds with a GIF from the aforementioned film: the long-awaited smooch on the pitcher's mound between Drew and her hunky high school teacher who just found out she's not a kid. (Sidebar, still a little weird.)

Tell us, writes Carmen. Was the kiss of this here caliber?

I laugh again. Well, maybe not quite so dramatic. But I was pleased.

Awww, says Hen. Our little Gretchen is all grown up.

It's completely stupid, but for a second, I hold the phone to my heart. Then I notice that it's four in the morning.

Okay, it's obscenely late, says Hen, apparently reading my mind from a whole state away. Let's all get some beauty sleep, shall we? Love you twooooo

Carmen writes back a string of hearts.

I send kissy faces.

And I pass out with the phone still in my hand.

SIXTEEN

The Will-They-Won't-They | A question that is, if we're being honest, not usually very difficult to answer. For more of a nail-biter, try a male lead who sucks at communication or is fervently opposed to eye contact.

"Oh, hey, Sam!" says Natalie, catching him in the hall after school on Tuesday. She just caught *me* a few seconds ago, wanting to talk about something yearbook related. So now I'm stuck here, in the closest proximity I've been to Sam since her big birthday dinner.

"Hey," he says, friendly-ish while looking completely ready to bolt.

"You going to the game tonight?" she asks.

He hikes up his bag. "Can't."

"Me neither," she says quickly. "My dad's short-staffed at the restaurant, so I said I'd help. Now I'm kind of bummed."

"Oh. Um." He shrugs, smiles. "That's too bad."

"Yeah it is," she says, shooting me a look like, *What the heck?*

He glances at her, then *right past* me. "Well, I should probably . . ."

"Yeah," says Natalie. And together, we watch him go. She sighs when he's out of earshot. "Oh, forget it. College boys, here I come."

Out of nowhere, Annika goes bounding past us like a tumbleweed. *"Three days, three days, three days . . ."* I laugh and make tiny hand claps, waving her off as she slips into a music room.

"Our New York trip," I translate when Natalie looks confused.

"So awesome," she says. "But what was I going to tell you? Oh, right. I can't stay today, and Ethan isn't here either. I asked him to get some shots of the game against Berwin tonight. He just went home to grab his gear."

"Oh, okay," I say, a little disappointed. I've been enjoying our afternoons at HQ lately. Pilsner and Grody have even started stopping by to hang. According to Pils, I'm one of the "bros" now.

"But I was thinking, do you have plans tonight?" she asks. I shake my head no, then wonder if I should have left myself vulnerable like that. "Cool. In that case, why don't you go with Ethan? Everyone will be there, so you'll pretty much have the whole school sitting in the stands. I was hoping to get moving on those quotes for the club captions, and this way, you can probably knock most of them out tonight."

My shoulders slump. *This* is why you always have plans. As a rule, any event involving *pretty much the whole school* is one I'm probably not interested in. Also, while I can't really follow *any* sport, in hockey you can't even see the ball—puck. Whatever.

Natalie has already moved along, though, her eyes on her phone, fingers flying. "I'm actually texting him now. He says he can pick you up at your house later if you want."

"Uh, sure," I say. Ugh. *She got me.*

"Look at that," she says, glancing up with a satisfied grin. "All my worker bees staying on task. Plus, you'll have a good time. I wish I could go. People got *so* into it last year."

"Tell me again why we have this Berwin rivalry?"

"Because it's *Berwin*," says Natalie. "And Carlton hates Berwin. Sports are very simple, Gretchen." I laugh. "Plus, it's kind of fun, right? We put on our team colors, scream our heads off with every goal. It's something we can all belong to—everyone is welcome."

"Except anyone from Berwin," I say.

"Well, yeah, fuck those guys," says Natalie.

A little before six thirty, Ethan texts to say he's on his way.

I wait in the foyer at the bottom of the steps, Nacho curled up against my leg—in solidarity, I think. I'm pretty sure he can sense my growing dread about the game tonight. I knew I'd have to face this assignment eventually. But still. Me and school spirit do not mix.

Nacho perks up with his listening face, and I grin and eavesdrop too.

In the living room, Mom and my brother are still bickering. He came by a little while ago to drop the twins off for a sleepover, and Mom was not pleased to see Mina in a Disney princess dress.

"I don't know what to tell you," I hear William say now. "I let them each pick one item from the toy store. It's what she wanted. I'm not going to shame her for being girly, Mom."

"I know, I know . . ." She sounds like she's letting up a little. "Have you at least been reading them those board books I got on Frida Kahlo and Katherine Johnson? They're good for Gus, too."

I smile, filing away a few of my own childhood memories as my phone goes off.

I brace myself to get up. But actually, it's Jeremy, with an innocuous *Cool cool* in response to something I said earlier. All week, it's been, *How are you?* and *Did you have a good day?* But never, *Should we meet up and do more of the kissing?*

Now Ethan's name pops up on the screen. Here.

With a glum sigh, I stand. "Bye, Nacho . . ." He yips out a pep talk. "Thanks," I say, before calling, "Bye, Mom! Bye,

William!" Outside, I kick a little snow on my walk down the path.

"What's with the face?" says Ethan as I slide into the passenger seat.

"Nothing," I say, brightening somewhat at the sight of him. He's dressed head to toe in dark green and white, our school colors, which have always made me think of snow dusted on pine trees. He even has a matching hat and scarf. "You're looking festive."

"Carlton, let's *go*!" he says, in a jokey, dog-bark kind of voice.

"And fuck Berwin?" I say like I'm being tested. I nod myself along. "Yep. Uh-huh. I hope they all have . . . terrible lives!" Ethan laughs as he starts to drive. "Sorry. Still working on my smack talk."

The rink smells like an actual armpit.

But no one seems to care. And Natalie was right: there are *so many* Carlton kids here. Now I sort of wish I owned something forest green, my plain black leggings and oversize gray sweater sticking out for once.

"Take this," says Ethan, draping his scarf around me. *How did he do that?* Ever since I told him about the Comithon, it's like he can read me or something. He frowns. "Why are you being weird?"

"I'm not being weird," I snap back. He levels me with a look, and I roll my eyes. "It's just a lot of people-ing, okay? And I never know how to insert myself into group conservations. It's like . . . playing jump rope or something."

He laughs. "Well, maybe try channeling some of that *Sabrina* edge."

"*Shhhhhhh*, don't say that so loud."

"You got this," he says, walking backward with his camera. "Godspeed!" I shake my head as he moves into the stands, occasionally tapping someone on the shoulder, prompting groups of friends to squeeze together and pose. Talking to people seems to come so naturally to him. Even with the game taking focus, everyone he approaches seems to want to keep him around, chatting away as he checks the LCD screen to make sure he got a good shot.

I draw a long breath, steadying myself. This shouldn't be so hard. But the longer I stand here, the more the skin-crawly feeling comes back, phantom eyes on me—though of course, everyone is watching the game.

Just do it, woman, the little voice in my head commands. I make tight fists at my sides before releasing them, zeroing in on a couple older lax girls nearby. I slide my phone out from my stretchy leggings pocket and open the recording app. Chin up, back straight . . .

"Hi. I'm Gretchen. I work for the yearbook and I was . . . just wondering if you'd like to be quoted about your time on the lacrosse team?" I extend the phone out.

"Uhh . . . sure," says one of them. "The experience has

been . . . like having twenty *extremely* hardworking, aggressive, kick-ass sisters."

"Aw," says her friend before leaning in. "Also? A bunch of us got *abs* this year. But maybe that's not important." I laugh under my breath as I back away and thank them, already scanning for another interview. I guess I've found a use for my lurker-girl skills, because I can more or less match the faces to the clubs and activities.

Next, I approach a guy from the school musical, who seems more than happy to offer a quote: "First off, I have to hand it to our crew, and our director, Mrs. B. Also Doug's mom for making all the costumes. I mean, they're the real reason we get to go up there and shine."

After that, I find a girl from model UN who's very ready to dish: "Let's just say for a bunch of wannabe *diplomats* we sure did have a lot of conflict. We had a bit of an . . . Ecuador-UK-China love triangle situation on our hands for a while there. The geopolitical implications were nearly catastrophic. . . ."

Before I know it, Deb, my cafeteria curiosity, is telling me about her time with the Mathletes (sans iguana) tonight: "You think this Berwin rivalry is bitter? We just got beat by a team called *Deez Hypote-nuts.* When the new season starts, they better believe we're gonna *Deez Hypote*-neuter them." She tilts her head toward the guy next to her, keeping her voice down. "That is, if *Josh* here doesn't forget to carry the one."

"You're . . . kind of awesome," I tell her.

"Thanks," she says, like she already knew that.

The more time that passes, the easier it gets. I talk to runners and singers and a few members of the robotics clubs, later re-introducing myself to Natalie's friends Sasha and Lexi (captains of the swim and debate teams, respectively), who I never really got a chance to talk to at her birthday dinner.

I also manage to find the *one boy* from Carlton's modern dance company. "It's a good thing I'm honest," he's telling me now. "The girls *still* always forget I'm straight and offer to let me change with them. I thought this was the twenty-first century; that we'd rid ourselves of the stereotypes! But nope. I might as well have *gay* stamped right across my forehead."

Pilsner and Grody flag me down in the stands when I'm just about done, asking to be recorded though I could easily get them later. For a few minutes, I humor them, holding out the phone with my lips pursed as they drone on about football and the *true meaning of grit.*

"Very inspirational," I tell them, sliding the phone away.

"You ever play a team sport, Gretch?" asks Grody.

"Nah. I've never really done a team *anything.* I'm kind of a *small circles* kind of girl."

"I guess that explains it," says Pilsner. "We were just talking about that. Like, where's Gretchen been hiding all this time?"

I laugh, sort of, though the comment oddly stings. The boys have already moved on, though, up on their feet, eyes on the ice.

I spot Ethan below, and hop down to join him. He's taking a few shots of the game, standing behind glass, just slightly off center from the net. "Get enough?" he asks, glancing over as a Carlton player sweeps by us.

"I think so," I say, feeling a sudden swell of relief. That wasn't so bad. Actually, it was kind of fun. "You?"

"Yeah, I'm just about done," he says, snapping a few more.

I flinch as two guys slam against the glass.

"This is a close one," says Ethan, lowering the camera. "No fights this time. That's disappointing. . . ."

The intensity in the rink has grown since we arrived, the score tied up, apparently. I listen in as the Carlton side shouts together in rhythm: "Mules are ster-ile!" *Clap. Clap. Clap-clap-clap.*

I frown. "Mules?"

"It's the Berwin mascot," says Ethan. "I guess . . . since mules can't reproduce?"

"Ah," I say, straining to hear the calls from the Berwin side, three syllables repeated over and over. "Wait. Did I just hear *ugly chicks*?"

"Yeah, that's . . . one of their chants about us."

My jaw drops. "I don't see why they have to bring *us* into it. Also, show me *one girl* on their side as pretty as Natalie." I shake it off. "I don't know why I'm dignifying this."

A bunch of guys go whizzing by us on the ice before . . . *something* happens. The Carlton side screams. A player holds his stick up in the air.

"Wait," I say, still looking for the puck. "Did we score? How does anyone follow this game?"

"We scored," says Ethan with a laugh.

I pump my fist, do a little dance, and start shouting, "Woo-hoo! Aww yeaaaaah! Fuck you, Berwin! How you like that, huh? You fuckin' pieces of shit!"

A few Mule parents look over, returning from the snack bar with cocoas in hand. I freeze and Ethan puts an arm around me, swiftly guiding us away. "Okay, that's enough. . . ."

By the time Ethan pulls up to my house, something about my mood has shifted—the last traces of our fun night turning almost bittersweet. We chatted at first, then fell into an easy silence, driving smoothly through the pitch-black night until a daze came over me.

"Hey," says Ethan as the engine cuts out. I'm staring straight ahead. "What's wrong?"

"I . . . don't know, exactly," I say with a weird little laugh. "I guess I was just thinking about some stuff Sam said a while ago. I think he might have been right."

"About . . . ?"

I shrug. "Just . . . how I am sometimes. I always thought I was protecting myself. I mean, it *is* high school, and there's a reason that *Heathers* movie exists." Ethan laughs under his breath as I strain against the seat belt, turning to him. "But I've been wrong about some things. Like . . ." I meet his eyes, almost ashamed to admit this. "I really hated it when Sam started hanging out with the football guys. You were, like, Neanderthals in my mind. But, like, evolved enough Neanderthals to be really arrogant and shitty to girls."

"Ouch," says Ethan.

"I didn't actually think that about you," I amend, truthfully. "I guess since I already knew you from yearbook. To be honest, I always saw you as someone I could probably . . ." He's looking at me funny.

"What?" he says.

"Just . . . be really good friends with."

"Right," he says. "I always thought that too, Gretchen. And I guess I am less intimidating than the average jock."

"It's really true," I say curiously. "Maybe because you're only a kicker? . . . Sorry."

"No, it's okay," he says, laughing a little. "It is a pretty unsung role. And to your other point, it's not like you were totally wrong. We do have players like that on the team. But then you get guys like Pils and Grody."

"Exactly," I say. "And they're, like . . . kind of the best. And almost . . . sweet?"

"Yeah, Grody's become super big on saying *I love you* to his friends. It used to make me awkward, but now I just say it back."

I clutch my heart. "See? I love that."

He grins fondly. "He and Pils both. They're . . . pretty devoted."

"Aw. Like how?"

He breathes in, thinking a minute. "Well, they definitely stepped up when we were in middle school." He hesitates, as if making a quick call in his head. "Right after seventh grade, my mom was diagnosed with breast cancer?"

"Oh. My God."

"She's okay now," he says quickly. "But during her treatments, I was really scared. My sister had this internship, and my dad was working at the store constantly to keep us afloat. My mom kept saying she wanted us all busy. But I just had to be home. I basically refused to go anywhere all summer."

I smile—that's sweet—and he shakes his head.

"Anyway, I don't remember having a big conversation about it, but at some point, Pils and Grody just started showing up at my house—like, every day. They knew I wanted to keep the place quiet enough for my mom to sleep. So we'd just sit around playing video games on mute. I swear, even the food they brought was quiet. No crunchy chips or noisy wrappers. We were still *very cool* about everything back then, so it's not like anyone ever asked, 'How are you feeling, Ethan?' But in a way, they kind of did."

When he looks at me, I realize I have tears in my eyes.

"Hey," he says, his face falling. "I told you, my mom's fine. . . ."

"I know," I say, tamping down this completely inappropriate

reaction. "That's just so . . . *nice!*" To my horror, the word comes out a squeak. "And I almost missed out on them—on *Pils and Grody*. And you . . . and Natalie . . . and who knows who else . . . Sorry. I didn't mean to change the subject."

"No, no," he says, his arms sort of flailing now like he isn't quite sure if he should touch me or not. "I just, uh . . . have this thing where I get super weird around crying girls."

I crack up, sniffing back snot. "Sorry. *God*. I guess I have a lot on my mind right now. Too much artistic introspection, or . . . something."

"Well, just . . . don't cry onstage," he says, making me laugh again. He reaches around to the backseat. "Hey, you want to see some photos before you go?"

"Sure," I say as he returns with his camera, leaning in. Our heads bump together as I watch the images flick by: group after group, people chanting and hollering, arms slung around shoulders. A sea of green and white. For a second, I want to dive straight into the photos—to feel so naturally, effortlessly a *part* of something.

"These are *beautiful*," I whisper, almost getting choked up again. Ethan's eyes flit to mine. "Sorry. Don't worry." I sniff. "The dam is closed."

SEVENTEEN

The "You Were Lying the Whole Time?" | It was all a ruse, but the feelings were real. It's really not that bad. Barely even creepy if you think about it.

"Can we talk?" I say to Jeremy Wednesday night, pulling him from the group before the show starts. He waggles his eyebrows at everyone, following me out to the hall by the exit.

"What's up?" he says breezily, hands tucked into the front pockets of his jeans.

I frown up at him. "Are things weird between us now?"

He takes a step back, and from the curious look on his face, I think maybe he respects my directness. "I hope not. Is this better?" He picks up my hand and quickly kisses it.

"Jeremy!" I look around, barely suppressing my smile.

"Oh, they know about us," he says.

Know what? I want to say. *What we are to each other? Could they maybe explain that to me?* But I guess I have no right to demand clarity on the terms of our relationship. Sometimes I actually have to remind myself of this: Jeremy doesn't even know my *name.*

"Listen, sorry to cut this short," he says, "but Dolores asked me to make a quick run for printer paper. For the ballots. I should be back in time for your set if I go now."

"Oh," I say. "Uh . . . okay."

"But, um . . ." He reaches out for a piece of my hair that's come loose, tucking it behind my ear. "More on this later?"

"Sure," I say, blinking strangely as I watch him go.

He glances back with that megawatt smile and I laugh, rolling my eyes.

Paula walks up beside me and slowly shakes her head.

"What?" I say.

"Oh, nothing," she says playfully. "Just haven't seen him make that face in a while. I think somebody's in *looooooove.*"

I scoff at her, then stop short. He's not, right?

I'm still thinking about it when Dolores calls me to the stage, but in a blink, I'm putting Jeremy out of my head, warming up the crowd with my plight-of-the-third-child bits, even adding some new flourishes to the learning-to-bike section: "'I'm okay, Mom and Dad! Survived the shark! But I think I'm gonna bike into this weird guy's van. . . .'"

I also bring back that tangent about Hen and Carmen, blathering on about their drama while my hair catches fire. This time, I go so far as to mime blasting myself with a fire extinguisher, slumping forward, heaving for breath. "'Wow . . . That must have been . . . really hard for you. . . .'"

To be honest, neither bit feels quite right this time around, now that Mom and Dad have been gingerly probing me about my college aspirations these past few days, and my text chain with Hen and Carmen has come somewhat back to life. It's not like that history has been wiped away exactly, but I guess the jokes feel too simple now.

Anyway, the audience doesn't know the difference, laughing along as I switch to a new bit I wrote late last night when I couldn't sleep.

"I went to a birthday party once where they played *Sleeping Beauty* for all the girls. I was maybe six, and when my mom found out after, she was *livid*, just bombarding me with questions. Like: 'So, honey, what was Aurora's personality like? Hopes, dreams, special skills? Did she have a really *exciting arc* through the film? No? Do you want to know why? *Because she was asleep!*'"

I pace a minute, enjoying the rumble of the crowd.

"At the time, I was utterly perplexed. But of course I get it *now.* If I think the messages in my rom-coms can be a little questionable, I mean . . . *Sleeping Beauty*: asleep, guy falls in love with her. *Snow White*: asleep, guy falls in love with her. *The*

Little Mermaid: conscious but can't say a word, guy falls in love with her. Even in *Cinderella*, the whole basis of their love is one quick spin around the ballroom without any substantive conversation. Do you think if Cinderella had looked up at Prince Charming while they were dancing and made a joke that went over his head, he still would have chased her? Or would he have just started to scan the room like, 'That one looks pretty quiet. . . .'" I squint out at the audience, still scanning. "'Oooh, that one's asleep. . . .'"

I can't believe how calm I feel right now, despite the adrenaline pumping through my veins. I get this weird happy shiver, then focus.

"And what's with all these stories made for girls where the *whole mission* is finding love? I mean, so much of the media my brother grew up on was like, *One boy must save the world. . . .*"

I listen a beat, pleased that the audience likes my movie trailer voice.

"And then the stories we got were like, *One girl must get a boyfriend. . . .*" I can't help but feel a bit giddy as the crowd laughs again. "I'm obviously not the first person to point this out. My mom has been yelling about this stuff her whole life, one drop in a sea of other yelling women. And while it was helpful growing up with her in my ear, some of these ideas can still really get their clutches in you. Like, I sometimes *do* still want to be the *fairest of them all*. I compete with other girls in my mind, for no reason besides my own insecurity. And it's not my *mission*, exactly, but getting a boyfriend is still *pretty* up there on the agenda. It takes up a surprising amount of mental energy. . . ." I flinch as I catch sight of Jeremy, stepping back in from the cold in his beanie and T-shirt.

I hesitate. Is this weird now? Me venting about my boy drama up onstage? But then I remember what he and I agreed on not too long ago: *All's fair in love and comedy.*

As if reading my mind, Jeremy winks.

"I've actually been torn between *two* guys," I tell the crowd with a slight smirk. "My longtime best friend, and a very handsome, occasionally infuriating door guy I met recently." Jeremy's grin widens. "In the case of my friend Sam, I'm starting to let it go. If I weren't worried about preserving some semblance of our friendship, maybe I'd try a creepy *Love, Actually* sign at his doorstep or something but . . . that would be a disaster. A part of me wants to hold it against him—that he doesn't see me the same way. All our shared history, the way we can make each other *die* laughing? That made me no more appealing to him, the way it did the other way around. Though, honestly, I know he isn't Prince Charming in that ballroom, searching for some airhead girl. He wants the real deal. But for him, that's just not me. . . ."

I look out.

"Sorry," I say, snapping awake. "I . . . didn't mean to go so deep there. But you know what? I have some herb jokes I've been meaning to test out on you all. . . ."

"Wait, what about the other guy?" a woman calls from the audience.

"Oh," I say, eyes flitting back to Jeremy. "He's . . . promising. Good kisser. I mean, *I think*. I'm not all that practiced. And, well . . ." I smile. "He challenges me. Which I like. He's sort of a question mark in a lot of ways, but I guess I am, too." We're staring at each other now, an unfamiliar look in his eyes—oddly humble, and full of warmth, and maybe even a tinge of sadness.

At once, something clutches in my throat, and I wonder if Paula was right.

I think maybe I've filed Jeremy into the wrong box. Like he was safe to try things out on—someone I assumed I could never hurt.

Could I hurt Jeremy?

Have I been reckless with him?

Oh God.

What if he wants something *real*?

I'm saved by the blinking light, my smile a little weaker as I say, "Well, I'm Sabrina Martin. Thank you, Portland!"

I think I hear Dolores whisper "'Attagirl" as we trade places onstage, but I'm focused on charging down the steps, swiping my jacket from a stool before quickly heading for the exit. I need air. I need to *think*.

But then I stop short, my eyes going wide.

Because there, standing up in back, is my mirror image: all black outfit, two buns, a new pair of glasses. But it's not a mirror. It's Sabrina—the *real* Sabrina, talking to Jeremy and gesturing wildly.

Dolores announces the next comic as the thoughts race through my head.

How did she find out?

Is there any chance this is a coincidence?

Oh my God, I'm wearing her pants.

I haven't actually seen Sabrina since the night we all met at the haunted house—when Sam and I were double Dwight Schrutes, and she and my cousin were still friends. To be honest, I kind of forgot she was a real person, Carmen's updates notwithstanding.

She looks upset.

Really upset.

"Is this one of your weird little games?" I hear her say as I inch closer. The ideal course of action would be to run away right now, but it's like my legs won't listen to me. "Girls around school have been comparing notes. Once we looked you up and found some of your comedy on YouTube, we sort of put it together. The 'yeppers test'? Really? It's like you want these things to go badly, so you'll have something to talk about. Is that why you kissed me in the first place? Is that why you set up . . . whatever this is?" she scoffs, sweeping an arm in my direction. "I don't even get it. Are you trying to get a reaction out of me? To cause a scene? Because if so, I mean, you're welcome, I guess."

"Sabrina," Jeremy says bracingly. "I . . ."

I'm so confused. They *know* each other?

She laughs, baffled. "How were you even sure this would get *back* to me? I only found the headshot because I online-stalked you and found you in a Twitter fight with some guy. And what's in it for you?" she says to me before doing a double take. "Wait . . . *Gretchen*?"

Jeremy has a pained look in his eyes, and when I turn to her, I'm so lost I forget to be embarrassed. "Uh . . ."

Her face falls. "Are those my *pants*?!" Her gaze darts between the shoes, the jacket, the glasses. "Oh my God. Is Carmen in on this, too?" She exhales, eyes wide. "With all this stuff missing I thought I was going crazy. But wait, no . . ." She clutches her forehead, whipping around to Jeremy. "Why would Carmen help *you*? Last I checked, you were *also* on her shit list. And I don't think she'd want you anywhere *near* her cousin."

I literally cannot keep up with everything I'm hearing right now, my eyes just ping-ponging between Sabrina and Jeremy.

"You're such an *ass*, you know that?" She comes closer to his face, up on tiptoe, as he stands there, taking it. "And you're so *weird*." She shakes her head, stepping back. "Like, who would even believe this if I tried explaining it? I literally just sat in the audience and live-streamed the whole thing so you couldn't somehow gaslight me into thinking I'd made it all up."

"Sorry, *what*?" I say, feeling a rip of panic.

But she shushes me, eyes still on Jeremy. "I realize I had a part in this, too, but I just want you to understand that if you hadn't pulled all your . . . flirty . . . *Jedi mind tricks* shit on me, I would still have a roommate who spoke to me." When I look close, I realize she has tears in her eyes. They're spilling over now, and I feel a sudden bolt of shock.

It's like the camera lens has twisted *just right*, blurred shapes snapping sharply into focus.

"You've known exactly who I was the whole time," I mutter softly, staring out at nothing in particular. A tiny laugh escapes me, and in my periphery, I see Jeremy's head drop, one hand rubbing the back of his neck.

After a beat he says, "I mean, I didn't know *exactly* who you were. . . ." He meets my eyes, wincing slightly. "I just knew you weren't Sabrina Martin."

I stand there blinking, rewinding and replaying. That first night, when he worked the front door, I was the only one he carded from our group of three. But it didn't strike me as weird at the time, the way he ducked Carmen like that, keeping his head down as she and Henrietta drunkenly danced on in.

I *knew* Sabrina's ID shouldn't have worked. Even if it weren't so poorly made, when you look close, I'm so obviously *not her.*

But I guess Jeremy knew that—he knew it instantly, in fact. And then he got curious.

I hear myself laugh—loudly, weirdly. Jeremy is a student of the universe, right? If he sees a weird situation, he does what he can to make it weirder. Like letting a high school junior playing dress-up have a little fun for the night—before turning her into research, a potential bit. To him, I was nothing but a joke.

I realize Sabrina is watching us now. "You two aren't *together*, are you?"

"Oh, definitely not," I say, staring at him through wide eyes.

"All's fair in love and comedy, right?" he says with a helpless shrug.

"So you were fucking with me," I say. "Is that why you kissed me?"

Sabrina swats him across the chest. "You *kissed* her?!"

"Ow!" he says, lowering his voice as a few people in the audience look over. "Hey. Technically, you kissed me."

"Okay, but do you honestly think I would have done that if I'd known you were Carmen's ex-boyfriend?" I scoff.

"Well, technically I *did* do that," says Sabrina, her indignation briefly dwindling.

Jeremy holds my stare. "Look. *Boyfriend* is a big word. Carmen and I didn't even hang out for very long, which is probably why you knew nothing about me. And sure, maybe this started off in a weird way. But I swear." He dips his head down, eyes pleading. "Whenever I tried to write about you, it just felt . . . *wrong.* And before you get on your high horse, don't forget, you lied to me, too. And to everyone else here for that matter."

"Not to manipulate anyone," I say, though my face is starting to flush. That part is true, and I have no good excuse. Then again, while I was busy floundering around, he *knew*. He let me flounder. He might have even enjoyed it. "At least *I* never meant to hurt anyone."

"Neither did I!" he snaps back.

Lenny looks over from strumming his ukulele onstage but keeps talking through the commotion. I'm feeling almost woozy.

"Look," says Jeremy, lowering his voice again. "What I'm trying to say is, it doesn't matter. The way I feel now . . ."

I realize the ukulele has stopped.

And *everyone* is staring at us.

"Oh fuck you, Jeremy," says Sabrina, turning for the door and calling out behind her. "Get help. Both of you. And stop using my name, Gretchen! And I want my shit back!"

The door closes behind her—too slowly. It feels like it should be a *slam*.

After a long, painful beat, Lenny says, "Okie dokie . . ." and starts the ukulele up again, people in the audience reluctantly turning back around.

I notice Paula and Isaiah whispering at the bar, sharing quick confused glances as Dolores comes over to them. She's frowning as they talk, like maybe she somehow missed all the fuss.

My insides begin to twist. I think I might throw up. . . .

"Gretchen?" says Jeremy. It's freaky to hear my real name on his lips. "Gretchen, *please* just hear me out."

"Don't," I say, shaking my head. "Not another word,

Jeremy. And *don't* fucking follow me."

I push past him and slip out the door, walking, then jogging, then *sprinting* toward my car. I'm moving too fast for these high-heeled boots, but I make it to the parking lot, only to feel my foot slip out from under me. *"God dammit!"* I shout as my tailbone hits the icy asphalt, a sharp pain searing through me. I yank off the offending boot and chuck it into a pile of gray snow several feet away.

After a few deep breaths, I get up, hobbling unevenly across the lot to retrieve it. Real Sabrina will be wanting that back.

Behind the wheel, I slip both of my feet into sneakers, head spinning. It's too much to process at once, but I try to stay calm—to arrange the facts more slowly in my head: Who saw us talking . . . Who heard what . . . But then I hear it—an echo of Sabrina's rant back there. *I literally just sat in the audience and live-streamed the whole thing. . . .*

"Oh God," I say, fumbling around for my phone. "Oh no no no no no no no . . ."

Hands shaky, I pull up Instagram and find the video, now saved to Sabrina's profile, with the caption *What the hell???* Just from that first frame, despite the makeup and glasses—you can tell it's me.

I brace myself, then hit *play.*

It starts in the middle, me talking about the third-child plight. "Then, when parents have a third kid, they're like, 'Wait, we have *another* one of these?'"

My stomach twists, and I skip ahead to the bit about Hen and Carmen.

"I feel like my hair could be on fire, and they'd be like, 'Okay, we'll get to that, but first, let's talk about my thing.'"

Skip, skip, skip.

". . . In the case of my friend Sam, I'm starting to let it go . . . A part of me wants to hold it against him—that he doesn't see me the same way."

And that's when I gag, pushing open the door to hang out over the asphalt, heaves coming up empty. After a minute, I straighten back up, trapping in the heat again.

I hear buzzing—a phone call from Carmen.

Ignore.

Time passes.

Hen's name flashes across the screen.

"Make it stopppp," I whine, ignoring again.

I lower my head onto the steering wheel with a whimper and the phone goes off *again*. I go to silence it, then I pause: *Sam*.

"No . . ." I say as the buzzing goes on. "Uh-uh. No . . ."

It *did* cross my mind, but I didn't let myself think it. Sam only hung out with Sabrina that one night—at the haunted house, then out for milkshakes and later at that awful party. Knowing him, he probably does follow her online. But what are the chances he would have seen this already?

"I'm sure he's calling about something else," I say, like my own barely reassuring imaginary friend. I think being left to wonder might actually be worse, so I answer, slowly lifting the phone to my ear. ". . . Hello?"

I can hear him breathing. My chest rises and falls. One second passes. Then another. Until his voice comes out baffled, and small: "You like me?"

I can't seem to speak now—or think, or move. It's possible I really will puke this time—or cry, or both. "Um," I say finally. But that's all I've got.

So I hang up, hold down the button, and wait for the screen to go black.

EIGHTEEN

The Everything-Is-Ruined-Now Montage | Also known as *fuuuuuuuuuuuuck.*

I turn to a new page in my notebook, fresh tears somehow spilling over. I seem to have an endless supply today.

After last night's fiasco, I doubt I have much comedy in my future. No club to return to. No stand-up sets to write. Still, it's a comfort to hold the pages in my hands as I sit here in bed—trying to wring out any possible levity, like water from a barely damp rag. I swipe at my cheeks, then scrawl out:

Gretchen's 10-Step Guide to Utter Fucking Misery

I choke out a weird sort of sob-chuckle, thinking back on my day.

1. *Cry in shower.*
2. *Hide under blankets.*
3. *Hide from phone for fear of verbal smackdown from Hen and Carmen. (While also clinging to the hope that they probably won't show that video to Mom and Dad?)*
4. *Fake an affliction that is severe enough to warrant skipping school but temporary enough not to interfere with tomorrow's New York trip. (The answer is cramps. Always cramps.)*
5. *Miss Sam.*
6. *Hate Jeremy.*
7. *Sneak out of the house when Dad leaves to run errands, in order to—*
8. *Drive to the Holy Donut to purchase one glazed, one cinnamon, before—*
9. *Also picking up a mashed potato pizza from OTTO, only to—*
10. *Pull over on the side of the road to eat/cry in the car while it rains.*

In retrospect, those last few items probably looked a lot like the Portland girl's equivalent of a good old-fashioned Ice Cream Sob. Also, I'm not ashamed to admit it: I totally looked up the song "All By Myself" and whimpered it under my breath for the drive home.

At least the house is warm for once, and I'm swaddled in my favorite plaid pj's. And, if we're really scraping for silver linings, I think my face is as puffy as it's going to get.

I glance at my phone, charging but still turned off on the bedside table. Some part of me really does want to power it back up again, the same way I might want to touch wet paint despite a sign, or flick my finger through a flame.

Nothing good is waiting for me there. I know that.

I flinch at the sound of a knock.

"Gretchen? It's Ethan. Your dad let me in. I hope that's okay? I . . . tried texting."

"Oh!" I say. "Yeah, yeah, come in."

He steps tentatively into the room, closing the door behind him. "I heard you were sick," he says, holding up a takeout bag, alarm flashing in his eyes. I must look *awful.* And he does get weird around crying girls. "Uh . . . well, this is soup. From that Vietnamese place you and Sam like." I wince at the name, and his face falls. "What?"

"He seriously didn't tell you about last night?"

"Uhh . . ." Ethan sets the food on my dresser, before lowering stiffly onto the foot of my bed. "Sorry," he says. "Is it okay if I sit here?"

"What? Oh, please, it's fine," I say quickly. For a minute, I just frown at him. "I guess it was classy of Sam not to tell anyone. I just thought, since you two are friends . . ."

Ethan hesitates. "I mean, I'm not sure he'd necessarily think to talk to me in particular. To be honest, I sort of avoid that subject with him. . . ."

"What subject?" I say. *"Me?"*

"Yeah," says Ethan with a shrug. "I . . . thought it would be better if I didn't get involved."

"Oh," I say, though I'm not sure I follow. Maybe I've been asking too much, or putting him in a weird spot. He didn't sign up to be my go-between with Sam. But he doesn't *look* annoyed with me. He just kind of looks . . . *off.*

Not that I know the first thing about reading people, apparently.

I flop back onto my pillows, pulling the covers to my chin. "Well, I'll give you the short version. Sam *knows*. About the crush, and my double life, and the comedy. All of it. And I'm so fucking mortified, Ethan." I cover my face with the crook of my elbow, only to fling my arm away as I sit back up again. "Oh! And it turns out my gnome carver is an *ass*. Like, full-blown manipulative *freak*. I'm annoyed we kissed now. Not exactly a story I can tell my grandchildren."

"Well, I'm not sure your grandchildren will want to know *any* of your hookup stories," he says. "If that helps."

I laugh, the weepy feeling coming back. "Maybe I should be a nun. I could pick up the whole religion thing. Because apparently, I'm only ever *remotely* attracted to jerks and guys who have no interest in me." Ethan gets a weird look for a second. "What?" I say.

"Nothing." He meets my eyes kindly, patting my knee through the blanket. "Hey, I gotta go. But eat your soup. And don't forget to have fun in New York. Last I checked, you were pretty excited about that."

"Yeah," I sigh. "It'll be good to get a break for a couple days."

"Anyway." He smiles, bobbing his head as he stands. "I know these things hurt, but . . . trust me. You get over them."

NINETEEN

The Transportation-Hub Chase Scene | One person hands an attendant a boarding pass. The other zigzags desperately through throngs of travelers, cutting lines, even buying one-way tickets. In theory, both of them should not be running.

"Can we please just talk about this?" I hear from behind me.

"Nope!" I call back.

This is ridiculous.

My parents said goodbye from the Amtrak parking lot, having stepped out briefly to let Nacho take a tinkle. The second they rolled away, I spotted him, leaning against his car in his nice wool coat and stupid preppy scarf. It was the eyes that did me in: no glint, no trace of that old Sam-and-Gretch humor.

And so I turned, and ran.

I'm still running, is the thing, my duffel bag bouncing awkwardly along the backs of my thighs. I peel through the automatic doors. "I've been humiliated enough for one week, thank you. I can't take any more right now!"

"Why weren't you at school yesterday?" he says, still on my tail. I should have known Sam would be stubborn about this. "I've been trying to call you."

"Sorry! Turned off my phone!"

This train station really isn't all that big, so I'm forced to make figure eights as I search for the least obstructed route out to the track.

"This is so . . . stupid!" pants Sam, sidestepping a row of waiting-area chairs between us like a shifty defenseman.

"How . . . did you even know . . . I was here?" I say, just as—yes!—a man with a massive cart of suitcases blocks Sam's way around, buying me a few seconds. "And shouldn't *you* be in school?"

"Your mom . . . told my mom . . . about your trip. So I skipped class. God dammit, Gretchen, just talk to me!"

I realize he's catching up, so I fake him out, cutting one way, then another, before making a fast break for the platform outside. When I reach the front of the train, I flash my e-ticket at a conductor and jump inside the car, tucking myself out of view in the tight metal vestibule. I feel victorious for about five seconds as I catch my breath.

Then I cry again.

"Oh God oh God oh God . . ." I shake my head, pulling it together. So what if I can never face him again? All good things come to an end, right? Maybe we just got there a bit quicker. I dab my eyes with my sleeve, letting out a big breath.

"*There* you are." Annika pops her head into the train. "I thought we were meeting outside. Also. Was that Sam on the platform?"

"Uh . . . yeah," I say. "Long story." I straighten up, taking in the sight of her. She's her same old eclectic self this morning: bell-bottoms, fuzzy earmuffs, and a coat that *would* seem like fur if it weren't traffic-cone orange. And yet, she looks entirely different right now, like she's lighting up from the inside. I'm actually really glad this weekend will be all about her. I'm good at focusing on other people's lives. Maybe I should go back to that.

"Let's find seats," she says with an excited squeal. I laugh. Annika doesn't squeal.

We pick a booth in the café car, piling bags and her oboe up overhead before plopping down across from each other—just as the train begins to move.

"Oh, there he is again," says Annika, pointing out the window.

I turn to meet Sam's waiting stare, and weirdly, I just hold it. And keep holding it. All of a sudden, it's like we can't bring ourselves to break apart. Maybe because we both know that any second now, the train will do it for us.

My breath grows shallow as we pick up speed, and then I'm craning my neck back to hold his gaze a little longer. A lump grows thick in my throat, and before a wall of trees knocks him out of view, he smiles, just barely, and waves goodbye.

Another hour into the trip, the trees are still whirring past, lidded coffee cups shaking on the table. Across from me, Annika is humming into her sheet music, which I find strangely comforting. It's like we've put our caf routine on wheels.

I take a few deep breaths before powering up my phone. I wish I could stay dark all weekend, but I promised Mom and Dad I'd send regular updates, and that I'd answer any time they called.

When my screen lights up, I cringe at all the unchecked messages. I don't need to open them to get the general idea: a whole lot of Holy shit and What did I just see? and What the hell, Gretchen? Pick up!

A new text comes in now, and I flinch.

But it's only Mom: a Boomerang of her waving Nacho's paw, with the words Bon voyage! I text back LOL—my first check-in complete.

Then I fling the phone down into my bag like a hot coal and press my temple to the glass.

"Gretchen. We're getting close," whispers Annika.

"Five more minutes," I murmur. This is the deepest I've slept in days.

"Gretchen."

"Shhhhh." I peek out through slits. I guess it's nighttime. "Whoa."

She laughs. "Sleepy, huh?"

We ate lunch in the Boston food court before boarding this train, at which time we discovered the quiet car and its blessed library-like atmosphere, free from any Candy-Crush-without-headphones-type monster people.

The silence has been glorious—delicious even.

"Gretchen, look," Annika whispers, lurching me from another half second of sleep. We're still moving, but the noise of the engine has cut out, overhead lights going off.

I flutter my eyes open in the dark and follow Annika's gaze to the window. We're swooping in on the skyline now.

And the whole city is shimmering.

"Well, this place is bananas," I say when we step outside Penn Station.

"Isn't it?" says Annika, beaming up at the starless sky.

Out on the street, people scurry around us in weaving patterns, manholes steaming and billboards flashing. I get a waft of trash smell, or maybe urine.

"Come on," says Annika, eyes trained on Google Maps. Ten minutes later, we're figuring out how to pay and work the turnstiles, until we're gripping metal poles with arms outstretched, bags at our feet, Annika's oboe case swinging from a strap.

When we finally make it up to our hotel room, the stillness

is almost jarring, our floor-to-ceiling window looking out serenely from on high. After a long beat, Annika turns to me with a huge, goofy grin, and somehow *I'm* the one who squeals.

We drop our stuff and kick off shoes, quickly bounding around the room to inspect it. "Do you care which bed?" calls Annika as I paw through tiny toiletries, absently twirling the cord of the hair dryer hooked to the wall.

"Nope!" I say, popping out. "Oooh, big TV."

"And mini fridge!" she says, trading places with me to check out the bathroom. "Though my dad says to just go to a bodega since it's such a rip-off."

I open the closet. "We have robes! Aw. We can lounge around like fancy spa ladies." There's an ironing board, too, and a coffee maker that smells vaguely of burnt grounds.

"Feel this towel," says Annika, coming up to me.

"Mmmm," I say as I hold it to my cheek. I toss it on a chair and close the closet door. "Holy shit. We're really here."

"Yep," she says. And with that we collapse back onto parallel beds.

"So," I say a minute later, propping onto my elbow. "What do we do first?"

She turns to face me, hesitating. "Actually . . . don't hate me, but the admissions lady I've been emailing said I could have a practice room tonight, if I want."

"Annika." I sit the rest of the way up. "How could there humanly, *possibly*, be anything left for you to practice?"

"I know. . . ." She winces. "It's just, if I slack now and then don't get in, I'm afraid I'll never forgive myself."

"But . . ." I frown. "Don't you at least need to eat?"

"Too nervous," she says, getting up to grab her purse. She pulls out a few bills for me. "Here. My dad said to cover a couple meals anyway, his treat."

"No, no. I don't need—"

"Please just take it so I don't feel guilty?" She gives the cash a shake. "I promise, I'll be more fun tomorrow when all I have left is my tour. And you can still have a fun night. Eat some good food, see the sights. . . . I'll be back in two hours. Three, max." When I shove the money away, she charges over to my bag and triumphantly fishes out my wallet as I my roll eyes. She frowns. "Who's Sabrina Martin?"

I blink for a moment as she studies the fake ID. A few days ago, this might have presented a serious dilemma. Now I just laugh. "My alias."

"Huh," she says curiously as she slips the ID back into my wallet, along with the money. "Well, definitely more on *that* later . . ." She picks up her coat and oboe. "Text me where you end up, okay? And do *not* just stay in the room. We're in *New York*, Gretchen!" When I meet her smile, it hits me how right she is. This is not a time for moping. And actually, I know exactly what I want to do tonight.

When she goes, I unpack a few things with the TV on, changing outfits and brushing teeth as ambulances whine softly in the distance. I wash my face, moisturize, and quickly run a brush through my hair. Then I flop down onto the bed and google "New York comedy clubs." There are lineups listed on different websites, and I actually recognize a lot of the names: up-and-comers known for shows like *Full Frontal with Samantha Bee* or *Late Night with Seth Meyers*. Some of the clubs have big headliners listed, too—big enough that I kind of can't believe the ticket prices.

One club has a show in an hour. I scroll down for the info, breath hitching.

Marnie.

Smack in the middle of the lineup.

I'm grinning now. If I can get myself to the Village in the next—I check—fifty-five minutes, I could see her act tonight. *In person. In New York.* I glance at my wallet, feeling sheepishly relieved that it's now filled with enough cash for a cab and a cover charge. The website *did* say twenty-one plus, but I still have Sabrina's ID. I wish I'd thought to pack the glasses, or some Angry Graphic Designer clothes. But hair and makeup should do the trick.

Time is tight, though, so I work fast—eyeliner, lipstick, buns, *good enough!* I stamp my feet into sneakers, swiping the room key and the rest of my things. And soon I'm pressing the elevator button, over and over, until I burst out into the lobby and onto the street.

"Shit!" A delivery guy on a scooter nearly takes off my

foot when I step down from the curb. I clutch my chest, heart pounding. *Nacho, we are not in Maine anymore. . . .*

It takes four tries before I manage to hail a cab, sliding into a back seat that smells overwhelmingly of old leather and air freshener. I crack a window and press my face to the glass, peering out as we wind through evening traffic, past hundreds of shops and restaurants, smoky meat carts, and the blinding lights of Times Square.

After a while, the streets get cuter, quainter, more like the New York you see in rom-coms, where—as Mom often points out—the heroine always lives, even if she has no money.

When the driver slows, I pay and thank him, slamming the door shut and running across the street. I've cut it down to the minute, the last person to file in.

"Hi," I say breathlessly to the bouncer. "Did I make it?"

"Just barely," he says, surprisingly sweet-faced despite his imposing stature. I hand him my ID with relief. Then he starts to laugh.

"What?" I ask as he shakes his head, still cracking up.

"You realize this thing is fake as shit, right?" he says. "And that you look nothing like the girl in the picture?"

"Oh," I say, cheeks flaming hot now. I suddenly feel extremely stupid. Because that's right. The ID never should have worked—not with anyone but Jeremy. In a way, I *almost* owe him for that.

Almost.

"Are you even eighteen?" asks the man.

I wince. "I will be in October . . . ?"

"Look. I have kids your age," he says, clearly amused, "so I'm not going to get you in trouble. But I *am* going to hold on to this."

I feel something quake inside me as the ID disappears into his back pocket—just like that. "Wait!" I blurt out. "I swear, I don't even drink. I just wanted to see Marnie James."

"And I sincerely wish I could let you in," he says, gentle but firm. "After your birthday, you're welcome to come back with a parent."

I look to the sky, grumbling, *"Great."* And then, feeling I should still be polite, I add, "Well . . . have a good evening."

"You too, kid," I hear behind me as he chuckles again.

I walk a few blocks before I remember to take my hair down, passing couples with linked arms, and dogs on leashes. Greenwich Village is still plenty chaotic, with all its shops and restaurants jammed up next to one another, but there's a calmness here too, all the people seemingly more content to wander.

Finding a napkin in my bag, I wipe off my lipstick, my footsteps slowing with the finality of it: Sabrina really is gone now.

And Gretchen has been left with the mess.

For a moment, I squeeze my eyes shut, as if that will somehow keep out everything waiting for me back home. Still—maybe, just for a little while, I can stay in the moment, steeped in the rhythm of this place and all its thrumming energy. At the very least, I should be appreciating the fact that it's *well* above freezing here—downright balmy tonight, which could explain all the stylish outerwear I've been seeing. I'm actually getting hot in my puffy coat, and so I take it off, hooking it under my arm.

After a long while, I slow my pace.

It seems I have walked in a loop, ending right back at the comedy club, a line already forming behind a velvet rope for the next show. My stomach begins to rumble and the pizza place across the street abruptly calls to me, a beacon of fluorescent light.

Inside, I order a couple slices and soon, I'm sliding onto one of two stools along the cramped counter in the window. "Mmmm," I say, hot cheese oozing across double paper plates. I pick up my first slice, then freeze.

Across the street, Marnie James has just slipped out from the club. I lower my slice back down onto the plate, vaguely shocked to confirm that she's an actual, human person. She glances left and right, looking too springy for this time of year in her plain white Keds and jean jacket, her messy hair pulled up in a ponytail. She's prettier in person, I think. Or rather, she has some kind of magnetism you don't quite get on-screen. She's crossing the street now, hurrying before a car comes.

She's getting closer. And closer . . .

Until she's right on the other side of the glass, reaching for the door. I turn, eyes wide as she grazes past me. "Hey, Gino! Can I get two pepperoni?" The two of them chitchat for a moment, and I listen in, trying not to gawk as she pays, tips, and thanks him. "Have a good one!"

When she passes me again, I think I briefly black out. But when I come to, it would seem I am speaking. "I'm really happy for you!"

"Huh?" says Marnie-fucking-James. I look up at her where she's paused there, right beside me, her hand still on the door.

". . . You know," I say, gesturing to the pizza box she's holding. "Like . . . from your comedy special?"

"Oh!" She smiles, a curious quirk to her brow. "Thank you for that. I'm not sure anyone's ever quoted *me* back to *me* before." She looks over my shoulder then, and I hear it—the soft pitter-patter of rain, then a crack of thunder, announcing a downpour. "Aw, crap," she grumbles, eyeing her shoes, her clothes, her dinner.

Through the window, we watch as people scramble in every direction, jackets and magazines held feebly overhead. Thunder rumbles again—the counter window like the inside of a carwash now.

When I look back at Marnie, she's fixed her stare on the second stool beside me, which I've thoughtlessly covered with my jacket.

"Oh, sorry!" I say, quickly moving it. "Full disclosure, I'm a pretty big fan. But I'll try my best to be normal."

"Hmm . . ." Marnie James looks out the window again, then back at me. "I mean, you're not planning on making a skin suit out of me or anything, are you?"

"Nah," I say. "I don't look good in beige."

She laughs—loud—and I think my life might be complete now. "What's your name?" she asks, settling in and opening her pizza box.

"Uh . . ." I stumble, as if not sure I'll get the answer right. I don't mean this in a romantic way, but *wow*, do I have a crush on her. "Gretchen," I say finally. *Nailed it.*

"Well, nice to meet you, Gretchen. I'm Marnie." She takes a bite, catching a bit of grease with a napkin. "But I guess you knew that."

"Uh . . . yeah," I say with an odd little chuckle. I gaze down at my own pizza, still too nervous to eat in front of her. "I tried to see your show tonight, but I got turned away. I'm only in high school. I actually go to *your* high school. I'm just here for the weekend."

"Oh, no way," she says, gooey cheese stretching sumptuously into a long line, which she breaks with her fingers. *Oh, screw it, I'm eating too.* "Portland kid, huh?"

"Yep," I say, finally taking a bite—and oh my God, *yes*, New York pizza should be *everyone's* love language. I swallow. "And, um. Well, you know the Chuckle Parlor? How they're having that whole competition to open for you?"

Marnie takes a swig from her soda. "Yeah?"

"Well, I'm in it. Or—*was.* My alter ego was. Anyway, I'm just really glad I still got to meet you." I shove some more pizza in my mouth, mostly to stop myself from rambling any more.

"Huh," she says. "I'm not gonna lie to you. I think I lost the thread here."

"Sorry," I say quickly. "Basically, I've been performing as this girl, Sabrina Martin? I know it's not cool to steal someone's identity, but she *did* make out with my cousin's boyfriend. Actually, I did that, too, but not knowingly. The point is, karmically speaking, it was sort of a gray area."

Marnie looks thoroughly confused now.

I take a breath, slowing down. "I was doing comedy as someone else, basically."

"Ah," she says. "Huh. That's kind of interesting. So was the girl you were playing sort of like a character? Like Dolly Parton or something?"

"Um . . ." I consider this. "Not *really*. I mean, my hair and clothes were different. But I pretty much talked like myself up there. And I definitely pulled from my own experiences. Like, too much. Like, might-have-just-blown-up-my-life too much . . ."

"Oooh," she says, cringing. "Sorry. Although, also: been there."

I laugh, taking solace in that. Marnie seems like she's doing fine. "Anyway, I'm sure it sounds really weird, but . . . when I was Sabrina, it was almost like I had this force field around me. Like, without anyone expecting *Gretchen* up on that stage, I could just be . . . whoever I wanted."

"Well, maybe that girl *was* Gretchen," says Marnie.

"What?" I say, turning to her.

"I mean, I've known you for all of five minutes, so take this with a grain of salt. But I'm not convinced we have just *one* authentic self. I'm pretty sure I've already been, like, ten different people. I mean, I'm always *me*, but . . . you know. We try stuff on, and that's cool."

"Huh," I say, nodding, grinning. I freaking *knew* Marnie James would be wise.

She looks vaguely alarmed now. "I want to make sure you understand, I'm, like, *barely* an adult, so you probably shouldn't be taking advice from me. I just got an accountant for the first time and I still don't know what a Roth is. Do *you* know?"

"Um . . . no," I say.

She laughs, finishing her second slice and tossing the crust down in the box. "I'll be honest. I'm not sure I could have done comedy at your age, with all the things I worried about back then. I started in a brand-new city. I think I needed that . . . *space*, to find my voice, you know? Not to discourage you," she adds quickly. "That was just me. And there's no . . . right or wrong time to start with stand-up."

"Well, I won't be going back to the Chuckle Parlor any time soon. My whole double life thing kind of . . . recently unraveled."

"Bummer," she says.

And then I feel it: a lull. The rain has started to slow, our pizza gone now. I wish I could keep her here—not in a skin-suit kind of way. "Well, anyway," I say, giving her an out. "I think it's really cool you're doing this for the club. Everyone is so excited."

She shrugs. "It was a favor to my uncle. He and the owner grew up together. I'm pretty sure he's in love with her."

"Really," I say. "You know, I'd like to see ol' Dolores settled."

She smiles, then nods to my balled-up jacket on the counter. "Hey, I think your phone's going off."

"Oh, shoot." I find it in my pocket and open up a string of texts from Annika.

I'm back in the room and you're not here

Are you alive???

Actually considering alerting your parents if you don't write back

Oh God they're going to kill me.

Tell me you didn't get on the subway this late

Gretchen. Oh my gooooodddd. We didn't even think to pack pepper spray

Answer me biotch!

(If you're actually hurt, sorry for calling you biotch)

I write back, Sorry sorry! Alive! and look up to see Marnie James tossing her trash into a bin. Something about this momentary return to my actual life is making the reality of this situation click in for me. *Did that seriously just happen?*

"Later for real this time, Gino!" she calls out.

"Bye, Marnie!"

Meeting my gaze again, Marnie James seems nearly as puzzled as I am by this brief aberration. "Okay then . . . Sorry. I . . . have no parting wisdom for you."

"Oh, that's all right," I say. "But, um . . ." I clear my throat. "Thanks for eating pizza with me."

"Anytime," she says, only to frown, as if hearing herself.

"Well, no. Probably not anytime," I say, filling in the obvious.

"Yeah, no," she says. "I mean, never say never, but—"

"But probably never," I say, making her laugh. She goes for the door, and I stay where I am, so as to avoid the awkward possibility of walking out the same way.

She winces, doubling back. "But . . . it *was* nice to meet you, Gretchen. And for what it's worth, whoever *this* girl is," she says, gesturing in my direction, "she seems pretty funny to me."

TWENTY

One Day in New York | An augmented unit of time that allows soul mates to meet and rapidly get to know each other. Unfortunately does not apply to delaying one's imminent doom.

"Just toast for me," says Annika to the waiter, her meager request the exact opposite of my double order: two eggs and blueberry pancakes—savory and sweet. As we hand off our menus, we yawn in unison, then smile. I feel a little bad about staying up so late, but Annika claims she wouldn't have slept anyway.

When I got back to the room last night, she was waiting up for me with a tube of green face mask and a cucumber she bought from the bodega downstairs, our hotel robes laid out on the bed. "Spa ladies on a budget," she said, making me laugh as she sawed at the cucumber with a plastic serrated knife. "This will get me into a good headspace for tomorrow."

We found a relaxing playlist online—the kind of thing

that evokes images of majestically swimming whales, and for a while, we breathed in silence, spread out on our parallel beds like green-faced Vitruvian men.

Then Annika said, "You were supposed to explain that alias thing to me." And so I did, feeling a little like I was telling a bedtime story. She was remarkably cool about it, her questions all matter-of-fact. Afterward, I felt better, though still just as miserable at the thought of returning home.

Now Annika is looking crisp and clean as she continues to yawn, in her nice black slacks and a white button-down, a fancy tan peacoat stuffed into the corner of the booth. She spent the first twenty minutes of the morning sweeping the top half of her hair into an elaborate braided crown, which I was pleased to see—it looks like her.

"So . . ." I say, noticing the time. "How you feeling?"

She flinches as a man comes by to fill our waters. "Sorry," she says to him, before turning to me. "Let's . . . talk about something else. I've been thinking more about your predicament."

"My boy problems?"

"Oh, that you'll figure out," she says dismissively. "I meant your art."

"My art," I say, raising an eyebrow.

"Yes. The comedy," she says seriously. "I know you say you can't go back to the Chuckle Parlor, but there must be a similar place somewhere nearby. Maybe a . . . Giggle Lounge, or a

Chortle Bar?" I hold back a laugh, but she doesn't falter. "For my own distraction's sake, *Gretchen*, I'm simply asking that we consider your next steps. Which begs the question: What is your life plan?"

"I . . . don't think I have one of those."

"Well, I have a rough concept I could run by you."

I sigh. "Of course you do."

She straightens up. "So picture this. You move to New York, hit the club scene for a while, slowly build a name for yourself. On the side, maybe you're writing, or auditioning for bit parts here and there. We'd be roommates, of course. Both working nights, and puttering around the apartment during the day. It's kind of the dream, if you think about it. We'd be like . . . twentysomethings in a TV show." She hesitates, as if sensing the pang of sadness coming over me. "After college, I mean. This plan can wait . . . five years."

"Oh," I say, shaking my head. "No, it's not that. Actually, my parents have been asking where I'd want to go if money weren't an object. Which is sweet, but . . . money *is* an object. And they're right: I don't want to be a doctor or a lawyer." I wrinkle my nose. "I just also don't know if comedy is realistically in my future."

"Oh." She looks a bit deflated by this. "But . . . last night a famous person called you funny."

"I know," I say. "Trust me, I'm still pinching myself. But when I try to really visualize cracking jokes on a stage, with people in the audience knowing who I *actually* am?" I shrug. "It's like my brain glitches out or something. It still feels impossible. And I already have all these people to come clean to. If I were to keep going, as me? I mean, how would that even be sustainable?"

"What, telling the truth?"

"Yeah, kinda," I say. "Not enough truth can be a problem. But . . . so can too much." She nods, as if conceding this point. "Plus, the whole thing is so out of character. I've never dreamed of my name in lights. I almost wish I could do the work without . . . being the vessel."

"You're telling me in real life, as Gretchen, you don't like it when people laugh at your jokes?"

"So maybe I like being the vessel a *little*," I say, rolling my eyes. "But still. Maybe this was only meant to be a moment. The stars aligned *just right* so I could . . . gain some perspective, and at least briefly switch out the script of my life. Like in movies where people trade bodies. They always go back, right?"

"But . . ." She seems flustered now. "That *was* your body."

"Okay, it's not a perfect analogy," I concede. "Anyway, I think I *would* like to do something creative with my life. In which case, staying local would probably be good, seeing as I'm unlikely to make any money and therefore won't want a mountain of debt."

"Okay," she says. "So . . . get your degree, and *then* have your adventure. Or transfer midway through, once you know what you want. I still think comedy could lead you somewhere, even if it's not your white whale. Maybe you'll go to . . . film school, or a performing arts program. Or maybe you'll just be, like, a dentist who does open mics on the side."

I choke on my water, finding this completely hilarious for some reason. "I'm not going to be a *dentist*, Annika."

"I don't know! I'm just saying. It sounds like our paths will be different. Mine is . . . *nauseatingly* narrow. If I want to be in the New York Philharmonic, there are, like, three schools I can go to. Ideally Juilliard. And if that doesn't work out, then I guess I have to get a new dream. Which is *why we're not talking about that*!" She takes a calming breath, right as her toast and my two breakfasts arrive. We nod our thanks, unwrapping silverware from napkins. She frowns. "What was I saying?"

"Our paths."

"That's right," she says, buttering her first triangle of toast. "For you, maybe it will be more . . . winding. I bet you could go all different ways and still end up in the right spot. And if you do choose to go back to comedy . . ." She shrugs. "Isn't the main thing to go out and live life? So you have something to talk about?"

I smile. "That was wise, Annika. You might even be wiser than Marnie. Oh, that reminds me. Do you know what a Roth is?"

She thinks. "No . . ."

"Well, apparently whenever we find out, that's when we're real adults."

"Huh," she says, taking a bite. "Maybe we can cheat the system and just never look it up. Also, listen to you, all casually using a celebrity's first name. *You know. Just my friend, Marnie.*"

"Oh, let me have my moment. I'm never going to feel this cool again."

"I don't think that's true," she says, chewing thoughtfully. "In fact, I think your coolness is on a straight upward trajectory, Gretchen."

"Thanks," I say through a mouthful of pancake. "Yours too. I mean, you're already cool. But throw a little Juilliard in there? *Woof!*"

"Don't!" she says. "For the rest of breakfast. No more saying the *J* word."

When the time comes, I feel a bit like a parent on the first day of kindergarten, adjusting the collar of Annika's peacoat and tucking a wisp of blond hair back into her pretty little crown. She hikes her music case up her shoulder, shivering though it's not particularly cold outside. Must be nerves.

"If I get in, you'll come visit, right?"

"*When* you get in," I say. "And *duh*. Now go!"

As she walks in through the main doors, she turns back with a look of such sheer purpose I could cry. She disappears, and I pick a direction at random—north, I think—passing bookstores, coffee shops, and markets. Soon, I reach Central Park, where I wind my way under huge, bare trees, passing joggers and skaters and old ladies doing tai chi.

I send a thumbs-up to Mom and Dad's most recent *Are you alive?* text, then slip the phone away. I tried not to look, but it was near impossible to glaze over all those mounting red bubbles—signifying missed calls and unchecked messages from Hen and Carmen. Jeremy. Sam.

This whole freaking city is a giant reminder of him. Soon, this will be his home. But there's plenty to distract me, too. I've decided New York is . . . *a lot.* Since I've been here, it's like my senses have been in overdrive—all layered and competing. I imagine myself a sommelier of smells: *I'm detecting notes of roasted nuts and horse manure, and maybe wet cement?* And then there are the sounds, even here in the tranquility of the park—far-off honks and helicopters, and children laughing as they scooter past. The sheer volume of people is shocking. And everyone gets so close to you, moving fast and grazing by. The grouchy Mainer in me could actually use some breathing room.

I get out my phone again to text Ethan.

You'll never believe it, but I actually sort of miss Maine right now.

He writes back almost immediately. It's our super attractive population, right?

Oh yeah, I respond. I mean, this city full of actors and models? Yecch. Someone get these people an L.L.Bean catalog.

He writes back a string of crying-laughing emojis and I add, It is pretty awesome, though. This trip is taking my mind off things. Sort of.

I see a bubble, then a pause, until he writes back, I'm glad.

For a second, I'm tempted to ask him if he's heard from Sam. But then I remember—he doesn't want to be in the middle.

Suddenly, I'm miserable again, wondering how it will feel to walk into school on Monday. Will Sam and I spend the rest of the year pretending to be strangers? Or will he find some quiet corner, where he'll pull me aside to gently let me down? I can't tell which sounds worse. And now I won't even have the club to get me through it. I don't think it's fully hit me how much I'm going to miss that place, and the people there.

I didn't even get to say goodbye.

An ache starts spreading from my chest, a doleful sort of panic, and I begin to walk, until I'm out of the park, heading straight for the hotel.

Up in the room, I block out the sun, kicking off shoes and climbing into bed. I pull the blanket to my chin and breathe in and out, willing my heartbeat to slow. Until I feel myself start to sink, a heavy black veil blotting out thoughts of Sam, the club, all of it . . .

I hear a click, sounds of rustling, the scrape of curtains drawing open.

"Hello?" I lift my head, vision blurred. It could have been two seconds or two hours. I kind of forgot I was here.

Annika is standing over me, her jacket off, the oboe resting on the desk behind her. "Oh my God," I say, alert now. "How'd it go?"

"I . . ." She shakes her head, somber, then grins. ". . . was a motherfucking genius up there." I breathe with relief. "I made that oboe my bitch, Gretchen," she says, hopping up onto the bed. "Those judges looked at each other and were all like, 'My God. We've never heard an oboe sound like that before!'" She shrugs. "I mean, they said it with their eyes. But they totally said it."

I chuckle through a yawn, sitting up.

"Anyway, chop-chop," she says. "I'm finally not nervous. Let's go eat everything in New York."

It's a big task, but we do our best: tacos in Chelsea Market, and soup dumplings in Chinatown. We even split a Reuben at that deli where Meg Ryan had her famous orgasm. Well, actually, at first, my order was: "I'll have what she's having."

"Wow," the waitress said dryly. "Never heard that one before."

Annika's excitement has helped buoy my mood. We've taken to seeking out photo-worthy stops—like the shop that sells nothing but pink soap, or the ice cream place that tops off all their soft serve with unicorn horns.

As we pass under the arch at Washington Square, we stop to watch a street performer singing her heart out. She's good enough to be the real deal and Annika is clearly moved. I can tell she will fit right in here in New York, surrounded by all these people and their big, dumb dreams. Maybe someday I'll have that kind of certainty. I hope so.

Time does bend, but not the way I want it to.

In a blink, it's Sunday morning, and after Annika's early school tour and a quick bagel run, we're back at Penn Station. On the train, I twist in my window seat, watching as the city shrinks away. Annika has already passed out beside me, practically from the moment we found seats, her head lolling onto my shoulder.

I'm really going to miss her next year.

Somewhere near Connecticut, I feel a switch flick, the dread harder to ward off. The stop in Boston is short, and as we zip up the coast on the next train, it starts looking more and more like home outside—the trees, the space, even the snow. I'm not ready for what's coming. Not at all. And yet somehow, it's a relief to see Mom, Dad, and Nacho, all waiting for me at the station.

"Well, good to have you back, kiddo," Dad says as we step inside the house. I smile up at him, only to freeze as I hear laughter coming from the second floor. It's Hen's and Carmen's, unmistakably.

"We were going to let them surprise you, but I guess they went upstairs," says Mom. "Hen's back for a few days." The way she says it, so visibly content, confirms for me that she and Dad still have no clue what went down last week.

"Awesome," I say, immediately queasy as my gaze flits toward the sound. I guess I might as well get the verbal smackdown over with now. Leaving my bag, I pad up to Hen's room, knocking on the door left slightly ajar. "Hey."

She and Carmen glance up from her bed, two phones and a magazine out. I walk straight to the futon in the window nook, sit cross-legged, and wait for them to let me have it. I even close my eyes for a second, but when I open them, both Hen and Carmen seem to be at a loss for words, which is . . . rare for them. I almost want to make a joke about it. But no. Probably not the time.

"Does this mean you're ready to talk to us?" says Carmen, obviously annoyed. "We tried calling you. Like, *a lot*."

"I know," I say, wincing. This all feels too abrupt. I knew I'd have to face them eventually, but I thought I'd have more time. "I guess you saw the video?" They nod. "And, Carmen, did you . . . talk to Sabrina?"

"Yep," she says. "We're on speaking terms again."

"That's good," I say.

"And between the two of us, we *pretty* much pieced it together. . . ."

"So . . . you know about me and Jeremy?"

Carmen puts a hand up. "I really don't need to . . ."

"I didn't know he was . . ."

"No, I got that," she says. "And I didn't think you would . . ."

"Cool," I say, peering down at my lap. This is by far the

most strained conversation we've ever had, and I don't like it. "Listen . . ." I take a breath. "The stuff I said in the video—about you two? I didn't mean that."

Hen laughs. "I mean, I think you meant it a *little*."

"Rude, Gretch," says Carmen with a hint of a smile. "But . . . kind of funny."

"So . . ." I say, frowning. "You're not mad?"

Hen teeters a moment. "Oh, I was definitely mad at first," she says, looking at Carmen. "Well, actually, no. First, I was confused. Then I was mad. But then I went back to confused?"

"This must not come as a surprise," says Carmen, "but we have *many* questions."

"Also," says Hen. "Are *you* mad?"

"Why would I be mad?"

"You said we wouldn't notice if your *hair* caught on fire," says Carmen. "That sounds kind of mad."

"Oh. Uh . . ." Now it's awkward again. "Well, I was obviously joking. But, in the spirit of honesty, I might occasionally feel sort of . . . overlooked?"

"You could have told us that," says Carmen. "I will admit, we can be dramatic sometimes. Hen *definitely* is."

"Hey!" says Hen.

Carmen laughs. "I'm just saying. I'm sorry if we've been a little wrapped up in ourselves lately. But we're also not *mind readers*."

"I know," I say. "And I understand, honestly. Now that I've

had some drama of my own . . . It can get pretty all-consuming."

"Speaking of drama," says Hen, her face lighting up. "You like *Sam*?"

I cringe.

"I assume you've been ignoring his calls, too?" says Carmen.

"Oh, for fucking sure," I say. "It's worse than that, actually. He showed up at the train station on Friday and I just . . . ran away! He was literally *chasing* me for like five minutes."

"He *chased* you?" says Hen. "Oh my God, that's so romantic!"

"Eh," I say. "I think it was more of a . . . friend chase?"

"That's not a thing," says Carmen.

I groan, lowering down onto the futon to assume the fetal position. "I don't know how I'm going to face him tomorrow. I thought maybe time would help. But no. Still horrifying."

When I look up, Hen and Carmen are on the move, descending upon me now. They wordlessly rearrange us, until my head is in Hen's lap, legs outstretched across Carmen's. "Okay, spill it," says Hen.

Carmen peeks down with a smile. "And start at the very beginning."

I give them a longer version than I did Annika. Every detail, in fact.

They gasp in unison when I tell them about the almost kiss with Sam, cracking up when I recount the night I went back to the club and bombed before straight-up *snort-laughing* through the part where I hid under the table at Natalie's birthday dinner. To their credit, no one interrupts, though Carmen does spit out, *"Shut the fuck up,"* when I tell them about meeting Marnie.

"So much is clicking now," says Hen, when I'm finally done. "Like, this weekend when we were calling you, I noticed how weird your voice mail message was, but I didn't actually put it together."

"Leading a double life is hard," I say, honestly tired just from explaining it all.

Carmen grins. "You know. I like stand-up for you. It weirdly makes sense."

"Right?" says Hen. "You're totally that person who notices everything. And you're always making us laugh."

"Well, thanks," I say, shrugging weakly.

"Hey, what's the deal with this Ethan guy?" says Hen out of nowhere.

"What do you mean?"

"I don't know. I feel like he kept coming up. My friend Ethan thinks this. My friend Ethan said that."

"Is he cute?" asks Carmen.

"Uh . . . yeah, actually. Why?"

"I don't know," she says. "Just . . . interesting."

"What are you going to say to Sam?" asks Hen, making me groan again.

"He's moving soon. Maybe we'll never speak again?"

Hen peers down with a chiding look. "He's *Sam*, Gretchen.

Your Sam. You know you can't do that."

I nod, just as Nacho runs in, joining our pile on the futon. "So, wait," I say to Hen. "I never even asked. What are you doing home? Don't you have class tomorrow?"

"Yeah, but Lizzy had to fly back last minute and I wanted to be here for her. Her dog is sick. They're probably going to have to put her down."

I gasp and cover Nacho's ears, his beady eyes meeting mine. "It's okay, buddy," I whisper, pulling him to me.

"Uh-oh," says Hen. "Are you two the closest siblings in the family now? I'm suddenly feeling very left out."

"Knock, knock . . ."

When I look up, Mom has walked in with Dad behind her, the two of them frowning down at me. I must be a sad sight, draped across Hen and Carmen, even letting Nacho get in on the action. "We're about to start dinner," says Mom warily. "But is everything okay?"

I hesitate, then sit up. "Actually, there's something I . . . want to come clean about." I bite my lip as I stand, suddenly doubting this decision.

"Oh, just show them," says Carmen. "What you said about us was way worse."

I laugh, swiping open my phone.

"So . . . there's a long backstory here, but . . . well, just watch."

I hit play and hand off the phone to Dad. It's too awkward to look, so I keep my eyes on the ceiling, my stomach doing flips when they reach the family stuff: "Let's discuss how me and my siblings all learned to ride bikes, shall we?"

When I let myself peek, my parents both have baffled smiles on their faces. "Well," says Dad at the end. "This was . . . unexpected. But hey. Funny stuff."

Mom bobs her head slowly. "I'm *confused*, but . . . very glad to see you're expressing yourself. And I *loved* that Prince Charming stuff."

"She really got your voice down," Dad says to her, before turning to me with a curious look. "But I have to say, Gretch. That's not *quite* what happened the day you learned to bike."

"What do you mean?" I say, honestly stunned by these reactions.

"I remember," he says. "Actually, it was the day you first met Sam."

"Oh yeah," says Mom. "They'd just moved up here that summer. Viv and I had been to one of Gabriela's yoga classes, and we all hit it off so much we invited over the whole family. Aw." She looks at me. "You two must have been . . . six? Neither of you had any idea you were about to meet your best friend. Or—" She frowns, eyes flitting to the phone. "More than friend?"

"Oh, we definitely don't have to talk about that," I say. "But what does this have to do with learning to bike?"

"Well," says Dad. "That day we were throwing this big barbecue. Viv, Arvin, and Carmen were there, too, and everyone was rushing around, trying to get the house nice before our guests arrived. But *you* . . ." He shakes his head. "You chose *that moment* to sneak outside with Hen's bike and start working at it. It wasn't long before Mom and I came and found you, but you'd already pretty much figured it out." He smiles faintly, and I think I see a flicker of emotion behind the mustache. "I remember when we got out there, we asked you why you did it that way."

Mom breathes in, looking at him. "That's right," she says, turning to me with a funny little pout. "You told us you didn't want anyone to see you fall."

Over dinner, Hen and Carmen take turns recounting the events of New Year's Eve-Eve, spooning cheese onto pasta before I jump in to explain the rest. Dad appears more impressed with me than anything. Mom, on the other hand, still seems pretty stuck on the fact that we all used fake IDs.

"I don't even drink," I tell her. "I swear. I've been throwing back ginger ales every night for weeks."

"Still illegal," she says. "In fact, all three of you are grounded."

"I'm in college, Mom," says Hen. "And Carmen's not even your kid. You can't ground us."

"Oh yes I can. You can be grounded for as many days as you stay, Hen. And Carmen, you can . . . just sleep over here and be grounded."

"Okay," says Carmen, shrugging happily.

"But wait. What if Lizzy calls?" says Hen.

"Well, obviously if Lizzy calls . . ." says Dad, looking hopefully at Mom.

"If Lizzy calls, I will grant you a variance," sighs Mom. "But the rest of the time you're grounded."

Hen pouts teasingly. "But what if I get a craving for a snack we don't have in the fridge?"

"Then we'll get takeout," says Mom, laughing despite herself.

"I think I'm going to like being grounded," says Carmen.

Hen frowns at our parents now. "You know, Gretchen was kind of right. You two really aren't that strict anymore."

Dad sips his beer, considering this. "I think as you get older you just sort of want to enjoy your life and let your kids be kids. But it's true. We may have gotten a bit lax over the years."

"And we'll keep talking about the college stuff, okay?" says Mom, reaching out to squeeze my hand.

"Yeah," I say. "All good."

"Poor William," sighs Hen. "I don't think he got any of your loosey-goosey years."

"Eh," says Mom. "We make it up to him with free childcare."

Are you back?

The text sits like a heavy stone in my lap.

"Fine, Aunt Lulu," says Carmen. "We can watch *Love, Actually* again." The couch is especially tight with all of us crowded together—two bowls of popcorn and one Nacho between us, four sets of pj's, and Dad still dressed for some kind of wilderness expedition.

A second buzz fills me with dread, but I look down anyway: Will you please just come over?

"What is it?" says Hen, straining see my phone across Carmen. "Is it Sam?"

"He wants me to come over," I say, queasy now. "Oh well. Can't. Grounded."

"Well," says Mom delicately. "I mean, maybe you can be un-grounded. . . ." I glare at her. "Honey, you're going to have to face him eventually. And selfishly, I like the idea. I think he'd be a great son-in-law."

"Oh my God, Mom," I say, rolling my eyes all the way back. "He doesn't even like me that way, but here you are talking about marriage."

"I reject this premise," says Hen. "You have no idea how Sam feels. He *chased* you. Like in a movie!"

"He *chased* you?" says Mom, touching her heart.

"Can we not?" I say.

"Personally, I think you should go now," says Carmen. "Talking in private will be way less awkward than trying to do it at school. If it's horrible and you have a huge meltdown, do you really want everyone seeing? Not that I think that's what's going to happen," she adds quickly. "Hen's right. You don't know how he feels."

I look at Dad, mid–popcorn bite, the only one yet to speak. "Oh," he says. "You don't want your dad chiming in on your love life, do you?"

"I mean, everyone else has," I say, shrugging.

He laughs. "Just go talk to him, Gretch."

"Dammit," I say, getting up. "You're all traitors. All of you!"

"You'll be *fine*," says Mom.

I don't even bother trying to glam myself up—just grab a sweater and yank it right over my pj's, stuffing my feet into boots and swiping my keys. I swivel back. "Wait. Should I have, like, a speech prepared, or . . . ?"

"I don't think that's really necessary," says Mom. She turns to Dad. "Did you ever make me a speech?"

"Don't think so," he says.

She smiles. "Just go be Sam and Gretch."

"Yeah," I say, nodding a few times. And with that, I step out into the snow.

Here, I text when I've parked outside the yoga studio.

A minute goes by with no response, and I wonder if that's a good enough excuse to turn back. But the apartment is lit up, and downstairs, a few yoga ladies are trickling out after the last class of the night. I know Sam is home. And on a normal day, I wouldn't think twice about letting myself in through the studio.

I take a few breaths behind the wheel, then get out and run

across the street, snow catching in my hair. Hand on the door, I repeat Mom's words to myself: *Just go be Sam and Gretch.*

"Sabrina?"

I freeze as I walk in. Amber is standing behind the desk. I honestly forgot she worked here. "Or wait. I guess that's not actually your name," she says, tilting her head, until something shifts—a click. "Oh my God. I *knew* you looked familiar. You're Sam's friend! Man, I can be such a dingus. Wait. Is Sam *that* Sam? From your sets? This just got *good*! Does he know?"

"He does now," I say weakly. "Since everything kind of . . . blew up."

"Right," she says, crinkling her nose. "Everyone was so confused after you left on Wednesday."

"Yeah, sorry about that," I say, just sort of squirming by the door now.

"It was pretty dramatic," she says. "The second the show ended, it was a big fight. So many people were pissed at Jeremy. And Paula *really* let him have it. Dolores, too. I don't know *what* he was thinking, messing with you and that other girl. You know, the . . . other you. Also, after you left, he still had to go on, and his set was *terrible*. He was so flustered. I really think he blew his chance at winning."

"Well . . . serves him right," I say. It's strange talking about Jeremy. After all those confusing feelings, he seems so suddenly unimportant. At least compared to what's waiting for me now. A silence swallows us up and I can't help but ask, "So . . . were people mad at me, too? For lying?"

"Um?" Amber thinks a moment. "Maybe. Or . . . I think they were more surprised? In retrospect, we all agreed you seemed young. And that your outfits didn't really match your personality. No one thought you were being malicious. But it was still . . . pretty frickin' weird."

I nod my head. "I'll take it."

She laughs, then stops short. "Wait, are you here to see Sam? Am I interrupting something?"

"Oh," I say, abruptly nervous again. "Possibly?"

She gets a giddy look, gesturing toward the studio. "Well, he's right on the other side of that door. I'll leave you to it. You and Sam can handle closing." She grabs a few things from a cubby, then slides into her Uggs. "Also, no Mercury tonight," she says with wink.

"Huh?"

"I'm just saying, the planets are on your side!"

Through the hanging vines of the window, I watch Amber scamper out to her car, the place now quiet. Actually, I hear music—that same old bossa nova CD of Gabriela's, which grows louder once I lightly knock and open up.

I poke my head in and smile. Sam is dancing around the candlelit room in his socks, pushing a Swiffer along smooth wood. His silly, unrestrained moves remind me of the kid he used to be, and I can't tell if it makes me happy or sad.

He jumps. "Oh . . . my God. Hi!"

I gape at him, suddenly unable to believe I *willingly* turned up here. "Hi."

"How, um . . ." He takes a few steps closer, searching my face. "How are you?"

"Fine," I say, definitely dying inside. "You?"

He shrugs. "Fine."

God, this is excruciating. "Look." I steel myself, kicking off my wet boots and padding my way in. "I really don't want this to be weird. . . ."

"Me neither," he says.

"I know so much has changed, but I still think of you as my best friend."

"Same," he says quickly. He gestures to the floor, and I follow his lead, until we're both seated, facing each other with legs crossed. It's total New Year's Eve-Eve déjà vu.

"So . . ." I say, after another long, painful silence. "I guess we're going to talk about this?"

He looks equally mystified. "It appears that way."

"I don't know where to start," I tell him honestly. "Should we . . . talk about the stand-up thing, or the you-and-me thing?"

"Both," he says. "Though the you-and-me thing is probably more . . ."

"Unbearably awkward?"

"I was going to say *pressing*, but sure." His laugh comes out strained. "And, I will say, on a more *bearable* note, you were good, Gretch. *Really* good." He catches my gaze, his gold-flecked eyes lighting up. "It was kind of amazing to watch. It was like . . . there you were, the exact person I'm always wishing you'd let other people see." I smile despite everything, an odd mix of ache and deep appreciation lodging in my throat.

I think I needed to hear that.

He frowns. "That said, I still don't really understand the whole fake-name, dressing-up thing."

"We'll . . . get to that," I tell him, feeling rattled again. "But, um . . ." I clear my throat. "I'm afraid I might actually black out from the awkwardness if we don't clear the air about the . . . other stuff."

"Okay," he says seriously. "So . . . how long have you felt this way?"

"Oh God." I cover my face with my hands, then peek out between tiny slits. "A few months?" I close my fingers again, speaking into the dark. "At first I hoped it would pass. Like it was a . . . cold or something. But then I found out you were moving away, and I guess I started to wonder if letting it pass was even what I wanted. Like maybe this was a sign, and it was *now or never*! But then I changed my mind *again* when I realized how *not* on the same page we were, and of course there was Natalie, who I really weirdly like for you? Even though it also sort of makes me want to cry. . . . Anyway, most of all, I just wish I'd never opened my big mouth, because I don't want everything to be ruined. . . ."

He reaches out to pry my fingers from my face. "Hey. Gretchen. It's okay."

I make myself look back at him. "Did I ruin us, Sam? Or . . . maybe we were already ruined. If we're being honest, we've been growing apart for a while, right?"

"I mean, maybe," he says. "But we could never be *ruined*. Things have changed and they will again—and again. But I feel like we'll always . . . come back around. I'm pretty sure friends like you and me can withstand a few bumps."

I nod, a wave of emotion coming over me. "I think I owe you an apology, Sam. That night on the phone . . ."

"No, please," he says, swatting the air. "I was being a dick."

"Uh-uh." I shake my head. "A lot of what you've been saying is true. I do judge. And I close myself off to people. . . ."

"Well, you were right, too," he says. "I do get kind of . . . *party-hardy* when I'm sad. And maybe sometimes I choose to be in groups, or around people who don't know me as well, so that they won't see through all my bullshit."

"But maybe it isn't bullshit!" I say. "I mean, what do I know? I'm not the authentic-Sam police. I don't even know who authentic Gretchen is. If she even exists."

An odd look flits across his face.

"What?"

"I guess I'm . . . realizing I have to come clean about my side of things," he says, taking in a long breath. "It . . . wasn't just you."

I frown. "Just me who . . . ?"

"Felt something."

"Oh" is all I can think to say. We're quiet for a minute. "But . . . I thought you liked Natalie."

"I did," he says. "Or, do? Doesn't matter. I botched that. And if we're being honest, I'm pretty sure you're the reason why."

I can't seem to produce a response to that, so I stare.

"I know you and I don't usually talk about crushes and stuff," he goes on, "but in the past, I've always been a strictly one-girl-at-a-time kind of guy. So feeling torn like that was . . . a lot. It mostly just made me want to hide from both of you."

I almost laugh, my brain and mouth finally synching up: "When did this . . . ?"

"Remember the night I told you I was moving?"

I nod, heartbeat picking up. "We were right here. . . ."

"Except . . ." He levels me with a look. "I mean, we definitely almost kissed, right? Or did I imagine that?"

"No," I say. "No, I . . . I thought *I* imagined it."

He puffs his cheeks, looking a little dazed. "Well, that was the night it hit me. That you and I could . . . maybe work as more than friends?"

"But . . . if you felt it too, why'd you act so weird after? Why leave me hanging like that?"

"Because, it's *you*, Gretch," he says. "My *best friend*. The person I've . . . shared more of myself with than anyone else, who can make me laugh so hard I shoot soda through my nose, and who . . . held my hand the day my dad moved out. Who watched the whole *Office* with me like thirty times! And never got bored!"

Somehow we both have tears in our eyes.

"It would change *everything*," he says. "And for what? For me to just move away? It's going to be hard enough leaving my entire life behind. I didn't want to lose you, too. And I mean, is that *actually* what you'd want? You and me, as boyfriend-girlfriend?"

As I peer into his eyes, I'm surprised the answer isn't simpler. "I . . . don't know."

"I don't *either*. And the most confusing part is, I still *really do* like Natalie." He cringes. "Sorry if that's weird to say. I'm trying to be honest. I seriously don't know how to feel. Or what to do, or—"

"Kiss me," I say.

"What?"

I sort of can't believe myself, but I don't break away from his gaze. "Let's just find out. Once and for all. No strings, no expectations. This moment doesn't have to count." I say it to myself as much as to him. "It will be a . . . purely objective experiment."

Sam's grin is dubious, but I can tell he's considering it. "I think you've finally lost it, Gretch." But he's coming closer. I'm coming closer, too—until we're hovering, his features growing blurry. His lips part. I feel him let out a breath. I close my eyes.

And then I feel . . . a mouth.

And spit.

Sam's spit and mouth.

When I open my eyes, he's staring back at me. We hover,

our gazes locked, each of us searching for confirmation, I think, from *way way* too close.

At once, we break apart. And now I can't seem to stop shaking my head.

Sam hasn't blinked yet. "That was . . ."

"Bad," I say, the word like a tiny exhale.

"Honestly?" he says, still looking completely dazed. "I felt more chemistry when my great-aunt kissed me at Christmas."

"I've had steamier nights at home with Ben and Jerry," I say.

I watch as a little smile starts to pull at his lips, our breathing audible against the sudden quiet. I guess the CD ran out.

Abruptly, I start to snicker, prompting Sam to choke out a snort. The fit overtakes us almost instantly—peals of slaphappy, stomach-stitching laughter. Like some kind of giddy, deranged cleanse.

After a minute, we stretch out onto our backs on the floor, shoulder to shoulder.

"Holy shit, that just happened," I say, actual tears now dripping down my face.

"Yep," says Sam, still panting a little as he turns to me. "Although . . . no it didn't."

"Oh, that's right," I say. "That never happened."

"Never," he says.

"Oh wow," I say to the ceiling, muscles relaxing into the cool wood. My whole body floods with a strange sort of joy, and I erupt in one last weird little giggle. "I can't believe how relieved I am. Are you relieved?"

"I'm relieved," he says through an exhale, his hands on his ribs.

"We should have done this weeks ago," I say. "It's kind of funny, after all that. . . . Poor Ethan. I'm embarrassed to admit I . . . kind of talked his ear off about you."

"You *didn't*," says Sam.

"Yep. About you and this other guy, Jeremy, from the club. But that was also a nonstarter. I guess it's what happens when you open yourself up to romance. You overthink everything, waste a bunch of air, and in the end, nothing even comes of it."

"You don't really believe that," says Sam. "For all your TV-yelling during rom-coms, I've caught you swooning just as often."

"It's true." I sigh. "What can I say? I love love."

"I can't believe you talked to Ethan about me."

I shrug. "He's such a chill guy. I'm sure he didn't really mind."

"Okay, but . . . you realize he's totally into you, right?"

I turn to him. *"What?"*

"He's actually been a little funny around me lately," Sam says thoughtfully. "Which I guess makes more sense now that I'm hearing this."

"No . . ." I say, frowning. "You're obviously wrong. Ethan doesn't . . . He's like everyone's favorite person. And I'm a total grouch."

Sam is clearly amused now. "I don't think I'm wrong, Gretch. I've got a good sense for these things. And you're not *always* a grouch. Anyway, I've seen the way he looks at you."

I sit up. "Oh no . . ."

Sam sits up too, wincing slightly. "Not into him, huh? It's the hair, right? Little mullet-y?"

"Shut up, I like his hair," I say, laughing. "I like . . . a lot of things about Ethan. It's just . . . shit! I've been blabbering about my boy problems to him for weeks." I palm the top of my head, remembering. "Oh God . . . He was the first person I talked to after I kissed Jeremy!"

Sam seems impressed. "Look at you juggling boys."

"Uh, I am an empowered modern woman," I tell him.

"But you said it's over with that guy, right? Was it another zero-chemistry situation?"

"Actually, no," I say. "There was some . . . definite sizzle. But there was also, like, no *there* there, if that makes any sense. Plus, he's a douchebag." I shake my head, thoughts snapping back to Ethan. "Seriously, how did I miss this? Now *I* feel like a douchebag."

"You're not a douchebag," says Sam. "You and Ethan are friends. And I think he enjoys being your friend. I just think he'd . . . also enjoy making out with you."

I feel my cheeks go crimson.

"What's this?" says Sam, grinning and gesturing to my face. "What am I seeing here?"

"I don't know!" I say defensively. "I'm processing!"

He smiles, getting up. "Well, while you process, want to help me close?"

"Sure," I say, heaving out a breath. I go over to a pile of yoga blankets in the corner, refolding the ones that weren't done right. Sam straightens up a stack of bolsters on a shelf, then darts out to the front desk to shut down the computer.

"What are you going to do about Natalie?" I call out. "I feel I should warn you. She has pretty much given up. . . ."

"But she did like me?" he says hopefully, walking in again.

"She did," I say, misting plants with a spray bottle, then popping out to the front to get the ones in the window. "And if you do win her back, you'll be in the same city next year."

"Right," he says as I pass him in the studio again, stashing the Swiffer in the closet. "That could be good. Really good . . ."

"I can't believe you aren't going to live here anymore," I say, turning around.

His shoulders slump. "Me neither. Will you visit?"

"Of course," I say. "Though you may have to share me with Annika, since she crushed her Juilliard audition and is totally getting in. Maybe we can all meet up. We'll get pizza."

"And feel happy for each other," he says, grinning. "I was just watching that Marnie James set the other day." He pauses, noticing my face. "What?"

I laugh. "Just . . . we have a lot to catch up on."

TWENTY-ONE

Plan-Making Time | Set your targets. Commencing Mission Happily Ever After.

When I reach our lunch table today, Annika is—*wait for it*—poring over her sheet music. "Huh," I say, sitting down across from her. "I always sort of assumed you'd mellow out when the audition was over."

"I assumed that, too," she says curiously, closing the folder. "I think this might just be my natural state of being."

"When do you hear?"

She sighs. "Not for a little while."

"Hey, Gretchen," says someone walking by—the modern-dance kid I got a quote from at the Berwin game last week. I wave to him, right as one of the lacrosse girls gives a quick nod in passing.

I noticed it happening the day after the game, too, and this pattern of acknowledgment seems to be persisting. In fact, that gossipy model UN girl I met last week caught me in the bathroom this morning and basically talked *at* me the whole time I was washing my hands. I guess there's some big beef now between Albania and Sierra Leone. Meanwhile, the musical theater guy I interviewed is actually in my art history class, and earlier today, as our teacher clicked through pasty boob-out ladies on the overhead projector, he turned around to invite me to an open dress rehearsal. So that's on the calendar.

I don't think I've made any new best friends yet, but I've already felt a change walking the halls between classes. I haven't gone skin-crawly once today. And I've felt . . . lighter. *Literally* lighter when Pilsner saw me coming after second period and legitimately *picked me up*, twirled me around, and gently set me down, just because he felt like it.

Now, as I look around the cafeteria, I feel something like appreciation for this place, which I guess is strange for me. I actually feel excited to get back to work on the yearbook. I hope we can capture all the shades of Carlton High this time, all the quirks and characters that make it interesting.

As I unwrap my PB&J, Deb from the Mathletes walks by and waves. I wave back.

"Okay, what's happening here?" says Annika, eyeing me skeptically. "Something's different."

"I guess I'm trying to get better at . . . people-ing?" I glance around at our backpack-barricaded table. "I hope that's okay."

"Oh no, that's good. I wasn't going to say anything, but I mean . . . I'm not going to be here forever."

"You better not forget about me," I say with a warning stare.

Annika breathes in through her teeth. "I don't know. The oboe fame *could* go to my head."

I laugh and look past her, suddenly catching eyes with Ethan from across the room. He smiles my way for a second, then turns as Grody says something on his other side.

I remember to exhale, rattled now. Somehow Ethan and I haven't run into each other yet today, and all the waiting is making me weird. I still haven't decided how I want to act around him, or what I should say. If Sam is right, and I'm just the dum-dum who didn't see the guy who was *right there all along*, well, then, I'm . . . definitely flattered. In fact, stealing another glance at Ethan now, I feel my cheeks grow stupidly hot again.

But I don't know. At the risk of sounding like Amber in one of her Instagram captions: I think I need a little me-time right now? There's still so much clutter in my head. And I have things to work out—big things.

After I got back from Sam's last night, I went up to Hen's room, and caught her and Carmen up on the latest developments. They seemed to especially enjoy the story of our kiss that *did not happen*, both of them giggling like schoolgirls as I, *okay, fine*, kind of hammed up the details for their amusement. By the time we all went to bed, I was practically on a cloud. I started thinking about how good it feels to make people laugh, and how that rush is probably the closest I'll ever get to a hit of hard-core drugs. As I began to drift, Sam's words started rattling around in my head. *It was like . . . there you were, the exact person I'm always wishing you'd let other people see.* And for a second, I wanted to cry.

Why has it always been so hard to let people see?

What am I so fucking afraid of?

When I look back at Annika, she's tumbled down into her music again, her free hand conducting, today's avocado rolls nearly gone—wasabi wisely set off to the side.

I smile, remembering the future she painted that morning in the diner: the two of us as cool creatives living on the fringes, sharing tight quarters and pouring our hearts out into our work. The vision might be a bit glossy, but it's a nice thought.

Maybe someday I'll be brave like that.

I let out a long sigh. I'd rather not think about any of it—not that my brain cares what I want. The fact keeps cropping up whenever there's a lull: the last night of the Comithon is this Wednesday. Three winners will be chosen, have their sets sent to Marnie James . . .

And I'll be sitting at home.

"Hey, Gretch," I hear from above.

I'm yanked from my thoughts as Sam takes a seat at the table. Annika looks up from her sheet music with alarm, but he grins and says, "Heard you killed it at your Juilliard audition." She's never seemed particularly impressed with Sam, but this clearly pleases her.

"What's up?" I say.

"It's Natalie," he says miserably. "I tried to pull her aside earlier, but it's like she's icing me out."

"Weird," I say. "That doesn't sound like her."

"I mean, she's doing it in a very Natalie way. She's still being extremely nice, but there's a wall now. Sort of like you said last night. It's like suddenly there's no . . . *there* there."

"Oh, there's a *there* there," I say, laughing at the tongue twister. "But you have to remember how annoyingly fickle you were. Girls hate that. It might take a few tries."

He nods. "I've been racking my brain for something romantic to do. Maybe we should watch one of your rom-coms after school?"

"Nah," I say. "Just cut the cool-guy act, and talk to her. But, like, *for real*." I think of Mom and smile. "Go be . . . Sam and Natalie."

"Huh. So no public singing or impassioned speech?"

I wrinkle my nose. "I mean, no one *actually* does stuff like that. Right?"

When I arrive at HQ, Mr. O is standing in the middle of the room with his to-go mug, car keys already in hand. "I'm in a hurry, Gretchen, so if you could be efficient with today's inane proposal, that would be great."

I mime deep thought. "You know, I *was* going to suggest a scratch-'n'-sniff element, but I guess it can wait."

He regards me a moment, dubious. "You seem . . . chipper."

"I am not," I say, and for some reason, I find myself looking anyplace but where Ethan is sitting.

Natalie looks up from the scanner as she presses an old yearbook page to the glass. "You really don't have to do these check-ins every day, Mr. O. I'm telling you: this squad here is a well-oiled machine. And we've had no trouble locking up ourselves."

"Yeah, Mr. O," Ethan says into his laptop. "This way, you're teaching us to take matters into our own hands." He glances my way, and I brace myself for some kind of awkward shock. But actually, everything feels normal. So normal, in fact, that I may have to yell at Sam later. I think he got me all worked up for nothing.

"I like that interpretation, Ethan," says Mr. O. "On that note, I'm leaving now. Make me proud!"

As he walks out, Natalie returns her attention to the scanner, still collecting images for our Randos of the Century collage. "So, for today, Gretch, could you type up those quotes? And after that, I've got my own stuff to do, but you and Ethan can pair up together to match them with the right team photos."

"Uh . . . sure," I say, dropping my bag on the carpet before pausing a moment. Is it just me, or has Natalie been conveniently pairing us up a lot lately? As if in answer, she glances playfully in Ethan's direction, then back to me. And then I sort of frown-laugh through the queasy feeling in my gut.

Ethan seems to be in the zone now as I go for the beanbag across from him. He looks up, probably because I'm looming like a weirdo. "Hey," he says.

"Hi," I say, sitting down and pulling out my laptop.

I open up the recording app on my phone to start scrolling through clips. For every title like "Rachel from field hockey," or "Brandon from debate team," there's a random one, like, "Nacho's internal monologue—surprisingly complex?" Looking back on these random bits feels a lot like going through old photos, the quick flashes like a time-lapse of my brain.

I put in my earbuds and hit play on a clip from a couple weeks ago, which I titled "Snow D-Day." Like always, my voice sounds higher than I think it is:

"If I do that 'Defective Mainer' bit I was talking about with Ethan, I could segue into how New Englanders love complaining about snow. There's a lot of pride to it. Like, snowstorms are our D-Day and surviving them proves some kind of rugged heroism on our part. . . . Maybe I could pitch it to the audience as a movie concept. Think *Saving Private Ryan*, only everyone's just shoveling."

I smile. That could have been good. I've missed this these last few days—the thinking, and planning, my mind feeling lit up, always scouring for little glimmers of humor or truth.

When I look over, Sam is in the doorway, appearing a bit

nervous. I shoot him a smile that says, *I know just what you're thinking now, friend from forever.* To which I add, *You've got this.* He nods my way, straightening up a bit. "Um, Natalie? Can we talk for a minute?"

She hesitates, then seems to soften. I watch Sam's body sink with relief when she starts to walk, following him out into the hall.

The door shuts behind them, and I remember I have actual work to do. So I open my laptop and begin transcribing quotes, filling up several pages until I run out of clips.

Looking up, I realize Sam and Natalie still aren't back. That seems like a good sign. I remove my earbuds, extending my leg out to kick Ethan's foot.

"Oh, hello," he says. "All done?"

"Yep," I say, quickly scanning his face for clues again. He doesn't *look* lovesick. Or even remotely uncomfortable for that matter. I don't how to feel about that.

"Hey, check this out," he says.

I get up and he scoots over, leaving me half the beanbag chair.

Now I have to wonder: Smooth move or courteous friend gesture? It's very hard to tell with Ethan. We've been close like this before—at Natalie's birthday dinner, and the night of the Berwin game when he swept me away from those staring Mules parents, his arm around me.

Huh. Ethan had his arm around me. . . .

But this right now is different. There's something. A small but very real current.

"Okay," he says, clearing out a few tabs. "So I tried drawing up your Mad Lib idea. I took some old senior pictures and photoshopped them into silhouettes—as placeholders for whoever people choose to include on their own pages. I realized, you know how sometimes kids exchange school portraits? We can make the boxes the same size, so if people want, they can paste their own friends in, and then fill in the blanks for each caption. You know, with *best butthole*, et cetera."

I laugh, amazed by how perfect this is. "This is exactly what I wanted, Ethan. This is exactly what I didn't even *know* I wanted." I freeze, hearing myself. But he doesn't seem to infer much from the comment.

"Cool," he says, clicking out of the page. On his screen, there are rows and rows of folders. One is marked *Gretchen*, from our headshot day, and for some reason, I feel my stomach tighten.

"Wait," I say as he starts to shut the laptop. "Could I . . . look through these again?"

"Sure," he says, handing the computer over. I sift through, frame after frame: me in my little buns, the makeup and glasses. There's one series with hands on hips, another with arms crossed. Throughout, my eyes are smoldering. Then there are the occasional ones where I break, barely holding in a smile.

You can feel how much fun we're having. I speed through the rest, until I land on what I'm looking for, at the bottom of the folder—the very last shot. It's me, back in my regular clothes in the café, looking straight at Ethan, mid laugh. I wouldn't say I look like a badass, but I look strong. Happy. Open.

"I like this one," says Ethan, leaning in.

I smile, turning up to him. "Could you send it to me?"

TWENTY-TWO

The Grand Gesture | Cheesy and completely over-the-top? Absolutely. But sometimes nothing less will do.

"Tape," I say to Hen Wednesday night as she and Carmen sweep the area like a security detail. We waited in the parking lot until Ted finished taking IDs and packed it in. Now the street is empty, and my heart is racing.

In the display case by the main door, my Sabrina headshot is still up with the others. I guess Dolores forgot to take it down. As anticipated, the case is locked, but that doesn't stop me from sticking my new picture to the glass, right over the old one.

"There," I say, stepping back. When I brought the photo to the print shop kiosk earlier, I chose a big, bold font for the name at the bottom: *Gretchen Wilder.* I actually get a little shiver seeing it now, looking *almost* official under the Comithon banner.

"I hope it doesn't snow," says Hen, peering up at the sky as the edges of the glossy paper flap around in the open air. "Your face will get all streaky."

"The idea seemed cooler in my head," says Carmen, frowning. "This actually just looks kind of janky."

I roll my eyes and add more tape. "I'm being symbolic, okay?"

The epiphany came on Monday—somewhere in the time between sharing that beanbag chair with Ethan and going to bed later that night. I guess *epiphany* is a strong word. There was no lightning bolt. No sudden *aha* moment. It was a fuzzy, slow burn of a thought: I can be whoever the hell I want to be. But also? I am what I am.

As Sam and I once discussed over Vietnamese soup, sometimes it's about holding opposing truths in our minds at once.

Maybe I can be bold, and new, and also exactly me. Maybe *Real Gretchen* is a moving target. Always in motion, evolving, a patchwork of contradictions. I don't really know exactly.

I just know I need to be here tonight.

The fact that I enjoy telling jokes to strangers may never cease to surprise me. I'm not brassy or sassy, and I wouldn't say I'm someone who gives no fucks. I actually give a lot of fucks. And if my heart rate is telling me anything, I'm still a nervous mess. But I'm starting to think bravery isn't some miraculous energy force I can hope will arrive one day. It might just be a decision, honestly. A matter of saying, *Fuck it.* Or *Why not?* And then simply doing the thing.

I take a moment to imagine it: charging up the steps to that stage tonight with no armor to protect me. I'm pretty sure I'm going to love it. But also? Some part of me will probably want to barf.

"Smile!" says Hen, snapping a photo on her phone—of me next to the taped-on headshot. "We'll want this someday. For when Carmen and I are just the little people you met along the way . . ."

"It's one night," I say, biting my nail as I check my texts.

"She's nervous," Carmen says to Hen.

"We'll distract you," Hen says to me.

"Oooh, I've got it," says Carmen. "This was supposed to be a surprise, but I bought us Rice Krispies ingredients for later, to celebrate." I smile at her, touched but still no less jumpy.

"I know it's a weeknight, but could we watch a movie anyway?" asks Hen. "Maybe something old-school. Have we seen *Sixteen Candles*?"

"Yeah," I say vaguely, still watching my phone. "But I think we were little so a lot of it went over our heads. I don't know how that one got past the moms. . . ."

"I want to say it was playing on TV?" says Carmen. "But you're right. Their brains would have exploded."

"Oh yeah . . ." says Hen. "That's the one with Long Duk Dong in it."

"And a pretty egregious Me Too situation," I say, frowning up at them. "I feel like that was even bad for the eighties. . . ."

"Sucks because I love Molly Ringwald," says Carmen. "She's totally one of my style icons. Well, except for that boxy dress she wears at the end of *Pretty in Pink*. They seriously built us up for that potato sack?"

"Awful," says Hen with a shudder.

I nod along, laughing under my breath. "Actually, I'm probably going to be pretty wiped tonight. Maybe we should pick something that . . . *doesn't* elicit TV yelling?"

"*To All the Boys I've Loved Before*?" says Hen, her face lighting up.

"Oooh, or *Love, Simon*," says Carmen.

We all swoon.

My phone buzzes and I jolt. A new message from Amber has appeared: Show's starting, and I am in position!

"That her?" says Hen.

I nod and draw a long breath as the two of them link arms with me.

We round the corner to the alley, and after a moment, the door swings open.

"Hi," Amber whispers, fixing her eyes on Hen and Carmen. She frowns, leaning out into the alley. "Wait a minute . . . I remember you two. No getting sloppy, okay?"

"We'll be on our best behavior," Hen promises. "We just want to see Gretchen."

"And maybe yell at Jeremy a little," says Carmen happily.

Amber laughs and braces the door, letting the three of us slip past her, until it gently clicks shut, blocking out the streetlight. My eyes adjust to the dark, and I'm hit with what I realize is now my favorite smell: cheap bathroom soap and sticky floor beer. "Okay, well, hang tight," whispers Amber. "I'll keep watch up front. Also, don't forget to announce me when you're done. I'm *slightly* afraid Dolores won't tap me back in if she's mad about this."

"You think she'll be mad?" I say, suddenly alarmed.

She shrugs. "I just know she was pissed when she found out Jeremy let you in with a fake ID. There was a whole speech about how this place needs to start running like an 'actual fuckin' bar' with 'actual fuckin' rules.' But whatever. I couldn't let you miss the last night of the Comithon."

"Thanks," I say, my resolve waning slightly. "But I don't want to get you in trouble. You could still win this thing."

"I don't think so," she says. "This crowd doesn't get me. I'm too esoteric."

I smile as she moves toward the other end of the hall—her guard post, I guess. I can hear Dolores greeting the crowd now.

"We're gonna go find seats," whispers Carmen.

"You've got this," says Hen as the two of them pull me in for a final squeeze.

I watch them tiptoe off into the audience, and then I pace. I've practiced and practiced these past couple days, but to be thorough, I should go over the beats again in my head.

The audience applauds for the first comic of the night.

"So I'm a preschool teacher. . . ."

I pause to listen, and in a blink, I'm completely lost in Paula's set. Soon, it's Isaiah's—and yep, same thing. "Everyone thinks they have a bad Tinder story," he says, making me smile. "Then they hear mine. . . ."

I don't even bother trying to focus by the time Haru goes up: "Here's what most people don't know about halibut. . . ."

Somewhere along the way, I slide down the wall to sit, fully giving up on the idea of preparing.

Lenny reveals his plans to propose to his girlfriend with an ethically mined opal later this month. He hopes the gesture won't be received as overly patriarchal. Next Lakshmi talks about the many, *many* drugs she intends to take during childbirth now that she's officially allowed to tell the world she's pregnant. And then Bill admits to using a Mary Berry voice whenever he bakes at home, switching off his Maine accent to say the word *layers* in a single syllable. The crowd can't get enough.

I get so swept up, eyes closed, feeling completely at home, that I'm not even all that nervous anymore—just listening contentedly as Dolores's gravelly voice winds up to the next act. But then she calls out, *"Jeremy Griffin!"* and my eyes shoot open, goose bumps forming under my sweater. And it hits me: I've never actually seen him do stand-up before.

I know I shouldn't care how he does tonight. I've kept him firmly banished from my mind this week. But curiosity wins out, I guess, because I'm getting up now, moving down the hall to catch a glimpse.

"How's everyone doing tonight?" he asks, prompting a raucous cheer as he grips the mic. I think he's already won half these people over with his looks alone, the stage lights working nicely for him, drawing into focus his height, the good hair, and the muscles under his T-shirt.

A few feet ahead, Amber turns back with an eye roll. I glower out at the stage, willing Jeremy to stumble again, like I'm told he did last week. I want him to suck. I want a *train wreck*. Although, I don't know. That might just be awkward for everyone.

As he flashes that gum-commercial smile out at the still-cheering crowd, a new thought turns my stomach: What if all that ego of his was justified? What if he wins this whole competition, and walks off completely unscathed? Guys like him win *all the time*. I'm sure someday, I'll make seventy cents to his dollar.

Maybe he'll even be my idiot boss.

"So I recently broke up with—" Jeremy freezes, his face falling suddenly. My view is partially blocked by someone's head in the audience, but I think he's looking at Carmen. And if I'm right, I'd bet good money she's smiling up at him in a way that is truly terrifying. "Oh wow," he says, taking a step back. "I . . . just remembered, I meant to open with something else tonight."

Under the lights, you can see his Adam's apple bobbing up and down. And he seems to be searching the room.

I retreat into the shadows. Because I think he's looking for *me*.

After another long beat, there's a puff of air against the microphone. "Okay, new plan. I need to come clean about some stuff. I have an . . . old flame in the audience. Possibly more than one. So this night is going *great* for me so far."

A few people laugh.

"Sorry," he says after a pause. "I'm just . . . kind of going through the joke Rolodex in my head. . . . I'm actually struggling to find any stories that won't make me look like a dick in this context. Maybe not a great sign."

There's another small murmur, but it's totally tense in here.

"Okay . . ." he says, sounding a bit miserable, actually. "The truth is, I . . . suck at love. And for a long time, I'm not sure I even believed it existed. I told myself to lean into that. It was better for my work anyway. You have to admit, relationships are sort of the kiss of death if you want to lead an interesting life. And I've never wanted to be one of those people who, when you ask what they're up to, they're like, 'Oh, you know. Sylvia and I are rewatching *Breaking Bad.* We're training for a 5K. . . .'"

The audience really does laugh at that. And actually, I kind of do too.

"Anyway, I hope it's not too late for me. I don't *want* to be this cynical. And as someone very special once said, while I may not believe in the fairy tale, I *might* believe in the rom-com. . . .

Maybe with a few added tweaks for plausibility."

I let out a breath of surprise, hearing my own words quoted back to me after all these weeks. It would almost be sweet if my *blood relative* who he *also made out with* weren't currently in the audience.

"Anyway. Enough with the sappy stuff," he says, abruptly shifting gears. "I recently found out the internet is like forty percent porn?" The audience laughs. "I guess the remaining sixty percent is mostly, like, streaming services and social media. And then this one *teeny-tiny* sliver is, I don't know . . . knowledge? Sort of puts my own shortcomings into perspective, honestly. People are gross."

I'm big enough to admit that Jeremy does get a few more laughs out of me. And yet, when he finally says good night, I'm relieved. It's clear he neither sucks nor is a rock star. He's somewhere in the middle. Just like the rest of us.

"All right, all right," says Dolores, snapping me out of my head. "Let's keep it moving, shall we? Up next, she's everyone's favorite yogi-slash-comedienne. Put your hands together for *Amber Bernhardt*!"

I flinch as Amber looks back at me. We share a quick nod and I wait for her to take the stage before following, feeling a little odd making this walk in my plain fleece leggings, frumpy sweater, and black Converse.

"Sooo, slight change," says Amber as I hurry up the steps. She grins at me from her place behind the mic. "I'm going to let this young lady here cut in front of me and then I'll be right back. Let's give it up for *Gretchen Wilder*!"

Her clapping is painfully audible over the murmuring of the crowd. There's a rhythm to this show, and we've clearly disrupted it. As we lock eyes, Amber gives a helpless shrug and darts off, leaving me there, alone under the spotlight.

Ted looks over as he dries a glass behind the bar. Dolores and the hostess pause a hushed conversation. In back, Lenny, Haru, Bill, and Lakshmi all peer out at me curiously. I spot Jeremy, too, but skip over him, my eyes landing instead on Paula and Isaiah at a table in the middle row.

Their faces are so inscrutable as I squint out at them, devoid of their usual warmth.

It hurts to know that I did that.

I lied and messed everything up.

"Hi," I say, straining to reach the mic. Without Sabrina's high-heeled booties, I'm much shorter than usual up here. As I adjust the stand, I wonder if this was mistake. Maybe I should have simply called Dolores and asked for a second chance, for a real place on the lineup, complete with a proper introduction.

But I think I needed the element of surprise tonight. I couldn't risk her turning me away. Not without proving to myself I could do this.

Not without saying what I need to say.

Standing tall, I brush my hair away from my face, letting it fall loosely around my shoulders. I feel my feet, flat on the ground, my roomy sweater like a warm hug, thankfully hiding all my perspiration. This part—the being me part—actually feels okay. And as my eyes adjust, I realize I'm not at all daunted by the strangers watching me. It's the familiar faces that make my stomach flip. I don't think they're angry exactly. But definitely . . . wary.

"For those of you who don't know me, I'm Gretchen," I say, clearing my throat. "I'm in this competition. Or . . . my alter ego was."

I smile weakly, eyes sweeping this place I adore so much.

"I know I haven't been honest about myself with a lot of you. But tonight, I come before you as I really am: a high school junior who, a couple months ago, never could have imagined herself standing up here, ready to bare her soul while sweating balls." That gets a meager laugh. "I thought I was a certain kind of person. With a predetermined role to play. I thought I could only do this if I became someone else. If I . . . lied to you."

The room has gone completely still—so quiet I can hear my own breath.

"I guess I should quickly add, for anyone new to the Chuckle Parlor: sorry this is turning into a night of big speeches. This isn't, like, a thing we do. Actually, the guy before me kind of stole my thunder." I look at Jeremy, standing off to the side, and catch a trace of a smile. "Anyway, I just had to tell you all how much I love this crappy club, with its random crooked curtain that leads nowhere. . . ."

I point behind me to the brick wall and the audience murmurs another laugh.

"I had to tell you . . . how much I love the *people* here." I briefly glance at Jeremy again. "Okay, *most* of the people here." I let out a big breath, my heartbeat picking up as I look around the room. "I love that pretty much from day one, even though most of us had just met, and we were supposed to be competing, we all supported each other—became *invested* in each other. We shared our truths and our quirks, our joys and our pain. I've come to care so much about you all, and I just . . ." I swallow, getting strangely choked up all of a sudden. "I really want to win you back."

When I finally let myself peek, Paula and Isaiah both have oddly excited looks on their faces, like they're expecting something big to happen. My heart sinks. Because of course. For all my talk of rom-coms up on this stage, I should have known: you don't *say* you're going to win someone back. You *win them back*! And I'm honestly so overcome right now, I really do wish I had a Creepy John Cusack boombox to hold over my head, or a marching band waiting to back me up, *10 Things I Hate About You*–style.

"Uh . . ." I bite my lip, thinking a moment. I *could* sing. . . .

The song pops into my head, and I don't hesitate—just close my eyes and let it out: "You're just too good to be true. Can't take my eyes off of you. . . ."

Wait. This might have been a weird choice.

"You'd be like heaven to . . . touch." Oh God.

"This really isn't necessary!" Dolores calls from the back. I open my eyes, breathing out a laugh. "Think you could maybe tell some jokes now?"

"Um, okay," I say with a happy sniff. "But just know I'd sing my heart out for you, Dolores. And Paula and Isaiah." They grin up at me as I continue to scan the room. "And Haru, and Amber. Lenny, Lakshmi, Bill . . . You too, Ted . . . Not you, Jeremy."

He smiles, and somehow, I do too.

When I land on Dolores again, she's pointing at her watch.

"Sorry," I say. "But real quick. I actually did practice this. . . ." I clear my throat, gazing out beyond the lights at her. "I'm just a girl. Standing in front of a . . . sort of grouchy club owner. Asking her to . . . let me come back here sometime."

"We'll talk," Dolores says gruffly.

I sigh, happy. "Talking would be great."

For my remaining minutes, I test out some new bits about home, first getting into my recent trip to New York and how those beautiful people have nothing on us: "Not *one* person had a hat that looked like a beaver. . . ."

Then Ethan's Mainer test sends me off on a weirdly intense tangent: "You know what? No. If you support bacon in clam chowder, I say fuck that, and *fuck you*! Whoa." I collect myself. "Too far. I apologize."

After that, I pitch my *Saving Private Ryan*–style New Englanders shoveling movie, even reenacting a dramatic scene with a full-blown slo-mo accent: *"Nooooo! You'll throw ya' back out, Johnnyyy! Just use the snooow blowahhh!"*

My cheeks actually hurt from smiling when I finally cut myself off at the sight of the blinking light. "Okay, well. I'm Gretchen Wilder," I say, beaming out at the cheering crowd. "Thank you, Portland!" I walk toward the steps, heart swelling. *I did that!* I feel like I could burst into song again.

Amber frowns at me from the base of the stage, and I quickly swivel around and go back the way I came. "And now Amber!" I say, leaning into the mic once more. "Sorry. Forgot the show wasn't over."

"Do you want to go yell at Jeremy?" I ask Carmen when the lights go up after Amber's set. I thought she was terrific. But she was right. The audience didn't get it.

"Surprisingly, no," says Carmen. "Apparently I just don't care enough."

Hen checks her phone, her face brightening. "It's Lizzy. I'll be right back."

She runs off and Carmen cranes her neck, eyeing the bar. "Actually, there's something I need to do, too. . . ."

When she gets up, I lock eyes with Paula and Isaiah a few

tables away. It's awkward for about five seconds. Then they rush over to swarm me with a hug.

"That was . . . something," says Isaiah with a baffled laugh.

I shrug sheepishly, looking back and forth between them. "I really am sorry. You must think I'm so weird."

"Eh," says Paula. "I'm over it."

I bring them in for another hug—I guess I'm a hugger tonight—but Isaiah pulls back with concern. "Wait. Nacho was real, though. Right?"

"Definitely real," I assure him. "It all was, honestly. Sabrina was . . . mostly an outfit. Or maybe an attitude."

"I get that," says Paula. "I have a kid in my class who wears a full Spider-Man suit whenever he's having too much separation anxiety. I say whatever works for you."

"Aw," I say with a little laugh. "Also, you were both on fire tonight. Way to make the competition boring. At this point, the only real question is who's going to get the third spot." The two of them share an odd glance. "What?"

"I'm . . . actually going to have to bow out," says Isaiah. "When I auditioned for that commercial, the casting people also had me read for a movie. I honestly didn't think much of it. But . . . turns out, I got it. Paperwork just came through. It's . . . well, it's fairly life-changing."

"Holy shit," I say, eyes wide. "What's the movie?"

"I'm not at liberty to get into it yet, but . . ." He hesitates, looking around. "Let's just say I have a scene with a . . . former talkative, celebrity-gossip-obsessed Dunder Mifflin employee?"

"No," I say, my heart practically stopping. "Mindy Kaling?"

Paula squeals. "We're going to have a famous friend!"

He laughs. "Anyway, the movie's filming in Boston, so I'll be around a little longer. But after that . . ."

My face falls. "You're leaving us, aren't you?"

Paula gives a sad little smile as he nods. "Off to LA . . ."

For a minute, we all look at each other, the excitement bittersweet.

But then some other comics from tonight start trickling over, and we open up our circle. I suppose my big speech might have been a bit dramatic for the Comithon participants I don't know as well. But Lakshmi, Lenny, Haru, and Bill all assure me they were touched. We exchange compliments for a little while, recapping the highlights from different sets. Isaiah doesn't bring up his news, as if not wanting to overshadow everyone's big night. I think we all know it's just a silly competition, but the stakes still seem high. You can feel it—all these different pairs of eyes occasionally drifting over to people from the audience as they cast their ballots on the way out the door.

When the basket fills to the top, we watch Dolores pick it up and bring it to the office.

She emerges a few minutes later, catching my eye across the room. "Wish me luck," I whisper to Paula and Isaiah before excusing myself from the circle.

"Dolores?" I say, my steps slowing as I reach her.

"Hi. Gretchen, is it?"

"Yeah," I say, feeling somehow more awkward now than I did singing to her up onstage. "I know. I'm really sorry. What I did was super strange. Trust me, I know. The whole thing just got out of control. And I never expected to love this place so much."

"Yeah, well, there's a lot to love," she says, shrugging one shoulder coyly. But then she softens a little. "So. How old *are* you?"

"Seventeen," I say with a wince. "Does that disqualify me?"

"Um . . ." She thinks. "I guess it doesn't actually matter. I just counted up the votes. You . . . didn't make the top three. Sorry. It'll be Paula, Lenny, and Haru going up there next week, now that Isaiah's out."

"Oh, that's okay," I say, disappointed, maybe, but not surprised. "Honestly, I kind of figured my big speech destroyed any chance I had at that. But . . ." I look at her, hopeful. "Maybe I could still . . . try stuff out here once in a while? When the regular open mic nights come back again?"

She looks me over, then breathes out. "If you can get me a note from your parents, I guess I don't see why not."

"Oh, thank you!" I almost hug her but decide not to push my luck.

"Dolores?" An older gentleman walks up to us then. "I don't mean to interrupt, I just wanted to say hi."

"Oh. Hi, Randy." She turns to me. "This is Marnie James's uncle."

I perk up with a smile. "You know what? I'm going to let you two talk."

As I start to walk away, I notice Jeremy hanging back in the hallway, eyes fixed on me. All week, he's been calling and texting. Now he's giving me space out of respect, I guess. I probably should face him eventually, but I still feel such an odd mix of emotions, looking at him now. My steps grow more deliberate as I weave through people. And when I reach him, I stop and take a long breath. "So you know, I'm still mad."

"Fair enough," he says, bracing the air between us. "For what it's worth, I am trying to make it right. I already called Sabrina and apologized. And I would have done the same with Carmen, but she—like *you*—would not pick up her phone. And now she seems . . . busy." He nods toward the bar, where she and Ted are back to making out like no time has passed since that first night.

I let out a laugh of surprise before remembering I'm still mad.

I glance at the exit that leads to the alley, where Jeremy and I spoke that same night in the snow. "I think the worst part might be that you encouraged me," I say after a beat, not quite able to look at him. "I *did* need a push; that meant something. So for it to have been a joke? It's kind of cruel, don't you think?"

"But it wasn't a joke," he says immediately, bending down to find my gaze. There's an earnestness there that surprises me. "Or . . . *joke* isn't the right word at least. Was I dishonest? Yes.

But, I mean, *come on*. You walk up to my line, you hand me an ID with a girl *I know* on it. And then you go up on a stage and blatantly lie to everyone about who you are? How could I not find that just the littlest bit interesting? That was a really weird thing to do."

"I know," I say, abruptly irritable. I realize I don't *totally* have a leg to stand on, yelling at him about the lying thing. But his lie still feels worse to me. He held all the cards, right from the beginning. He never should have let it get this far.

"Look," he says. "I meant it when I said I saw a spark in you. And I tried to tell you this last week. As much as this might have started off as a game for me . . . somewhere along the way, I changed. I mean it." He takes a step closer, holding my stare. "I fell for you, Gretchen." I take in a clipped breath, gazing up into those deep blue eyes, so intense and pleading. It would be so easy to give in to those eyes.

But somehow, I just snort.

"What?" he says, his face falling as I start to laugh.

"Sorry, I honestly didn't mean to—" I snort again, and I can tell that it's here now: that mood that hits me once in a while, when something is so funny I can't stop.

"Gretchen!" he says. "Come on . . ."

I can barely breathe. "Oh, Jeremy, just stop it," I choke out. "Come on. You've kissed my cousin!"

"Okay, I know that's not *ideal*," he says, "but there's something here. Tell me you don't feel it, too." I'm actually growing kind of hysterical now, fanning my eyes to keep them from watering. Jeremy's jaw tightens. "Okay, seriously, what's so funny?"

"What you said . . ." I shake my head, struggling to get the words out. "It's literally the plot to, like, half the movies I like. The guy is always some jerk who's been messing with the girl as part of, like, a bet or something. But by the end, he's like, 'Sorry for manipulating you this whole movie; I love you now,' and she's all, 'Oh okay; well, in that case, that's fine.'"

I feel another fit of giggles coming on as he stands there, arms crossed over his chest. "May I remind you: *we were both lying!*"

"Oh my God, I know!" I say, actual tears coming out now as I nod my head. "And I like that plot, too! Where they're both—" I catch my breath, finally calming down. "Oh, I don't know, Jeremy." I shrug. "This was fun, but . . . maybe a web of lies just isn't actually a great foundation for a relationship."

He sighs, brows knitting together. "I'm really not a bad guy, you know. . . ."

"I weirdly believe that," I tell him. And for his sake, I hope my aunt Viv was wrong. Maybe reformed bad boys *can* be a thing. "But . . . I don't know what to tell you, Jer. This time, you still don't get the girl. Ted, on the other hand." I nod across the room, to where the making out has grown a little ridiculous, to be honest. "Ted gets the girl."

Jeremy laughs under his breath, and I'll hand it to him: he's taking this well.

"So . . ." he says after a drawn-out beat. "I don't know what your plans are after tonight, but you probably won't see me around the club for a while. I've been thinking I might want to take some time off. Clear my head. Maybe try out screenwriting or something."

I smirk up at him. "A new filter through which to observe?"

"You're never going to let me live that down, are you?"

"Nope. Too eternally douchey."

He laughs. "Well, for what it's worth, it's been fun watching you grow at this, Gretchen. I really do think you have potential."

"You, too," I say. "And I'm glad I finally caught your set this week. It was . . ."

"What?" he says when I hesitate.

I smile, shrugging. "Pretty decent."

TWENTY-THREE

Super-Happy Time Dash | Three years since the wedding. Six months since that sprint through the rain. Or maybe just two and a half weeks after a stand-up set.

Saturday night at Willard Beach Coffee, Ethan cleans the espresso machine for the last time. "I know you were making next to no money here," I say from my perch on the counter, "but I'm still a little bummed the old barista's coming back." I take a swig from my PSL. "I'm going to have to start paying for these."

Ethan runs a hand through his hair and sighs out at the empty place, the door locked, the hanging sign flipped to *Closed*. "I guess it's time for the next gig. . . ."

"Speaking of," I say. "I told my mom about you."

"Oh?" He seems pleased.

"This is actually kind of embarrassing. She wants to hire

you. As a photographer for Nacho's birthday party coming up? It's . . . *Gatsby*-themed."

"Um, a thousand times yes," he says, removing his apron as he walks over to me. He leans into the counter, and I'm abruptly aware of my legs, dangling on either side of him, close but not quite touching. He eyes my phone, now buzzing on the counter a few feet away. "Do you need to get that?"

I shake my head quickly, not wanting to spoil the moment, though I probably should check soon to make sure Paula doesn't need another pep talk. Her last message came in maybe twenty minutes ago—a screaming Kristen Wiig GIF, which I think was meant to encompass both her feelings on opening for Marnie tonight and the fact that Isaiah just sent us a picture of his folding chair on set. Anyway, even if she's nervous, I have absolute confidence in her. And I'll be bringing a whole squad with me to cheer her on later.

"So," says Ethan, our eyes locked at the same height.

"So," I say, biting back a smile.

This seems to be a game we're playing—neither of us wanting to be the first to admit what's happening here.

Now that I feel this way, it's strange to me that I ever didn't. The realization came on slowly, then felt abruptly obvious. And then I worried I might have missed my chance.

The day after my big speech at the club, I recounted the whole thing to Ethan as we returned our cart of yearbooks to the library. Walking the empty halls, I heard myself going on and on about how, despite my weird peace agreement with Jeremy, I was *definitely not interested*, and how I was *so relieved* that Sam and I were *just friends*. Ethan nodded along in his thoughtful way, seeming vaguely delighted to hear about my embarrassing public singing moment. And maybe a bit disappointed when I told him that I hadn't made the final three. When I was done, he didn't seem to want to talk about my love life. He just smiled and asked, "So when do you go back?"

My phone's buzzing has stopped, and now we're just looking at each other in the quiet empty room. There's been this palpable anticipation between us these past couple weeks. I'm *pretty sure* I'm not making that up.

At the movies last weekend, while Sam and Natalie cuddled, and Pilsner and Grody loudly shared two different kinds of M&M's, Ethan reached over and took my hand in the dark—ever so casually. And when we all decided to carpool over to Natalie's after, with one too few seats in her Mini Cooper, I very coolly volunteered to sit on his lap.

I'm telling myself he'll break eventually. In fact, his expression is serious now. I wonder if this is finally it. My breath catches as he reaches out, brushing my bottom lip with his thumb. "Sorry," he says, a glint in his eye. "You had a little . . . PSL."

My face falls.

"Hey, are you free tomorrow?" he asks, grinning. "I was thinking we could bundle you up and hit the outdoors. Want to go skating?"

I pretend to think. "Nope."

"Sledding?"

"Nope again."

"Ice fishing?"

I frown. "You go ice fishing?"

"Nah," he says. "I just wanted to see you to make that face."

I laugh, somehow extremely happy and frustrated all at once. I think I'm going to lose our little game. He snaps his fingers. "Hey, what about—"

And that's when I kiss him—a quick, soft brush of the lips that makes my head spin. When I pull back to scan his eyes, it's clear that he felt it too. In the space of a blink, there could have been a thousand swirling cameras.

So that's what that's about.

"Oh thank God," he breathes, pulling me into him. I wrap my arms around his neck, unable to keep from smiling. "What is it?" The words come out mumbled against my lips.

"Nothing," I murmur. "Just happy." And it's true. Waiting like this was *killing me*. Which, actually . . .

I pull back, frowning suddenly. "Ethan!" I shove him. "Why did this take so long?"

He shrugs. "Sam said you were processing."

My jaw drops. "He told you that?! Oh, he's in *big*—" Ethan interrupts me with another kiss and I soften, only to shriek.

Outside, Pilsner is puckering up against the storefront window, his palms pressed to the glass. Under the streetlight,

Sam and Natalie are cracking up while Grody does that thing where he pretends to make out with himself, his back to us, hands going everywhere.

"I guess we should have seen this coming," says Ethan.

"I'll get it," I sigh, but I don't actually want to move. So I don't.

Ethan grins and leans in again, ignoring our audience. And when our lips meet, I get such a rush, I forget to care about the wolf whistles outside.

"Ugh! Finally!" I hear Natalie say as someone calls, "Ow! Ow!"

"Okay, but we really are cold!" chimes in Grody after a minute.

We laugh and pull apart.

"To be continued?" says Ethan.

"Definitely," I say, and I hop down from the counter to let them in.

OUTTAKES

From the recording app of Gretchen Wilder

"Testing, testing. Hello, me. Me here . . ."

"Jokes, jokes, jokes . . ."

"Oh, actually. I recently came across the phrase 'balls out.' That could be something. I should run the origins by Sam. . . ."

"Real talk. Were we too dismissive of the mullet?"

"You know what herb isn't polarizing? Fennel. Nobody likes fennel! . . . Yep, this is comedy gold."

"My boyfriend is legitimately proud of the fact that he *might* be related to Britney Spears. Possible bit there?"

"Okay, so no text from Sam yet. But apparently 'balls out'

means 'with maximum effort.' So, what . . . A guy was trying so hard at something he . . . took his balls out?"

"Sidebar: I'm actually afraid Ethan may be planning a prom proposal, just as an excuse to dance. He's had the song 'You Drive Me Crazy' suspiciously in his head. This is what I get for wishing for a marching band moment."

"Maybe the open air is comforting for balls? And that . . . somehow lends itself to productivity?"

"Oh, note to self: pitch Dolores my teen open mic night idea. I've been gauging interest around school, and I feel like Deb from Mathletes would *kill.*"

"Well, whatever. Clearly, we as a society are just really into balls—oh hi, Nacho! Awww. Look at you all ready for your party. Do you look stunning in your flapper dress? Yes you *do!* Yes you *do!* Annnnd I did the Mom voice. This one stays between us, little dog bro."

ACKNOWLEDGMENTS

A lot of people told me the second book would be hard, and those people were right. Luckily, I had the extremely brilliant (and patient) Donna Bray in my corner, helping tease out this flicker of an idea until it came bursting to life. I'm so grateful, and I had so much fun. Thank you.

I'm also hugely grateful to my agent, Jennifer Mattson (who is also extremely brilliant and patient). I couldn't ask for a better sounding board, coconspirator or champion.

I'm so appreciative of the many great publishing minds who helped make this book happen: Tiara Kittrell, Alison Donalty, Corina Lupp, Alice Wang, Aubrey Churchward, Ebony LaDelle, Sabrina Abballe, Patty Rosati, Mark Rifkin, Laura Harshberger, Jessica Gould, Kristin Eckhardt, and the rest of the Harper team. And thanks to Taryn Fagerness, my foreign rights agent, and Ana Hard, for this beautiful jacket art.

Thank you to my real-life handsome architect husband, Bobby, who brings out my silliest self, and who can both read my mind *and* raise one eyebrow. (And who put up with all the times I made him riff with me until I found the punchline.)

And to my parents, who have always encouraged me to believe in myself and go after things, even when they're not particularly practical. (And who each read a silly number of drafts for this book. We're a very collaborative family.)

Big shoutout to Nicole Panteleakos, my CP and friend, whose notes this time around were mostly of the "ahahahahaha" variety. (Thank you for that. Those were the exact notes I needed to keep going.)

A big squeeze to the rest of my friends and family. I appreciate all the support and joy you bring to my life. There's a reason I like writing big, lovable casts.

And finally, thank *you*, dear reader, for picking up this book. For what it's worth, I think you're most likely to be whoever the hell you want to be.